T0149886

THE SECRET BROKERS

Other Books by Alexandrea Weis

Realm

By the Multi-Award-Winning Duo
Alexandrea Weis with Lucas Astor

The Magnus Blackwell Series
Blackwell: The Prequel (A Magnus Blackwell Novel, Book 1)
Damned (A Magnus Blackwell Novel, Book 2)
Bound (A Magnus Blackwell Novel, Book 3)
Seize (A Magnus Blackwell Novel, Book 4)

The St. Benedict Series
Death by the River (A St. Benedict Novel, Book 1)

Forthcoming from Vesuvian Books
By Alexandrea Weis with Lucas Astor

The Chimera Effect
4 for the Devil
A River of Secrets (A St. Benedict Novel, Book 2)

ALEXANDREA WEIS

THE SECRET BROKERS

The Secret Brokers

Cover design by Deranged Doctor Design

ISBN: 978-1-944109-20-2

VESUVIAN BOOKS

Published by Vesuvian Books
www.vesuvianbooks.com

Printed in the United States

10 9 8 7 6 5 4 3 2 1

CHAPTER ONE

Slush from a late winter snowstorm splashed the side of the sleek limousine as it came to a stop at the curb. Dallas August tucked the jacket of his fitted tuxedo closer to stave off the bitter chill. He pushed open the limo door and peered up at a four-story brownstone in the center of the Chelsea Art District of Manhattan. A grin curled his lips. It was time to play the game.

That kick of power coursed through him, diverting the blood to his muscles and energizing his pulse. Dallas relished the sensation. He used to get it with each new job, and even though he never went into the field anymore, he couldn't run his business if the thrill wasn't there.

I've still got my edge.

The glistening entrance of The Flint Gallery had black-tie waiters carrying trays overflowing with flutes of champagne. The glare of diamonds and gem-clad watches blinded Dallas as he snapped up a drink and strutted past a who's who of esteemed guests from New York's high society.

He caught his tall, lean figure in the glass doors and ran his hand over his short-cropped dark hair, brushing off flakes of freshly fallen snow. The hungry looks he got from a few women did fan his ego, but he brushed it aside and concentrated on what he came to do.

"Your name please, sir?" a young woman asked behind a sign-in table.

"I've got this, Jenna," a stunning brunette insisted, coming alongside Dallas.

Every nerve in his body electrified at the sight of her.

"Yes, Ms. Kelly." Jenna went to assist the next guest.

Dallas did a quick appraisal of Bridget Kelly's black velvet gown and how it flared at the knees. Her long brown hair cascaded over her right shoulder, and her smoky eye shadow emphasized her cat-green eyes. He approved. Perhaps she had what it took to make his team.

"You look nice this evening, Bridget."

"Nice?" A line appeared between her brows. "You realize what this dress costs?"

Dallas's chuckle carried in the air. "You've only been with the organization for two weeks and already you're asking for a raise?"

"Not at all, Mr. August. I was just …" She shyly smiled. "I was told you never liked hiring people from my former employer, so I was rather surprised you gave me this chance."

Dallas swirled the champagne in his glass, surreptitiously checking the guests standing around them.

"My predecessor was the one who was finicky about where his people came from. I'm always open to hiring recruits from The Bureau."

"Your organization was whispered about at Quantico a lot."

His little organization bugged the crap out of the higher-ups at The Bureau. He enjoyed their grumblings about his team interfering with investigations. He considered it payback for all the shit they'd given him when he left their anal-retentive world to join the ranks of spies who made a living outside of the government.

He clutched his drink and then dropped his voice. "Did you do your homework on your target?"

Bridget nodded. "A comprehensive database search on tastes, preferences, favorite restaurants, and—"

"Are you ready to make first contact?" Dallas looked her in the eye. "Or is tonight purely for research?"

"I didn't buy the dress to watch him from a distance, sir."

"Very good." He combed the gallery floor. "Where is your target?"

"Mr. Garvey arrived five minutes ago with his assistant. I greeted him at the door."

He eyeballed what was left of his champagne, still doubtful of the girl's abilities. "Our client wants the file in his London offices as soon as possible. Do anything you can to get your hands on it. And I do mean anything."

Bridget glared at him. "Is that why you're here? To remind me of the job?"

He was glad to get a rise out of her. "Maybe I like art."

"I can handle this."

Her attitude set off a gut-reaction to reprimand her, but he refrained. "I check on all my recruits during their first assignment. Pass this test, and I will have more jobs for you."

Bridget's brows rose, adding to the defiance in her gaze. "Six years with The Bureau means I'm not a rookie like the rest of your operatives. I have lots of field experience."

He'd seen her "know it all" demeanor before. It was the hallmark of anyone transitioning from the government way of doing things to his. Even he'd copped an attitude in his early days with the organization, but he'd changed his tune, and so would she. Experience was the best way to break any seasoned spy. He would give her a taste of his world where there was no backup, no agency protocol to follow, and no rules.

"Being an agent for The Bureau doesn't compare to being a specialist in my organization. Agents have limits; specialists don't. Now find Trent Garvey and get the information."

Bridget's plastic smile hinted at her compulsion to comply to keep her job, but her unwillingness to be too accommodating glistened in her eyes.

"Yes, sir."

She marched away, her heels clicking on the floor.

Dallas was confident her stubborn streak would prove useful.

He finished his champagne and set out across the showroom, taking in the faces of the guests. It never surprised him to find at least one former client or current client at these affairs. Tonight, there were quite a few, but he didn't acknowledge them. His business required the utmost discretion.

Bored with the colorful paintings and inane conversations around him, Dallas checked his stainless watch, wondering how much longer he should wait before the real reason for his presence at the gallery appeared. Babysitting his newest acquisition, the beautiful Bridget, had been a good cover, but he had other business.

The flute jostled in his hand when a petite blonde grazed his elbow.

"I beg your pardon," she murmured.

He held up his empty glass. "No harm done."

The blonde's hungry gaze went up and down his lean figure. "Funny. You don't look like a man who's into art."

Her flirty manner enticed him. "I have a lot of interests."

"I bet you do." She inched closer, dipping the cleavage of her low-cut dress into his line of sight. "I was sent to get you, Mr. August."

Damn! Just when it was getting interesting, work beckoned.

"Perhaps I could tell you about my interests later, over a drink?"

"I doubt my employer would approve."

Her flowery perfume coaxed him closer. "Where is your employer?"

She eyed the staircase in front of them. "Upstairs. There are some private rooms."

Dallas let her guide him to the straight flight of stairs, keeping an eye on the area around them. There were sure to be others watching, but he doubted they would question him. That was the good thing about setting up meetings with potential clients at such events—everyone was too busy talking or drinking to notice.

She trotted up the steps. He took a moment to delight in the curve of her little round ass beneath the snug dress. He liked them petite. They reminded him of *her*. Then the scar she'd left on his heart tore a little.

Damn. You need to focus.

A landing cluttered with loud artwork representing a variety of styles—contemporary, pop-art, and art deco—momentarily distracted him. They headed along a deserted but brightly lit corridor with several blinding spotlights. Dallas dissected the area, trying to detect anything out of the ordinary.

"There seems to be no one around."

She took his hand. "He doesn't want anyone to disturb your meeting."

Dallas pretended to admire a collection of charcoal skyscapes of various famous cities, checking for an escape. Whenever entering a room or building, always plan your getaway. It was one of the first things he'd learned at Quantico.

The woman suddenly stopped at a black door.

With no men following him, no guards posted outside, and no escape routes detected, a flutter in his belly roared to life. The girl had been sent to retrieve him. It was nothing more than the opening to an intricate game of chess, but why? Some of his clients fiercely protected their privacy, but this seemed a bit much for an initial meeting.

Her hand went to the doorknob.

"Aren't you going to tell me your name?" he asked.

"There's no need, Mr. August."

He played it cool as the door opened and kept his attention on what appeared in front of him. He tensed as he scanned a cozy sitting room, which was filled with white leather furniture, its cream-colored walls covered in pop art of fifties-era actresses. A trim man in a Brioni tuxedo waited on a red rug made up of intricate geometrical patterns.

Dallas scrutinized his polished Italian leather shoes, Cartier watch, and then his face. Darryl Keen wasn't the imposing presence he'd expected.

Known as a Whiz on Wall Street, Keen's investment company had made a fortune during the market's recent volatile nosedives. Several government investigations into his business practices had yielded nothing. Mr. Keen was about as slippery as they came.

"Come in, Mr. August."

Dallas relaxed when he saw no one else in the room.

He gave a quick nod to the blonde. "I presume she works for you."

She smiled and waved him inside.

"One of my staff. She handles my appointments," Keen told him.

The click of the door begged for Dallas to turn around and make sure they remained alone, but that wouldn't build much trust.

"Why here?"

"Parties are an opportune time to talk business." Keen walked toward Dallas. "If I had gone to your office, or if you had come to mine, people would have found out. I want to keep my association with you very low key."

Dallas studied Keen's cold brown eyes. "You said little in your email. What business are we here to discuss?"

"I want to hire your little organization to help me with a problem."

Dallas bristled at the word *little*. His specialists covered the globe, working jobs from Alaska to Zimbabwe. Over a hundred men and women at his disposal hardly qualified as *little*.

"What do you know about my organization?"

"Your people are the best at getting secrets. Whether from a business partner, mistress, lover, colleague, a friend, or even children, your specialists have a variety of talents for prying secrets out of just about anyone."

"Who told you about me? I usually work on a referral basis."

"A friend. He said you took over ownership of Simon La Roy's organization after he was found dead. Nasty business."

Dallas didn't let an inkling of his apprehension show. He hadn't wanted to take over the reins after Simon's death, but fate had insisted.

"The police never found Simon's killer, but they blamed Greg Caston for his murder. Greg ran an organization similar to Simon's. He used his art galleries around the country as a cover for his specialists." Dallas casually toed the edge of the round red rug. "But you already knew that."

"The news chalked up the murders to a business rivalry gone bad." Keen stepped behind the bar. "With Caston dead, you took over the only spy business in town, and got all of Simon's money, too." He lifted a bottle of vodka and held it out to Dallas. "Vodka straight, right?"

"Ice, if you've got it."

Dallas strolled toward the bar, impressed by Keen's research. A client taking the time to check up on you meant business—big business.

Keen lifted the lid on a stainless ice bucket. He dropped two cubes into an old-fashioned glass and added a measure of vodka.

"I have someone on my management team who's leaking information to a competitor. I want it to stop."

Dallas took the glass from Keen's outstretched hand. "You must have staff you can trust to weed out plants. Might be cheaper than hiring my people."

Keen reached for a bottle of scotch. "I don't trust anyone in my organization. I want someone on the outside looking into this. See if we have an infestation."

"You want a man or a woman for the job?"

"A man. Most of my upper management are men, and a woman might make them curious." Keen poured three fingers of scotch into a glass. "I want to find if they're cheating on me, not their wives."

Dallas peered into his drink, hiding his smirk. Husbands who cheated were easy sources for information. He wouldn't have half the business he did without cheating spouses.

"I'll need more to pair the right specialist with this job. It's not as easy as you think."

"I can get you whatever you want."

Dallas removed a business card from his inner jacket pocket.

"This has my cell and private email. Contact me with the details in a few days. Dates, times, addresses, and all the names of those you suspect. Once I find a specialist to help you, we'll talk about my fee."

"I'm sure we can work something out." Keen put the card on the bar. "What if I want you to handle this personally? You were once the best. 'Simon La Roy's right-hand man,' they said."

Dallas set down his drink. "My days in the field are over."

"It's a shame Simon La Roy is dead." Keen took a sip of his scotch. "Then you would still be out in the field." He contemplated the amber liquid in his glass. "Can you assure me the person you will find will get me what I need?"

"You'll get your information, Mr. Keen, not to worry." Dallas glanced back at the door, itching to check on Bridget. "If you will excuse me, I have other matters to attend to."

"Trent Garvey knows you planted that little brunette on his tail." Keen lifted the right side of his mouth in a half-smirk. "She's not very subtle."

Dallas hesitated and then asked, "What makes you think I planted her?"

Keen raised his brows, appearing amused. "I saw you chatting with her at the door. I know she's yours. My question is who hired you to put her there?"

"Client confidentiality. Surely, you understand." Dallas walked toward the door. "And you're right; Bridget is very conspicuous as a spy."

"You have someone else here, don't you?"

He eased the door open. "Contact me when you're ready, Mr. Keen."

Dallas snickered under his breath—go to supervise one job and get another. That was the way of it. His was one of the few businesses that did well, no matter how good or how bad the economy.

He set off down the hallway that led back to the stairs.

The pretty blonde came toward him. "I hope everything went well, Mr. August."

He relaxed as he took in her exquisite oval face. "That remains to be seen, Miss …?"

She flashed him a slight smile and turned away.

Dallas eyed the curves beneath her dress again as she moved past him. When she darted into the room he had just come from, Dallas cursed.

"For a second, she reminded me of …"

Then that funny ache returned—the one he got whenever he thought of her. He didn't want to acknowledge it. Giving in to one's emotions was a sign of weakness, and there was no room for weakness in his world. Besides, she was a non-factor in his life. She wasn't his to love anymore.

Before he reached the first floor, Dallas saw a panic-stricken Bridget eyeing him from across the crowded gallery. A short, bald, round man with thick-rimmed glasses had his arm around her, leering at her cleavage.

That didn't last long.

If Dallas didn't humble her now, her arrogance would get her killed. Mistakes were the only way he got his rookies to listen.

A waiter came up to him, carrying a tray. "Champagne, sir?"

Dallas took a crystal flute. "You're on, Stokes."

Ray Stokes, with a wicked glint in his blue eyes, displayed an unabashed smile. "Already made my move while she was distracted with him."

"Make sure you get the file before you leave his place." Dallas took a sip of champagne. "Get the girl out of here before she draws too much attention."

Stokes dipped his head, hiding his mouth. "You should have told her he was gay."

Dallas sighed. "She didn't do her homework."

"Good thing I did." Stokes chuckled. "See you in the morning, Mr. August."

Stokes glided away, heading toward Bridget and a laughing Trent Garvey.

He was glad he'd heeded his instinct. Thankfully, Stokes would get what he needed.

Dallas hurried across the gallery floor and set the glass on the sign-in table. It was time for him to get back to his office. There was still a lot to do before he could call it a night.

Cold slapped his face when he stepped outside. The myriad of guests had moved indoors, leaving the entrance deserted. The street appeared desolate without the line of cars dropping off the invited elite. A lone streetlight shone on the icy sidewalks as he retrieved his phone from his jacket pocket and sent a quick text to his driver. About to put it away, he caught a glimpse of an older message he'd saved. It was nothing earth-shattering, just a reminder of the life they had shared.

He swiped his thumb across her name, bringing the satisfaction of his evening to a crashing end.

> Can you pick up some eggs on the way home? Love you.

The beam of headlights of his approaching car reminded him of his job. He yearned to be free of her, but he also feared losing what she'd given him—hope for a normal life.

CHAPTER TWO

T he gray morning cast a veil over the sprawling high-rise buildings while Dallas took in the view from his office window. The trees in Central Park still had a thick dusting of snow and the business at the ice rink remained brisk. Nevertheless, winter would soon end, and Dallas would no longer be able to blame the constant ache in his chest on the cold. He turned and gazed down at the cream-colored carpet, struggling to push the memory of her soft skin from his mind.

He'd been sent to learn Nicci Beauvoir's secrets and had fallen in love with her charm, grace, and practical personality. She'd been the reason he'd walked away from Simon's organization. Their year together had saved him. Dallas had trusted another, and to a ghost like him, living in the shadows where lies are the only truth, it had given him a taste of the real world. But in the end, she'd left him to marry a man he'd worked beside and considered a good friend. He wasn't bitter, but he wasn't whole.

"Nicci," Dallas whispered, remembering the taste of her lips.

"You say somethin', Boss?"

His muscle-bound security guard lumbered toward his desk, a .9mm Smith and Wesson pistol holstered at his hip.

"I've told you before, Cleveland. Don't call me boss."

Cleveland laid the morning newspaper across Dallas's desk with a concerned gleam in his eye. His impressive size, and the way he seemed to entangle himself in Dallas's personal life like an overzealous mother hen, made him impossible to ignore.

"You look like crap," he scolded in his baritone voice. "You didn't sleep again, did ya? Not like anyone could sleep in this museum, anyway." He motioned to the office wall where numerous framed photographs remained as homage to a short man flourishing a decorative wooden cane. "Maybe you should get rid of Simon La Roy's things. Kinda creepy bein' surrounded by a dead man's shit."

Dallas ignored Simon's beady brown eyes staring back at him.

"Simon turned a sideline into a multi-million-dollar business. We should at least leave his pictures up."

"I thought you hated him."

"He may have been a worthless piece of shit, but I still respect what he accomplished." He rubbed his hand across his brow, pushing all thoughts of his former boss from his mind. "Did Stokes come in yet?"

"Not yet. I just checked his office."

Dallas gathered up the bills scattered across his modest wooden desk. He'd refused to use Simon's fancy hickory one, sending it to storage instead.

"Tell him to come in here when you see him. I've got some things we need to go over."

Cleveland crossed his massive arms. "You sure you don't want to hire another assistant? Stokes is a strange dude."

Dallas tapped the bills into a neat pile before setting them down with a decided thump. "I could give a damn if he's strange."

Cleveland pinched his face. "What's eatin' you?"

He leaned back in his chair, not in the mood. "I'm ... beat."

"It's more than that. You've lost weight, and your eyes got dark circles beneath 'em." Cleveland clucked like he usually did when scolding Dallas. "You're still thinkin' about that girl, ain't ya? The one we rescued back in N'awlins from Greg Caston. That writer, Nicci Beauvoir."

Tension careened through him. "Nicci Beauvoir is dead, remember? You were there when we faked her death, gave her a new identity, and sent her off to start a new life."

"Yeah, a new life with your former best friend."

The pain of the loss of the two people he'd cared about most squeezed his throat. "You promised not to discuss what happened last summer with anyone. That includes me."

"Yeah, I know what I promised. But Nicci—whatever her new name is—she sure ain't dead to you." Cleveland's rugged jawline softened. "And if you treated her like you treat me and everyone else in this here organization, I can see why she left your sorry ass for the other guy."

"What in the hell is that supposed to mean?"

Dallas gathered his calm before he spoke again. He could tolerate Cleveland's grilling sessions on any subject but her.

"I treat you and everyone else in this organization very well. The only reason I came back to this job was to save the people who would be destroyed by Simon La Roy's death."

"That lie workin' for ya yet? 'Cause if you ask me, takin' this job was the easy way out. You didn't want to fight for that girl back in N'awlins. God knows you don't want nobody to know what you're really feelin.'"

It was arguments like this that made Dallas wish he'd never taken the formidable man on when he found him working for Greg Caston. His size and knowledge of firearms had been perfect for his organization. It was just his compassion that irked Dallas. He didn't know how to respond to an employee giving a shit about him. In his world, one wasn't supposed to care.

"Are you finished?"

"I know I'm only supposed to be a security guard and all, but if you ask me, you chase people away faster than a jackrabbit can haul ass across a field. You don't want to spend the rest of your life alone, do ya? Maybe if you were a little nicer and not jump on everybody like they was—"

"You're right." He leaned over his desk, resting his weight on his knuckles. "I hired you to be my security guard, not my analyst." Dallas motioned to the office door. "If you have nothing else for me, you can go back—"

"There's a man here to see you. Says Lance Beauvoir sent him."

Dallas hesitated, running through a list of who would know to mention his old friend. Lance was one of the few people he trusted, but he was the kind to call before sending a referral. Dallas relaxed his hands as he considered his options.

"Does this man have a name?"

"Don't need none. His face is on the front page." Cleveland pointed at the newspaper on top of Dallas's desk.

Dallas scanned the paper, the one he insisted on ordering despite Cleveland's objections and hints about getting his news from the internet. The round face staring back at him from beneath the bold headline was one of America's most notorious crime bosses.

"Carl Bordonaro?"

Cleveland nodded. "He's waitin' in that fancy room with the old Egyptian stuff."

"It's the drawing room." Dallas glanced at his watch, juggling appointments in his head. "And those are ancient Greek vases, not

Egyptian."

"Like I give a shit." Cleveland turned to the doorway. "And if the two of you be wantin' coffee, then gets it ya'self. I'm the security guard, not the goddamn butler."

Dallas rubbed his hand over the back of his neck. *What the fuck is Carl doing here?*

After their last dealing together in New Orleans, he'd never imagined the underworld crime lord would seek him out. And Lance would never send someone so infamous his way without a heads up. The inconsistencies awakened a fire in his belly.

He headed for the open door and pounded the floor in the hallway. The ajar door of the drawing room brought him to a grinding halt.

His breath quickened before he eased the door open and stepped inside.

A short man waited by a glass cabinet displaying a long-necked Greek vase. His bald head and pasty face resembled his newspaper photo. Standing beneath the display spotlights, he seemed rather grandfatherly and nothing like his menacing reputation. He had his thick, black-rimmed glasses right up against the cabinet, inspecting the amphora inside.

Dallas shut the door, and the click reverberated.

Carl Bordonaro faced Dallas, his freshly pressed dark gray suit contrasting sharply against his unshaven morning stubble.

"Loutrophoros?" He thumbed the display cabinet.

Dallas eyed the black and red vase. "I have no idea what it's called."

"Used for weddin's and funerals in ancient Greece, I believe," he said in his thick New Orleans accent. "Quite a collection the little guy had."

16

Dallas grimaced at *little guy*. Simon would have hated it.

"He was an avid collector of art and antiques." Dallas kept a defensive tone from his voice, so as not to upset his guest. "I got the impression you never left New Orleans, Mr. Bordonaro."

"Oh, I leave all the time." He waved a nonchalant hand in the air. "The feds try to keep an eye on me, but there are ways to get around their tails. Lots of ways." He held his hand out to Dallas. "And you can call me Carl."

Dallas took his hand, weighing his firm handshake. It matched his intimidating history.

"I've heard you've avoided prosecution for the past fifteen years. That's quite a feat."

Carl puffed out his chest. "Yeah, five arrests with no criminal convictions. I'm like a good Louisiana politician—immune to a federal indictment."

Dallas let go of his hand. "How's Lance?"

"Still drinking and sleeping his way through most of the women in the city. You know Lance. I don't think he'll ever change, but that's what I like about him. He may appear as a buffoon to others, but beneath it all, he's a devoted friend who knows everyone in New Orleans, and can get anythin' done."

Dallas cleared his throat, eager to get to the reason for the meeting. "What have I done to deserve this unexpected visit?"

"It's not what you've done, my friend. It's what you're about to do."

A nervous tingle coursed through his hands. "About to do? I'm not sure if I like the sound of that."

Carl moved toward a chair upholstered to match the sapphire and cream in the wallpaper.

"Seems you have worked yourself right in here. Lance told me you had very little opposition to takin' over Simon's business."

Dallas took an adjoining chair, the apprehensive tingle getting stronger. "Many of Simon's past associates were more than pleased to hear of his death. The man had only enemies—myself included."

Carl sat back and folded his hands over his protruding belly. "Glad I helped get rid of his sorry ass last summer."

Dallas politely smiled but kept up his cool gaze. "Which is, I'm sure, why you're here."

"When you asked me to dispose of Simon's body, and set up his rival, Greg Caston, with his murder and Nicci's Beauvoir's death, it entitled me to ask you for a favor."

Dread, like a stone sinking to the bottom of a pond, settled in Dallas's stomach. He'd never assumed he would owe anything to Carl for his services, but that Carl believed he did meant Dallas had a problem.

"Why aren't you asking Nicci and her new husband for this favor? They benefitted from everything you did. I didn't."

"Because they have new identities, live a quiet life, and are out of the game for good. This favor is somethin' you and your organization are good at. I could entrust this job to any one of my associates, but none of them are skilled in gatherin' exactly the kind of information I need."

Dallas stared at the plump man, fearing he was about to be pulled into a dangerous situation.

"What kind of information are we talking about?"

"Simon La Roy was known around the world as the man to go to when one needed secrets uncovered. As his successor, you're the man to see. With our past dealin's together, I figured I could trust you."

A job.

Dallas relaxed, and the businessman in him took over. This was something he knew and could handle.

"Who's the target?"

"Target?" Carl snickered. "Odd choice of words. I don't want her killed, Dallas."

"Forgive me." He dipped his head. "Target is the person who we're sent to investigate."

"Of course." Carl rubbed his stubby hands together. "There was a former associate who knew a great deal about my business ventures. His name was Earl Yeager. Three years ago, Earl was diagnosed with cancer and spent his last days in a hospital bed. I paid to have private nurses see to his comfort. One nurse, Gwen Marsh, became very close to Earl—so close, in fact, he may have told her a few secrets about me. If certain federal agencies got a hold of those secrets, it could cause problems for several important men throughout the country." He clasped his hands and squeezed. "These businessmen want this nurse killed, to make sure she doesn't talk, but I can't do that."

Dallas studied his white knuckles. A man such as Carl didn't pass on eliminating a problem unless he had a very good reason.

"You can't or won't. There's a difference."

Carl shook his head. "I've known Gwen since she was adopted from China as a baby. Her father and I are old friends. I attended her christenin', her first communion, and all her birthday parties. Now can you understand my dilemma."

Dallas sat back, slightly amused. He wasn't about to condone a senseless killing of an innocent woman, but why Carl had come to him made no sense.

"You have people who can question her. What can my

organization do that your people can't?"

"I can't afford for any of my people to interrogate her or know where she is. I can't trust anyone right now. I also owe her father. I promised him I would do my best to protect her." He pointed at Dallas. "You're the best I know. I want you to go and find out what the girl knows. Not one of your people. You're the only one I can trust."

"Me?" Dallas recoiled at the suggestion. "I'm not a field man anymore. I have to run this organization. I can't just hop on a plane and—"

"I'm not asking." Carl's brown eyes twinkled beneath his glasses.

Dallas carefully considered his options. What he asked meant a lot of clients would be put out, and specialists would be left in limbo while on assignments. Then again, if he displeased the mafia leader by refusing the assignment, he would end up with a bankrupted business or a bullet to the head.

Dallas leaned forward and rubbed his face, knowing he had to take the job.

"Tell me about the girl."

"Do you like animals?"

He recoiled, rocking back in his chair. "Animals? I thought you said she was a nurse?"

"Yeah, Gwen's a nurse, but she's also an animal lover. She lives on a farm outside of New Orleans where she keeps rescued racehorses."

Dallas already hated the sound of it. He couldn't leave his office for some farm in Southeast Louisiana.

I must be mad.

"I don't know anything about horses." He tapped the arm of

the chair. "Tell me more."

Carl's cocky smile grated his nerves.

"Gwen is thirty-four, divorced, with no children. Her ex is a physician from a wealthy Houston family, so her divorce settlement left her more than well off. She bought a fifteen-acre farm in Folsom on the north shore of Lake Pontchartrain. She retired from nursin' after the divorce, but she took the private duty gig as a favor to me."

Dallas stopped tapping and hesitated as he analyzed what Carl had told him. "But if you're such an old family friend, why don't you just talk to the woman yourself?"

"I already have. But that ain't enough—you and I both know that. The people I'm lookin' to pacify wouldn't take my word that the girl knows nothin', but they will take yours. You're a third party, an outsider, and you run this organization, which has quite the reputation." Carl paused and cast his gaze to the Oriental rug. "Until other interested parties can be—let us say, distracted—from the girl, I need to know she's safe. And with you, she will be."

Dallas stood, wishing to retreat to the safety of his office where he could think. He had other clients and specialists to take care of before he could consider heading out of town. He had to find another way to appease Carl.

"Let's pull her out of there and put her somewhere I can keep an eye on her."

Carl waved Dallas back to his seat. "Then she would look guilty, and I'll be caught in a finger pointin' game with those other interested parties. No, the girl must stay put on her farm and not be seen changin' her routine. Anyway, there's someone already watchin' her, and if she were moved, a lot of problems would suddenly develop for me."

21

A swell of cold took over his limbs. "Who's watching her?"

"Some former associates of yours—the FBI."

Dallas shook his head, not sure what to believe. The FBI monitoring any civilian meant they were important, or the information they carried was worth a hell of a lot to the Department of Justice.

"Why is the FBI involved?"

"They're not officially involved, but are callin' their surveillance of Gwen a courtesy since her father's testifyin' for them against one of my biggest competitors—Devon Robertson." Carl examined his fingernails while twisting his lips together. "The feds picked him up on corruption charges. Now, I won't say the information I planted on Robertson got him arrested but … I needed him out of my hair. I gave Gwen's father my blessin' to testify and promised to keep him and his daughter safe."

"So you set this whole thing up? You leaked information to the feds, got your competitor arrested, and now you want me to help out while this woman's father testifies." Dallas's neck stiffened as he considered the ramifications. "You've created a shitstorm."

Carl cocked his head. "I don't see it that way. I sped up the process of removin' a pain in the ass from fuckin' up my business."

The new element of danger raised the stakes for Dallas. If the FBI had their men watching Gwen Marsh, Dallas would have to be very careful to avoid raising any red flags. It wouldn't take more than one call to dig up his past employment with The Bureau and piss off a lot of individuals who would love to get even for his betrayal.

"That's the reason why you can't go in and take her away." He turned away, reviewing his diminishing options. "You should have said that from the beginning. If the feds are watching her, moving her or getting anyone close to her will spook her agents. They could step in and take her anywhere they please."

"Now you get my dilemma." Carl rose slowly from his chair. "I need someone close to the girl, makin' sure she doesn't get snapped up by the feds and keepin' her alive until I can learn what she knows. I have assurances from the individuals who want her eliminated that you will be given a certain amount of time to learn her secrets, but I need you to move quickly."

"How long do I have?"

"Until the end of Robertson's trial. Two weeks, give or take."

"Damn it." Dallas dug his fingernails into his palms, fighting to suppress the assorted curse words he wished to spew. "Do you know how hard it is to set up a target and then gain their confidence? What you're asking takes months, not weeks. How can I get this woman to confide in me in two weeks?"

"In my experience, there are only two methods to get a woman to talk quickly—torture and sex. I leave the choice up to you."

He directed an angry scowl at him. "I don't torture people."

Carl narrowed his dark gaze. "I know."

Resignation settled in his bones. "I'll need to put some things in order and do a lot of digging on the woman. I can fly down to New Orleans in a few days."

Carl patted his arm in a fatherly manner. "You need to be in New Orleans tomorrow mornin'."

"Tomorrow?" He set his piercing stare on Carl. "Are you asking me or telling me?"

The composed older man reached into his jacket pocket and handed Dallas a business card.

He took the blank card and turned it over. It had a phone number scrawled on the back with a 504-area code—New Orleans.

"I'll make arrangements for one of my men to meet you at the airport. Just leave the flight details on the voicemail at this number."

Dallas crushed the card in his hand, already regretting his decision.

"I'll need to do my homework. Can you get me pictures, a list of friends, contacts, a work history, and family names? To build my cover, I'll have to—"

Carl silenced him with a wave. "You don't need that shit. I told her I was sendin' you for protection. She can tell people you're her new handyman."

Dallas hated not having control of any situation, and this one had already gotten way out of hand.

"I prefer creating my cover."

"Maybe next time." Carl sighed. "Gwen won't have anythin' to do with you unless you're recommended by someone she knows. She's well aware of the danger she's in."

"That will make it harder for me to get her to talk."

Dallas pressed his hand into his brow. His mounting misgivings had brought on a throbbing headache.

"There's not a whole hell of a lot to do in the middle of nowhere." Carl offered him a cheesy smile. "But I'm sure you'll come up with somethin'."

CHAPTER THREE

Dallas returned to his office, and the stench of stale coffee blended with the dusty, warm air compounded his irritation. To quell the fire coursing through his system, he kicked his desk chair. It didn't help. The problems Simon's death had created weren't behind him, not by a long shot. He settled his gaze on the wall where pictures of his former boss still hung, watching over him. He'd acted like a rookie and let Carl get the upper hand. If he wasn't careful, he could end up becoming his pawn. Dallas had to find a way to get ahead of the situation and win back his edge.

He retrieved his phone, scrolled through his contacts, and hesitated as he stared at Lance Beauvoir's number. Calling Nicci's uncle would open the door to memories he wished to forget.

I hope you know what you're doing.

Dallas dialed Lance's number, and as he waited, he sat at his desk and drummed his fingers.

"Hello?" The familiar gravelly voice sounded groggy.

"Get out of bed, you son of a bitch. You're going to do some digging for me today."

A heavy sigh came through the speaker. "Do you know what time it is? Why can't you put this in a text?"

"You're gonna get me killed one of these days, Lance."

"Let me guess," Lance grumbled. "Carl came to see you."

"A heads-up would have been nice." Dallas paused and lowered his voice. "You need to get me some information on this

Gwen Marsh woman Carl wants protected."

"Gwen's an acquaintance. I can tell you everything you need to know."

Dallas rubbed his hand over his chin. Lance was very well-known among gamblers, thieves, hustlers, and the social set in New Orleans. That he knew Gwen didn't surprise him—Lance knew everybody.

"Start at the beginning. Tell me about the ex-husband."

Female giggling erupted in the background.

Women—another thing in which Lance excelled.

"Let me get some pants on first." Lance's loud sigh filled the speaker.

Muffled voices dimmed as a door clicked closed.

"All right, the girl's gone downstairs. I can talk now."

Dallas scanned the bills and paperwork needing his attention, and shook his head. "Do you know the kind of position you've put me in?"

"Carl asked me if I thought you were good at what you did. I said yes," Lance told him. "He never mentioned anything else. What's this all about?"

"How well do you know this Gwen?"

"She's the daughter of Ed Pioth—another old friend. She kept her married name, Marsh, after her divorce for legal reasons. She and her ex share quite a few investments. Her ex is Doug Marsh, the big heart surgeon out of Houston—the one doing all the work with artificial blood."

Dallas eased back in his chair, hoping to relieve the knot forming between his shoulder blades. "Never heard of him."

"He's a real prick, but worships the ground Gwen walks on."

Dallas reached for a pen. "Then why the divorce?"

"Gwen insisted," Lance said, sounding disgusted. "Doug wanted the fast-paced city life, with his wealthy friends and backers for his research. When he got offered a prestigious job in Houston, Gwen stayed in New Orleans. She wanted a quiet life on a farm surrounded by her animals."

Dallas tapped the pen on his desk as he pictured days surrounded by flies, sawdust, and manure.

"What's she like?"

"Smart and has a great sense of humor." Lance's smooth, deep voice overflowed with admiration. "Her old man lives in New Orleans, not far from my brother. He had two sons with his wife, Nancy, before adopting Gwen. Other than a love of Johnny Walker Red and a great body, there isn't much more I can tell you."

Dallas sighed and put his pen down. "What about friends, habits, and preferences? Is there a man?"

"Been at least a few years since she and Doug split, but I've never got wind of a man. No friends that I know of—as I said, she keeps to herself on that farm. As far as the rest goes, you're on your own, Dallas."

The weight of his frustration dug into his neck and back. The rushed job, lack of proper intel, all pointed at the kind of sloppy work he couldn't tolerate from his specialists.

"I'll be in New Orleans in the morning."

"Let me know if there's anything else you need." Lance's matter-of-fact tone turned warmer. "It's good to hear from you again. Even if it is too damn early."

"Keep your phone handy just in case." Dallas turned to his computer screen.

"Will do." Lance cleared his throat. "Now if you don't mind, I have a lovely, young, and very naked woman waiting in my kitchen for me to make coffee."

He hung up, and Dallas's exasperation returned. He'd not learned enough to prepare for the assignment. He'd need more—lots more.

The walls closed in around him. This wasn't where he'd planned to be. This wasn't what he'd busted his ass to accomplish. Instead of overcoming the past, he'd been thrown right back into it.

"Shit!" He tossed his cell phone onto the desk.

"You still in a good mood." Cleveland came in his office door. "I saw that mafia guy leave. I figured the meetin' was over."

Dallas set his fingers on his keyboard, ignoring the imposing man leaning over his shoulder.

"I'll be leaving in the morning for New Orleans. Something has come up and I'll be gone for several days."

"N'awlins?" Cleveland put his face in front of Dallas, and his rumpled brow blocked the computer screen. "You said you was never goin' back there."

There were times Cleveland's overprotective nature drove Dallas insane.

"Is Stokes in yet?"

Cleveland arched away, frowning. "Yeah. Came in 'bout five minutes ago."

Dallas returned to his computer screen. "Tell him I need to see him. He'll have to keep an eye on things here."

Cleveland watched over his shoulder as he typed a name into a search engine connected to the FBI database. Images of an Asian woman, slender, tall, with long dark hair and intense brown eyes, appeared on the screen. He read from a list of stats giving height, weight, education, family background, finical stats, and arrests.

"Gwen Marsh?" Cleveland's decidedly deep voice rose higher. "What you gonna do with her?"

Dallas pointed at the woman's face on the computer screen. "You know her?"

"Know her?" Cleveland's throaty laugh filled the room. "She and her husband, Dr. Marsh, came to Greg Caston's gallery in New Orleans all the time. I heard Dr. Marsh hired a few of Greg's spies to dig up shit on some other surgeons giving him a hard time. Mr. Caston tried to date Ms. Marsh after the divorce, but she would have nothin' to do with him. Me and the boys got a good chuckle watchin' him chase her."

Dallas shook his head, blindsided by the information. "How in the hell do you know all of this? You were Caston's security guard, not his social secretary."

Cleveland's glower pushed his eyebrows together. "Don't you remember what a small town N'awlins is? Everybody knows everybody's business down there. As far as Caston bein' interested in the woman ... Hell, any man would've gone after her. Damn fine creature, if ya ask me. I don't have a thing for Asian women like some of my friends do, but yeah, I could see me takin' her on. But her mouth would cut any man in two faster than a sawed-off shotgun."

Dallas raised his eyebrows, impressed with his ability to ramble.

"Anything else you would like to add?"

Cleveland shrugged his mountain-like shoulders. "Nah, just wonderin' whatcha up to with Ms. Marsh?"

Dallas turned back to the computer. "That's none of your concern."

"Yeah, it'll be my concern if you get yourself mixed up with that woman."

Dallas didn't glance up from his keyboard, ignoring his warning. "What makes you say that?"

"You do know she's an animal freak. And you know what animals mean, don't ya?"

Dallas played it cool. "I have no idea, but I'm sure you'll enlighten me."

"Animals mean bugs." Cleveland's voice echoed throughout the room. "We both know how you feel 'bout insects. I'm just wonderin' how you gonna get near that woman without a can of bug spray in ya hand."

"I don't like bugs. So what? It's not going to interfere with my plans."

"Dallas, do you know what bein' on a farm in Louisiana means? Everythin' that can fly, creep, crawl, or walk will be out to eat your skinny ass."

Dallas pulled up a selection of pictures on Gwen Marsh. "I liked it better when you called me boss."

A few tense seconds ticked by, and then Cleveland's heavy footfalls carried across the room.

"I best be gettin' to the store and buyin' you some Deep Woods Off and shit, 'cause boy, ya gonna need it."

The *thud* of his door closing settled his jumpy nerves. He took advantage of the quiet and studied the photos of the woman, trying to get an idea of who she was. The image he had so far remained muddled, but he needed more to form a plan to get her to confide what she knew in him. The fuzzy shots taken by the FBI, her driver's license photo, and other pictures of her told him nothing he didn't already know—reclusive, distrusting, and probably spurred to hostility when pushed.

A knock then the *whoosh* of his door opening made Dallas spin around.

Ray Stokes rested against the doorframe, a smirk on his meaty lips. His double-breasted black suit, splattered with melting snow, was a much better fit than his waiter uniform from the previous night.

His dutiful assistant, Cleveland, appeared at the office door, nursing a mug of coffee. The way he glared at Stokes made Dallas cover his grin.

"Well, hello, Cincinnati," Stokes teased.

Cleveland peered down his nose at Stokes. "You'd better start calling me Cleveland or I'll drop your ass when you least expect it."

Dallas rubbed his forehead. "Boys, it's too early for this."

Stokes strolled into the room, passing Cleveland at the doorway. "Just lightening the mood. Your overgrown teddy bear looks as if he's ready to smother me."

He crossed to Dallas's desk, running his fingers over dirty blond hair. With his striking, sharp features and toned figure, he would have made any woman swoon. Probably one of the reasons Dallas put up with his hijinks. Stokes was versatile as a specialist, pleasing both male and female clients without hesitation.

Dallas checked his watch, his patience wearing thin. "Where have you been?"

Cleveland pointed a V with his fingers at his eyes and then directed his hand at Stokes in the universal, "I'm watching you" sign. He then closed the door.

"He needs to lighten up." Stokes pitched a flash drive onto Dallas's desk. "Here's the file you wanted from Garvey."

Dallas put his hand over the flash drive. "What about the girl?"

Stokes rested his hip against the desk. "I put a little something in her champagne to make her drowsy and then sent her home in a cab."

Dallas inserted the flash drive into his computer. "Any problems?"

"No. Once I got into Garvey's apartment, the rest was pretty routine. He kept the files on a private server I accessed from his home computer."

"I'll let the buyer know we have the information." Dallas opened the files stored on the drive and scanned them. "I'm going to need you to watch over things for a few days. I have to go out of town."

"Out of town? Last time you said that you quit the business."

Dallas yanked the flash drive from his computer, annoyed by the reminder. "That's not going to happen. I've made my choice."

"You sure you want to leave me alone with Chattanooga out there? He might shoot me."

Dallas rubbed the back of his neck. "Play nice with Cleveland. I don't need to be worrying about you two bickering while I'm away."

"Why are you leaving?" Stokes asked, his brow furrowing.

Dallas pushed away from his desk, unable to sit still any longer. "It's a job."

"Then send a specialist. You're not a field man."

Dallas quashed an urge to pace. "I have to go." He pointed at the newspaper on his desk. "It's a command performance."

Stokes picked up the paper. His gaze honed in on Carl Bordonaro's picture.

"Damn, and I thought I had problems." He dropped the paper on the desk. "And how do I contact you, if you're in the field?"

"By phone. Text if it's not vital, call if it is. No names. If it's about a specialist, stick to the code names we have on file."

Stokes shook his head while heading to the door. "I hope you know what you're doing. This place will be in deep shit if you get yourself killed."

He waited until his assistant had left his office, and then Dallas slammed his fist into the newspaper.

The outburst relieved the fury that had been building since Carl's visit, but it also warned he had lost his ability to detach himself emotionally from any situation. This was a bad sign. How could he head back into the field and get the information needed when he couldn't rein in his emotions?

Dallas stared at his fist still pinned to Carl Bordonaro's picture, then retracted his hand and ran it through his hair.

I'm in trouble.

CHAPTER FOUR

A jazzy tune from a brass band greeted Dallas when he set foot in the warm, humid airport terminal. The rest of the country might have been fighting the brutal, gloomy cold, but New Orleans managed to stay balmy. He made his way along the concourse, removing his jacket and rolling up his shirtsleeves.

A slow smile spread across his lips. He was back in the city he'd grown to love. Despite the outcome with Nicci, he still felt drawn to the quaint nonchalance of the people here. His memories of the city by the Mississippi River were a mix of bitter and sweet, but he still treasured them.

He strolled to the end of the terminal, and as he approached the security checkpoint, a familiar face popped up beyond the double glass doors.

"Dallas!" Lance Beauvoir shouted and held out his open arms.

He quickly took in the faces of those scattered around him, alarmed by the greeting. The last thing Dallas needed was for the entire city to know he'd returned.

He approached the dark-haired man in the dapper gray suit and held out his hand.

"I presume Carl sent you."

"I volunteered." Lance gave Dallas's hand a reassuring squeeze.

Despite a lifetime of excess alcohol, and a penchant for gambling, Lance Beauvoir appeared to be the embodiment of youth. He'd lived a reckless life by avoiding the responsibilities of the family business, Beauvoir Scrap Metal. His mischievous green eyes corrupted every woman he met, but his best assets were his plethora of connections. From mafia kingpins to police chiefs, Lance had saved Dallas's ass from a wide variety of troubles in the past.

"I've already gotten your car." Lance handed Dallas a remote. "I pulled it into the garage on the second floor, right in front of the elevators. It's the red Mercedes E550 Coupe. You can't miss it."

Dallas put down his overnight bag, inwardly groaning. It was typical Lance to get a car that attracted attention. Despite his notorious friends and questionable liaisons, the man knew nothing about being inconspicuous.

"I'm supposed to be a handyman." Dallas weighed the black remote, sensing his mission was off to a terrible start. "Besides an expensive car won't impress a woman who owns a farm."

"Horseshit. She's a woman. An expensive car always turns the ladies on." Lance patted Dallas's shoulder and nodded to the stairs ahead. "Let's get your luggage."

Dallas lifted his overnight bag and fell in step beside Lance.

At the top of the stairs, leading to the baggage claim, Lance halted and gave him a thorough once over.

"I know how you feel about coming back here. It can't be easy after everything you went through with Nicci. But shutting out what happened doesn't make the pain go away."

Dallas pressed his lips into a thin, angry line. "Shutting out what happened is how I get by."

"I've been where you are. I know how hard it was to watch your fiancée run off with your best friend, but she's happy. Even though she and David had to change their identities, and live as hermits, they've made a life."

He dropped his gaze, unable to look at Lance. "I don't begrudge them their happiness. I knew she loved David before I came along. When he reappeared, I saw how she was with him. She'd never lit up like that for me."

"Don't make the same mistakes I did—don't waste a lifetime preoccupied with what could have been when an opportunity for a different kind of happiness comes along. It may not be the happiness you wanted with her, but it will be the happiness you need with someone else."

Dallas wanted to laugh at the advice. "What has it taken? Five ex-wives to help you forget about the woman you loved?"

"You're not me, Dallas. Yours is that self-destructive kind of heartache—that's why you bury yourself in a world where no one knows you or gives a damn if you disappear."

Dallas wished he could argue that he was none of the things Lance described, but he'd always been that way. It was only under the spell cast by Nicci that he'd changed. Now, he was right back to being the hardnosed specialist. Or, at least, he hoped he'd slipped back into his former life. He wasn't so sure.

"Between Carl Bordonaro and the mountain of problems Simon's death created, there isn't a whole lot of time in my life for anything other than the world I've buried myself in."

"You never know—Ms. Right could be around the next corner, waiting to sweep you off your feet and send you headlong into your first divorce." Lance hurried down the stairs to the baggage claim.

Weary travelers plodded next to him while questions circled his head. The return to the city, Lance's arrival, and the job bothered him. It was as if he were heading into a trap with no means of escape.

Dallas emerged on the lower level and took in the black baggage belts sitting idle, the colorful posters of New Orleans destinations, and the pungent smell of diesel.

"There is one thing I'm curious about, Lance." He eyed the people standing around the baggage claim area. "Why did Carl insist I handle this job? Why not let me send a specialist?"

Lance gleaned the arrival boards posted above their heads. "After everything he did to hide Simon's murder, he figured you owed him because you're the one who got the organization. Carl prefers it when people owe him—he says it keeps them honest."

"So, I'm to be Carl's whipping boy."

"More like information boy." Lance chuckled. "Don't knock it. The street runs both ways with Carl. Prove he can trust you, and he'll always take care of you."

They walked up to the first empty belt, where a small crowd waited patiently for their bags. The nippy breeze coming from the tarmac on the other side of the opening cleared the disgusting smell from the air.

Dallas dropped his overnight bag to the ground. "That doesn't make me feel any better."

"Friends like Carl are a must in your business. I don't need to tell you that."

He took in the deserted carousels, wondering why the airport appeared so empty for a Tuesday morning.

"But it's my business, and I need to be back in New York running it. Not here."

Lance frowned at the immobile baggage carousel assigned to Dallas's flight. "If I were you, I'd be a hell of a lot more worried about how you're going to win over Gwen."

He removed his phone from his jacket pocket. "I have a few ideas on how to handle her."

Lance's voice turned cold. "You don't handle a woman like Gwen Marsh."

"What would you suggest?"

Lance leaned in and dropped his voice. "Seduce her."

His gaze flicked to his phone, anxious to get out of there. "Sex isn't part of the game plan."

A blast of beeping came from behind the far wall and the conveyor belt groaned, coming to life.

"Why not?" Lance asked loud enough to be heard over the din. "I thought that's what your kind did."

Dallas waited for the noise to settle before he replied. Five more minutes with the man and everyone in the airport would know what he did for a living.

"I don't need to have sex with a woman to get secrets from her."

Lance's face sagged. "Then what's the fun in that!"

"Gwen Marsh is just another assignment, nothing more. I'll get close to her and gain her trust."

"Her trust?" Lance slapped Dallas's shoulder. "Boy, are you in for a surprise."

A blast of cold air whipped around Dallas as he walked across the loading zone to the five-story garage connected to the airport terminal. Despite the warmer temperatures, the breeze cut right through him, or perhaps it was the constant edginess of being back in the city. Then again, Lance's antics weren't making matters any easier.

He stepped from the garage elevator, and the smell of exhaust and dust overpowered him. Their footfalls carried throughout the low-ceilinged garage as they made their way across the lane to the rows of parked cars.

A red Mercedes waited in front of them, gleaming under the yellow garage lights.

Lance beamed as he waved his hand over the hood of the car. "Nice, huh?"

Dallas dropped his suitcase by the passenger door. "You're going to get me killed in this thing."

"If you get killed, it won't be my doing."

Dallas glared at him over the top of the car. "Yes, it will."

Lance popped open the trunk with the remote and retrieved Dallas's suitcase. "If you're still mad at me about Carl giving you this case, don't be. This could be good for you and your business."

Dallas lifted his overnight bag into the trunk. "I don't see it that way."

Lance shut the lid. "You will."

Dallas didn't argue and went to the driver's side. Once in his black leather seat, he pressed the *start* button, eager to get on the road.

The engine roared to life.

"How do I get to Gwen's?"

"Her farm is about an hour from the city in horse country, outside of the town of Folsom." Lance plugged an address into the car's navigation system. "You'll need to head across Lake Pontchartrain and follow this thing until you get to her farm. It's on a dead-end road and surrounded by woods."

"That has tactical advantages and disadvantages." Dallas

examined the directions coming up on the display.

Lance opened the glove box. "That's why I got this." He held up a Sig Sauer P226 pistol. "There are three extra boxes of ammo in the trunk along with a Sig P229 for concealed carry purposes, in case you need it."

Dallas took the gun. He racked back the slide, inspected the chamber, and then felt the weight.

"Any idea what a woman like Marsh might keep in her house?"

"Probably a BB gun, knowing Gwen." Lance rolled his eyes. "She's a big gun opponent, despite being raised with two brothers who make Dirty Harry look like a model citizen."

Dallas sat back in his seat, going over what he knew about his target.

"The FBI's file on her was pretty standard, and her DMV photo didn't give me a lot of insight into her personality. Anything else you can tell me about her? Things I should watch out for?"

"She's got a foul mouth and scowls a lot." Lance pointed at Dallas. "Kind of like you."

Dallas put the gun back in the glove box. "I'm surprised you didn't try to sleep with her."

"I did, but she wouldn't have anything to do with me. She won't have anything to do with any man." He held up his hand. "And no, she's not into girls. I checked. When a woman turns me down, I usually like to find out why."

"And what did you find out?"

"The marriage to Doug Marsh was arranged to help Doug get into some pretty prestigious hospitals." Lance tossed his head to the side, appearing indifferent. "It seems the good doctor is into boys."

"How did you come by this information?"

"I made some calls yesterday when I found out you were coming. I got word from a guy who happens to be good friends with Dr. Marsh. He let slip Doug Marsh wasn't too happy when Gwen wanted the divorce—the guy is big time into his image. Probably why Dr. Marsh pays male escorts to come to his fancy house in Houston under cover of darkness."

The news gave him some new insight into the woman, but she was still difficult to pin down. Dallas hated evasive targets—they made for disastrous assignments.

"She went along with the marriage for what, money?"

"I doubt it. Her old man has plenty." Lance shook his head. "Gwen never appeared too serious about any man, until Marsh came along. As far as I can figure, she doesn't like people."

Dallas nodded as he considered her quirks. "That would explain her love for animals. They replace the people in her life."

Lance feigned a shiver. "Try not to go all psychological on me. Anything sounding remotely like psychobabble gives me the creeps."

Dallas put on his seat belt. "If you get anything else on her that I can use, let me know."

"I do have one other thing," Lance offered with a dubious gaze. "She's rumored to have killed her mother."

His surprised jolt added to Dallas's mounting reservations about the case. "I found nothing about it in my research."

"Gwen was six when Nancy took a shotgun and blew her face off. The crazy woman had her daughter help her get ready to commit suicide. For years, people thought Gwen pulled the trigger. But the police said a six-year-old couldn't have held the shotgun in the position needed to create the fatal shot."

Dallas scrubbed his face. "That's exactly the kind of shit I need to know—the things that make a person vulnerable."

"Gwen's not vulnerable. She's a grounded, practical, and very together woman. A lot more together than ... Well, a lot of women I hang out with. I guess something like that in your childhood either rips you apart or pulls you together."

"She's ripped apart." Dallas caressed the leather steering wheel. "The mother's suicide, the fake marriage, the lack of close relationships ... there's a pattern here. She's troubled, probably deeply troubled. That gets me an angle to use to get close to her."

"What? Therapy?" Lance chuckled.

"No." A charge of self-assurance blazed through him. "Empathy."

"What empathy? Your parents died in a boating accident— you were almost married twice to women you loved. And as far as I know, you have few friends and no pets."

Dallas was glad to see Lance had done his homework.

"It's all part of the cover."

Lance groaned and reached for the door handle. "Your cover? Let me know how that works out for you. In the meantime, may I suggest another approach?" He climbed out of the car.

"What?" Dallas asked, leaning over to look at him.

"Why don't you just let the woman get to know the real you? You'd be amazed how far you might get if you show your true self." He gave a wave and shut the door.

Dallas sighed, relaxing his shoulders, and then put the car in gear.

That's not how I operate.

CHAPTER FIVE

Brown pelicans darted across the top of Lake Pontchartrain and hovered close to his car during the long drive across the Causeway Bridge. The tedious expanse of road gave Dallas time to think about Gwen Marsh. The more he put his years of experience with targets against Lance's advice, the more confident he felt about his approach. Simon La Roy had taught him never to share the details of his life with any target. Such information was immaterial and could be detrimental to the job.

Unfortunately, Dallas had not heeded Simon's advice with Nicci. She'd attached to his heart like a clinging vine. One day he would be rid of her, but for now, her invasive tendrils still stung. The pain had lessened some, but not his grief. He would never open up to another as he had done with her. He was better off alone.

His phone rang from inside his jacket pocket. He eased it out and eyed the number.

"What is it, Stokes?"

"Crappy flight?" Stokes sounded his usually upbeat self. "Or is all that humidity and cayenne causing your pissy mood?"

There were days his assistant's constant cheeriness got on Dallas's nerves.

The white caps on the choppy waters of the lake caught his attention. "Something must be up for you to call and not text. What is it?"

"We have a situation with Sugar Hill," Stokes said in a

businesslike manner.

His grip tightened on the wheel. The code name was for one of his best female specialists.   If she had a problem with an assignment, he should be the one to handle it. And she would never reach out unless something had gone wrong.

"What is it?"

"The target is getting possessive. She wants to pull out early. She's going to get the information needed, but extraction might be messy."

Dallas longed to punch something. This was why he could never leave the office.

"How messy?"

"She's being followed by his security people around the clock. We should set up a getaway."

Getaway. It was a term used when specialists needed somewhere to hide after an assignment, especially one that went bad. Dallas had been setting up more getaways than ever lately. In a world where information was the new currency, targets became vengeful whenever they discovered the double-cross. Legal ramifications had never bothered Dallas—it was the deadly ones that scared him.

He did a quick mental checklist of the safe houses in his possession across the world—thirteen in all. They were small apartments set up in the less touristy parts of cities such as London, Paris, Dubai, Hong Kong, Amsterdam, Vienna, and even New York.

"Get her to the safe house in Berlin for a few weeks to lay low. That should take her off the grid for a while." He paused and ran through the usual procedure when setting up a getaway. "Notify Mac to get a new passport and ID. Deposit her fee into her Swiss account early, then she'll have cash. Tell her to use the secure email to check-in. I want to know she's okay."

"Will do." Stokes paused. "I have two new client calls for you this morning. Referrals. I still have to do backgrounds on both of them, but they're anxious to get something rolling. Keen sent you an email as well. He sounds insistent."

"Email me the names, numbers, and background checks on the new clients when you get them. I'll call when I can. Ignore Keen. He can wait." Dallas saw the end of the long bridge coming into view, grateful to get off the damned thing. "Did you get taps on the Marsh woman's phone?"

"All done, but no activity yet. Our guy says it's been dark since he started monitoring the line. Same thing with her computer—all quiet."

Dallas unbuttoned the top of his shirt. The woman's lack of communication was unusual. "Keep an eye on it. I want to know who she calls or emails."

"I will let you know as soon as I do."

He wiped the perspiration from his upper lip and turned a few knobs on the dash, wanting to shut off the heat. "Anything else?"

"Chicago is breathing down my neck about inventory and access codes for the penthouse."

Dallas finally found the right switch and hit it with his fist. *How could two grown men act like five-year-olds all the time?*

"You and Cleveland need to work together while I'm out of pocket. I need to know everything won't fall apart while I'm gone."

"Just get this job done quickly." Stokes sounded unusually grumpy. "This organization can't run long without you. You've got six specialists out in the field with three more prepping to go. Your specialists trust you and only you. They don't want me and Cape Canaveral covering their asses, and you know it."

Dallas cracked a grin, glad to see Stokes had a tipping point like everyone else.

"Just hold down the fort and put any new clients off until I get back."

"I'll do my best."

Dallas slowed the car as he came to the end of the bridge. "Call me with any emergencies and Stokes …" He tapped the screen of his car's navigator. "Play nice with Cleveland. I hate to think what he will do to you if I'm not there to intervene."

"I make no promises." Stokes hung up before Dallas could reply.

There weren't a lot of people he trusted in the world, but Ray Stokes was one of them. Dallas had often used Stokes as a backup when he'd been the second-in-command under Simon. Now he was the one in charge, and his responsibilities kept him up at night. Then again, a lot of things kept him up at night. But being on the road and worrying about his specialists escalated his worry.

Pine trees soon replaced the blue water, and houses dotted the landscape as his car maneuvered the expanse of highway beyond the long bridge. The woman's farm was close, and his fingers tingled with the rush he used to get when starting a new assignment. But Gwen Marsh wasn't a typical target, and how to get the information he needed from her remained elusive. Winging it was not something Dallas did, but he could think fast on his feet. He felt confident he would figure out something once he got a good look at the layout.

How hard can this be?

☙❧

Dirt from the narrow road that led to the farm wafted up in clouds around Dallas's car. The dust blocked the full scope of Gwen's farm, but when a stiff breeze blew across the hood, the land came into view. Tall trees surrounded rolling hills still covered in grass and seemed to touch the sky. He had left brown and desolate landscapes in New York and remained in awe over how winter barely grazed the South.

He scanned the road in and out, scouted for clearings leading to the property, and ways any would-be-thug with murder on his mind could enter the farm. A fence ran the perimeter of the farm, and an open metal gate marked the entrance. Not far from the gate, he spotted the black sedan.

He swallowed hard, curbing his spiraling apprehension. Carl had warned him about the FBI keeping tabs on Gwen, but he hadn't expected this. The car stuck out against the fence and surrounding scenery.

Courtesy surveillance means they don't give a shit.

In his days with The Bureau, being seen while on surveillance wasn't tolerated unless you weren't there in an official capacity, then the rule book went out the window. The team assigned to this car—there was always a team—wasn't there to protect Gwen, but to let her father know they had held up their end of the bargain.

He slowed as he neared the black sedan, trying to get a peek inside, but the tinted windows made it impossible to see the faces of the agents. He didn't stop to introduce himself. He wasn't there for them.

Dallas watched the black car in his rearview mirror as he drove through the gate. No one climbed out to stop him, which confirmed his suspicions—they weren't there to protect Gwen. Otherwise, he never would have made it on to the property.

This assignment felt so steeped in bullshit he didn't know how much more he could stand.

His gnawing irritation eased up when he approached the main house. The Acadian cottage surrounded by a long porch had an old tin roof that glistened in the mid-day sun. It sat next to a shady oak with thick limbs that reached for the green field around the home. Painted a dusty shade of blue and with french windows trimmed in white, the structure appeared well-maintained and freshly coated with paint. There was a garden with fresh red mulch set against the raised porch. Azalea and crape myrtles branches brushed against the porch steps. To Dallas, it appeared to be a modest home exemplifying the tastes of the reclusive woman who lived there.

He turned and gazed at a slight ridge, which was sprinkled with more thick oaks. A red barn set against the backdrop of a clear sky sat on the highest point.

Around the barn, square paddocks with white fencing contained horses that grazed and batted their long, sweeping tails. Dallas could make out a sloping pasture behind the barn where the sun sparkled on a large pond in the center. A shady spot of pine trees was on the side of the pond. The cleared land ran to a line thick with trees and brush that shaded the outline of the pasture.

An imposing, rectangular metal storage building, to the side of the barn, reflected rays of morning sun off its slanted roof. The red tractor parked in front of two fenced kennels still had a mowing attachment hitched to its rear despite the chilly weather.

A gravel-covered driveway took him to the front of the house. He parked next to an old, blue Ford pickup sitting under the oak's shade. The wraparound porch appeared inviting with a few potted plants and statues of forest creatures placed along the worn floorboards.

Then he spotted the sign hanging on the front door—*All Visitors Will Be Eaten.*

"Yeah, she's not the friendly type."

He reached for his door handle, but before he could get out, a deep throaty bark erupted. The *thud* of paws on his window kept Dallas from climbing out of the car. The black muzzle of a huge fawn-colored dog pressed against the glass, leaving streaks of slobber that had him recoiling. Dark eyes glared at him as if sizing him up for a meal.

Dallas instinctively reached for the gun in the glove box, but then decided shooting her dog might not make a good first impression.

The animal didn't growl or bare his teeth. Dallas waited for the beast to do something, but he remained, blocking his way out of the car.

Now what?

He eyed the passenger door, and was about to move to the other seat, when a shrill voice interrupted him.

"Harley!"

A woman in overalls, her silky black hair pinned in a ponytail and running the length of her back, approached the car. Her graceful stride and the ease of movement captured his attention as she went up to the dog. She didn't show any fear, and her no-nonsense demeanor intrigued him.

She grabbed the creature's collar and urged him away from the car.

"Sorry." She gazed in the window. "You can come out now. Harley won't hurt you."

He became momentarily mesmerized by her eyes. They weren't brown but hazel and reminded him of the autumn leaves.

Dallas opened the door while the mastiff sat quietly to the side, slobber dripping from his thick lips.

"Is he the one who will eat all visitors?" Dallas pointed to the sign on her door.

She inspected his black slacks and rolled-up shirt sleeves. "The sign is for nosy salesmen and Bible-beaters looking for a handout. Which one are you?"

The pictures he'd seen didn't do her credit. She had the oval face and beautiful velvety skin prized by Asian women, but her pink lips were fuller, her cheekbones more prominent, and the long curve of her jaw made him suspect she wasn't pure Chinese.

After everything he'd gathered about the woman, and her past, Dallas expected Gwen Marsh to appear cold and withdrawn. However, this woman seemed vulnerable, and her delicate femininity was nothing short of intoxicating.

"You must be Gwen Marsh."

Her disapproving gaze lingered on his features. "You're the bodyguard, Dallas August, right?"

"Bodyguard?" His sharp tone let her know how much he hated that word. "I thought I was supposed to be your new handyman."

She pointed at his car and raised her eyebrows. "In that?"

Dallas silently cursed. This was not how he wanted to begin with her.

"The car was someone else's idea."

"You're a little small to be a bodyguard. I thought you guys were all big and muscular."

"Oh, we bodyguards come in all shapes and sizes." He studied her guarded stance. "I was under the impression that—"

"Let's cut the crap." She stepped back, slicing her hand through the air. "You're here at Carl's insistence. I don't need protection and I sure as hell never wanted it." She motioned to the black car parked by the fence. "I've got all I need."

"Yes, I noticed them on the way in. But unlike the FBI, I plan on keeping you safe."

"I appreciate that, but …" She hesitated, looking as if she fought to regain her composure. "If we're going to be stuck with each other for the next two weeks, I'd say let's not kid ourselves. We're never going to be anything more than what we are—Carl Bordonaro's hired hands." She glanced back at the barn. "I wanted to put you in the guest apartment above the barn, but I guess you'll have to stay in the house with me." She faced him, her lips twisting into an unflinching frown. "I don't cook, do laundry, or pick up after you. Are we clear?"

Lance had been right. She had the audacity of a pit bull, and he wanted nothing more than to put her over his knee, but the angrier she got, the more beautiful she became. He could see why Lance found her so damned alluring.

"Fine." He went to the passenger side door. "I can cook for both of us."

"Cook? You? This I gotta see."

Dallas attempted to find the outline of her figure hidden beneath her baggy overalls. "I think we should set some ground rules before we continue."

Her eyes went wide. "Are you kidding?"

Dallas rested his arm on the open passenger door, carefully choosing his words. "While I'm here, I need to have you in my sights at all times. You're not to go off or leave without telling me first. If Carl wants me here, then he has a damn good reason for being concerned about your safety. I suggest you work with me." He reached into the car and opened the glove box.

Gwen Marsh let out a harsh breath behind him. "If this is any indication of what two weeks with you are going to be like, then I think we'd better …" She went quiet when he emerged from the car with the pistol in his hand.

She pointed at the weapon. "Is that necessary? I don't want a gun in my house."

Dallas held up the firearm. "If I'm going to protect you, yes, it's necessary."

He tucked the gun into his waistband and eased around to the back of the car. He'd dealt with a lot of resistant targets, but her hostility was unexpected. She already knew too much about who he was and why he was here, putting up roadblocks he would have to work hard to overcome.

He caught a peek of her standing to the side, taking in his every move. He didn't react, didn't play into her resentment. Dallas retrieved his luggage, then carefully placed the gun inside the overnight bag, mindful to keep all firearms hidden from her.

"I suggest you show me to my room, and then we can take a tour of your grounds, Ms. Marsh. I want to get the layout of the place in my head."

She hiked her hand on her hip, exuding the toughness to which Lance had alluded.

"Call me Gwen. I don't think I could stand listening to Ms. Marsh from you. Am I to call you Dallas, or do you have another name to go along with that fancy car of yours?"

The edginess she inspired had Dallas wishing he was back in New York.

"Dallas is fine." He picked up his suitcase. "If you don't mind, Gwen, lose the attitude. It'll make things a hell of a lot easier for both of us."

"The attitude is non-negotiable. If you don't like it, I suggest you sleep in the barn." She turned away and climbed the porch steps.

Harley came up and sat next to him, a muffled *humpf* coming from his muzzle.

He tugged his overnight bag over his shoulder. "Yeah, women are a pain in the ass."

CHAPTER SIX

The warmth of light-paneled walls, a yellow throw rug, and a shaker-inspired bench impressed Dallas as he stepped into the home. The essence of coffee and chicory teased him while the bright morning sun coming through the living room windows chased away the chill. The rays spread across the pine floorboards and to a plush beige sofa set before a mammoth stone hearth. Above the mantle was a charming ocean scene along a rocky shore. The detail of the work entranced, but the piece felt a little extreme for such a cozy, intimate room.

The glint of stainless hinted at a modern kitchen adjacent to the living room, and next to it, a dining area with a heavy oak table and chairs. A breakfast bar covered in white tile sat between the two spaces. A glass-enclosed room connected to the far end of the living room basked a desk, neatly arranged bookcases, and a few filing cabinets in warm sunlight.

Gwen waved at the straight, unadorned staircase next to him. "There's a guest bedroom upstairs on the right. You'll have a private bathroom. Go put your bags down, and then I'll show you around." She raised the edges of her mouth not so much in a smile but a sarcastic smirk. "Unless you'd like to frisk me or search the house for bugs?"

Dallas retrieved his suitcase, mystified by her crappy attitude. "I'll meet you back out on the porch in five." He headed up the stairs.

"Oh, and watch out for Lawrence," Gwen called.

Dallas stopped halfway up and turned to her. "Lawrence?"

"Your roommate. A rescued tomcat who thinks the guest bedroom is his. I'll leave you two to work out the sleeping arrangements." She hurried out the front door, appearing uninterested in his thoughts on the matter.

Good thing I sleep with a gun.

The paneled wall alongside the staircase had faded outlines where small frames had once hung. Dallas ran his fingers over the empty spots, wondering what the images contained and why they had been deemed unsuitable.

Perhaps they were pictures of her ex.

He rounded the second-floor and stared down a short hallway with two doors on each side and an open linen cabinet at the end. A runner with red flowers covered the floor and a painting of Jackson Square in New Orleans—the quality was exceptional— hung on the wall surrounded by a gold frame.

Probably from her days at Greg Caston's Gallery.

He pushed open the thick cypress door to his right, and the overpowering scent of lavender and something reminding him of cat litter wrinkled his nose.

He stepped into the bright room. A double window behind the queen-sized sleigh bed had lemon yellow curtains that matched a throw rug on the floor. Another painting of two women sitting in a French Quarter courtyard sat above an oak dresser.

A mound of gray fur reclined in the center of the yellow bedspread stirred. Dallas glared at the reason for the unpleasant smell in the room. The creature didn't move or respond, but merely opened one green eye and stared at him.

Not a fan of felines, and dead set on not sharing his room with one, Dallas marched up to the bed and plopped his suitcase on top of it.

"I got some bad news for you, buddy."

But the cat didn't budge. Even when Dallas pushed his case closer, the animal didn't move a muscle.

"Why don't you find another place to sleep?" Dallas nudged his suitcase into the cat's side.

Lawrence beat his tail against the bedspread, challenging Dallas with his one open eye.

Dallas shoved the cat across the bedspread with his luggage, ready to show him who was boss.

The animal got up and stretched its front legs as if it didn't have a care in the world. Then it smelled his suitcase and climbed on top of it. The cat circled before finding the perfect spot to rest.

Dallas glowered. "We're gonna have a problem, aren't we, you little shit?"

Lawrence yawned, not looking at all put out by the stranger, and continued his nap.

Dallas's patience teetered on the edge of exploding. He could tolerate Gwen's snippy attitude because she was a target and could be controlled, eventually. But the cat was another story. He'd encountered a few animals on assignments, all of which he'd ignored, but he'd never been forced to share a room with one. He would have to deal with the bothersome creature after his tour with Gwen. He needed to concentrate on her, flush out her weaknesses, and not let a pampered feline distract him.

He slipped the overnight bag's strap from his shoulder and tossed it next to the suitcase. "If you pee on anything ..."

Lawrence didn't acknowledge him, having become comfortable on top of the case.

Dallas hurried down the steps, cursing the cat, but along the way, a few more empty spaces on the wall caught his eye.

On the first floor, he stepped into the living room and scanned the walls. There were more empty spots by the hearth. Next to the sunroom, it appeared as if an entire gallery of framed photographs had vanished.

This was more than wanting to remove photos of her ex—the elimination of pictures appeared to encompass the entire house. He touched a faded spot on the wall in the living room, debating if the change was for his benefit. Gwen Marsh had secrets, but it was his job to uncover those secrets before someone else beat him to the punch.

☙❧

Dallas took in his surroundings, noting all ditches, high points, and the vast woods around them as they crossed a patch of tall grass on their way to the barn. He assessed every way in for an intruder—there were quite a few. In a perfect scenario, at least four or five of his men would have been assigned to the property, working in shifts to keep Gwen safe. With only him and two agents at the gate, there were several ways Gwen could be dead before he got what he needed. His only chance to keep her safe was to stick close and never let her out of his sight.

She said little as they walked, only pointing out structures when he asked about them. She didn't appear nervous or have the jerky movements of someone who knew their life was in jeopardy. If anything, she came across as composed and unflustered. Her plucky, almost bold, stride surprised him. He knew seasoned field agents who were more skittish on assignment.

Does she understand the danger she's in?

"There are fifteen-acres," she said and looked over her shoulder. "Ten cleared acres for the house, barn, and a shed, while the remaining acreage had been left undeveloped."

Dallas surveyed the tall trees and thick brush at the edge of the field. The shadowy covering, dense foliage, and access to the main road offered plenty of places for any would-be assassin to hide in wait. He would have to limit his concerns to the house and barn, making sure she never ventured into the woods without him.

"What about deliveries and workers?"

"Feed, hay, and animal supplies are delivered twice a month on Thursdays. Harold is usually the driver. The feed store is called Cole's—it's in Folsom, and I have a standing order with them. If I ever need extra, I notify them. UPS and FedEx arrive when there are special orders for medicine or other equipment. I have one worker who comes every week on Thursday to help with chores and do some minor repairs. Any other repairs or services are on an as-needed basis. If I make any changes to that schedule, I'll let you know."

He liked the concise way she'd answered his question, sticking to the pertinent details and not straying.

"What about family? Anyone I should be expecting?"

Gwen shook her head. "My brothers are stationed abroad and my father never travels out of the city. Since the trial started—"

"Yes, Carl told me about that." Dallas halted in the high grass, keeping his attention on the black sedan by the gate. "Your father is testifying for the prosecution."

Gwen knitted her brow. "You do know that Devon Robertson was one of Carl's biggest enemies. He hated the man."

He shaded his eyes, wanting to see if there was any activity in the car. No one had stepped out to check his credentials or ask questions. It struck him as odd, and very unlike FBI protocols.

"Devon Robertson ran a crime organization comparable to Carl's. And probably the reason Carl is delighted with the trial."

Gwen snickered. "My father sold liquor to Devon's gambling dens and brothels for years. He witnessed all the illegal operations firsthand. It was the reason the feds wanted him to testify. He's their key witness. My father told me it would create problems, but he assured me Carl would take care of us. I didn't figure on getting saddled with a security guard for the duration."

Dallas raised his eyebrows, entertained by her annoyed tone. "Would you prefer if it were only the feds assigned to keep an eye on you? Because I can promise with their lazy security, you'll end up dead before the trial is over."

She waved off his concern. "At least they stay in their car and don't bother me."

Dallas considered a quick rebuttal, wanting to remind her that her snarky comments were not helping either of them, but refrained. He needed Gwen to believe that the trial was the real reason he was there. She didn't suspect why Carl had hired him, and that would help him when the time came to get the information he needed.

He pressed his lips together, tempering his reply. "Perhaps when the bad guys show up, you'll be grateful I'm here."

He expected a wide-eyed stare or at least a modest amount of hand wringing, but she remained as stoic as ever. Her deadpan gaze never wavered. It was as if she didn't give a damn about her situation, or perhaps, he'd underestimated her ability to be intimidated. If she had grown up with a man like Carl Bordonaro in her family, she might have seen more than he could fathom.

Perhaps I've been handling her the wrong way.

"Why did Carl Bordonaro think you needed my protection since you seem to think you don't?"

She grasped the straps on her overalls. "Carl believes Devon Robertson will do whatever it takes to make sure my father stays quiet. That's why Carl insisted on sending a professional to babysit me instead of relying on the feds." Her attention returned to the black car by her front gate. "I was warned the FBI might put a surveillance team on me, but they've never asked me any questions."

"Yet," he added, lowering his husky voice. "If the feds put a tag team on you, they're going to talk to you. They're just waiting for the right moment."

"How would you know that?"

Dallas dropped his gaze to the long grass, concealing his bitterness. "Experience."

He was about to walk away when she touched his arm.

"What kind of experience would you have with the FBI?"

He glimpsed the black car. "More than I care to remember."

The churning in his belly spurred his desire to get out of the feds' line of sight. He hurried toward the barn, betting he'd left her curious.

Tell a target anything they need to hear to get the information.

It was the second rule Simon had taught him. The first being, don't get killed.

❦

Acrid manure, oaky wood shavings, and the sweetness of hay slammed into Dallas as he stepped into the shade of the barn. His footfalls resonated in the wooden rafters beneath the tin roof. Birds had created a jumble of straw nests woven into the thick beams above the central aisle. There were four stalls on each side, and at the end of the aisle, a rickety door secured with a simple hook had hay bales stacked in front of it. At the rear of the barn were more open doors to allow the breeze to cut through, sending a few stalks of hay and shavings bouncing along the floor.

He took his time down the aisle, peering into each of the stalls. A few of the red doors had hulled out scars where the wood appeared gnawed. Some had chew marks climbing the doorframes.

Gwen came alongside him, and several horses poked their heads out, sniffing him.

A palomino twitched its lips; a red gelding with a white strip down his nose pawed the ground when he saw Gwen. The sleek dark bay pricked up his ears and warily inspected him. Dallas didn't care for their skittish reaction to him. Animals were always a troublesome variant when on assignment. They seemed to instinctually know when someone was up to no good.

The breeze kicked up, and he got a heady whiff of the pungent odor. He pinched his nose.

"You'll get used to the smell soon enough." Gwen held out her hand to a tall, strawberry roan. "This is Fred. He came from a race track outside of Lafayette. He paced around his stall most of the night, and when race day came, he was too tired to run, so they shut the door on him."

He waved at a passing fly. "Shut the door? I don't understand."

Fred nuzzled her hand while she stroked his forelock.

"When a racehorse is no longer profitable, many owners shut their stall doors and starve them to death. When the animal is dead, they pay off the vet to say it died of undetermined causes. Then

61

they can collect the insurance."

He took a moment and looked at each of the horses, mystified by the cruelty.

"You mean they actually starve them to death?"

She played with Fred's muzzle, not appearing moved by his reaction. "Only a few horses win races, but no one ever asks what happens to the losers. The lucky ones are discovered by people like me. I get anonymous tips from caring grooms on the track when they have closed the stall on an animal or marked them for termination. I go in, offer to buy the horse, and haul them away. The owners don't care who takes the poor creature, as long as they can make some money off the deal. Every horse in here has been rescued from a race track. I fix them up and get them new homes."

His admiration for the sport of kings fizzled. "I never knew that went on. I thought they all ended up in a pasture somewhere." He swatted at another fly.

She arched an eyebrow at him. "No one knows what happens behind the scenes, except those of us who do rescue. Sometimes we can get them new lives as jumpers in the show ring, or find people willing to take a disabled horse."

Dallas went to the tall bay in the next stall. "Disabled? They all look pretty healthy to me."

"Yeah, they look good, but on the inside, they're suffering. These animals have been through years of drug abuse to increase their performance, and it has done a lot of damage to their kidneys and livers. I can't tell you how many horses I lose to kidney disease. There are no regulations on what trainers can pump into a horse, and no one gives a damn about the long-term effects." She came alongside him and lovingly stroked the bay's head. "Thousands of these beautiful animals die every day in the racing industry. But I guess the cruelty of people shouldn't be a big surprise to someone like you."

Dallas studied her with a critical squint. "Meaning?"

Her brow smoothed, but the animosity lingered in her gaze. "Carl didn't tell my father much about you except that you were the best at what you do. Was he talking about protecting people, or did he have something else in mind?"

He stepped back, sizing up her tenacious stance. "Define 'something else' for me."

"You look like someone more used to killing people than protecting them."

He waited a few seconds before responding. Silence could be as debilitating as torture when setting out to learn a person's weakness.

"If I were a killer, Gwen, we wouldn't be having this conversation."

She folded her arms and stared him down. "What did Carl promise you? Money, power, some fantasy fulfilled if you get me to talk?"

Dallas stepped to another nearby stall and kept up his aloof mask. "Talk about what?"

She came alongside him—her tone dark and icy. "I'm not an idiot. The FBI can protect me just as well as you. Carl Bordonaro wants something from me. Something he's sent you to get, so let's not pretend anymore. Why are you here?"

He'd hoped to win her over, and knock her off her high horse, but his attempt hadn't worked. She was tough, but he was a professional, and an expert in the game of lies.

"Carl hired me to protect you. If you have anything to say, then I suggest you call him. I'm not Carl Bordonaro's interrogator."

"But you're someone's interrogator, aren't you?"

He gazed around the barn, keeping his annoyance in check. "Show me the rest of your property before it gets dark."

Dallas swatted at yet another passing insect.

Gwen mirrored his piercing stare and masklike expression. "Careful the flies don't bite you. Horseflies leave nasty wounds that can get infected."

The thought of becoming lunch for a horsefly forced him to roll down his shirtsleeves and head for the barn doors.

"The storage and supply sheds are this way," she said over her shoulder. "But there's nothing in there but extra feed, a tractor, and an ATV."

"I need to see everything."

"There's the manure pile behind the shed. Do you want to check that out, too?"

He stopped and went up to her, already tired of her attitude. "Not unless you think the bad guys are hiding in it."

"If that were the case, then you could just smell them coming and shoot them with your fancy gun."

A pain popped up in his head, and he pressed his fingers to the bridge of his nose.

"Just show me the shed, Gwen."

Her brazen posture sagged. "Suit yourself."

She kept more hidden behind her prickly gaze than any other target he'd met, but he had tactics to overcome her resistance. Dallas considered Gwen Marsh his re-introduction into the world his specialists inhabited every day. The experience would help make him a better boss when he returned to New York—better than Simon La Roy had ever been.

CHAPTER SEVEN

The collection of horse-themed coffee mugs running along the top of the white cabinets fascinated Dallas. The rack for copper pots above the cooktop in the center island, the fancy Italian bread maker, Viking appliances, and Cuisinart on the counter made his inner cook tremble with excitement. The kitchen was warm, inviting, creative, brimmed with basil and rosemary, but nothing like Gwen. If anything, it epitomized his dream—a place he'd planned to own after retiring from the organization.

She sauntered in, no longer wearing her overalls but having changed into a pair of jeans. The distraction of her slender figure briefly took his mind off the kitchen.

"You must like to cook." Dallas motioned to her expensive knife set. "Not a brand one usually sees in people's kitchens."

Gwen rested her hand on her hip while her upper lip rose into a sneer. "Do you spend a lot of time in other people's kitchens?"

Dallas leaned against the kitchen island, not letting her get to him. "What do you cook?"

A guarded glint settled in her eyes. "Food, of course."

He stifled his knee-jerk reaction to challenge her snide comment. He drew in a frustrated breath and redirected his focus to her cooking skills and not her obstinacy.

"What kind of food? Italian? French? Chinese?"

She fidgeted, placing her hands in her back pockets.

If he didn't know better, he'd swear she'd gotten flustered.

"How do you know so much about cooking?" she asked in an almost sweet voice.

The change in her, the slackening of her stern features, heightened his wariness.

"I grew up cooking in my mother's restaurant."

She flipped her hair behind her shoulder. The way it caught the light reminded him of black silk.

"How did you go from helping your mother at the family restaurant to doing what you do?"

The question sounded genuine, but the short time he'd spent with Gwen made him believe otherwise.

"Are you interested in hearing about that?"

Gwen shook her head and cracked the faintest smile. "Not really."

She changed when she smiled. No longer icy and evasive, she warmed like the sun breaking through on a cold winter's day.

"I'm not a cook." She motioned to the appliances on the counter. "My ex bought me these things, hoping I would pick up the skill. When I left him, I figured there was no point in letting him keep them."

That sounds like something an ex would do.

She went to the refrigerator and opened the freezer door.

He stayed behind her as she sorted through a bevy of neatly stacked frozen dinners. Then she selected one and took it to the microwave.

"That's what you're going to eat for dinner?" he demanded, stymied by her choice.

She glimpsed the package of lasagna in her hand. "Yeah. What's wrong with it?"

Dallas couldn't fathom why in a room filled with a cook's

paradise of gourmet appliances she had settled on that.

"It's unhealthy. Full of sodium, and, from my experience, tasteless."

Gwen set the microwave timer. "As far as I'm concerned, it saves me time so I can get back to work."

He pointed at the frozen dinner. "I'm not going to eat that."

She waved to the pantry door. "There's a tasteless collection of canned soups if you prefer something else."

Dallas marched past her and opened the refrigerator. He retrieved the eggs, cheese, and milk from the top shelf.

"Tomorrow, we will go to the grocery store and restock your fridge." He carried the ingredients to the island countertop. "If I'm going to stay here, I'll require something to cook."

"What do you mean *we*? If you want to go to the store, then you go alone."

He selected a copper pan from the rack above the island and then aimed it at her like a gun. "Wherever I go, you go. Even if it means tying you up and throwing you in the trunk, we will be going to the store together."

Gwen didn't say anything. She ripped open the package, retrieved the plastic tray, and flung it in the microwave.

She kept an eye on her dinner as it cooked, tapping her foot while her cheeks reddened. "Fine. We'll go shopping, but I have to feed the horses first. Animals get fed before the humans around here."

Dallas grinned, delighted he'd won one concession. He had a long way to go with the stubborn woman, but it was a start.

"Your animals probably eat better than you do."

Gwen tried to maintain her angry gaze, but the more she stared at him, the more he could see a quirky smile sneaking across her lips. Finally, she broke out into a fit of laughter.

Her small nose crinkled. "Are you always like this? You're such an asshole."

A rush of relief came over him. She could relax and laugh, even if it was at his expense.

"I'm an asshole? You should take a look in the mirror."

"You're trying way too hard to push my buttons." She wiped her hands together and settled against the counter. "I know I come across as angry, but it's with my father and Carl for putting me in this situation. I've been venting my frustrations on you, and I shouldn't have done that. I promise to try and be more civil if you promise to stop scowling all the time."

He hunted for a hint of sincerity in her face, but instead, he became distracted by Gwen's beauty. The softness of her skin, the curl of her lips, and the depth of her eyes bewitched him.

Alarm bells went off in his head. He chastised himself for thinking of her in that way—for thinking of any woman in that way. He needed to keep his distance.

Dallas went to the stove, no longer interested in appeasing her. "I'm just doing my job."

The tension reigniting in the kitchen made him want to kick himself. He should have handled that better, but any woman who awakened anything remotely close to what he'd felt for Nicci would get shot down.

An irritating beeping erupted from the microwave, adding to his unease. Perhaps the past had affected his ability to do his job more than he cared to admit.

Before he could apologize for his behavior, Gwen's stony manner returned. She grabbed a nearby towel and took her dinner from the microwave.

"I have paperwork to do," she said with an abrupt clip in her voice. "If you need anything else, I'll be in my study."

She was almost to the kitchen entrance when he asked, "Bowls?"

Gwen paused at the doorway but didn't glance back at him. "Try the cabinet next to the stove. I think that's where they are."

"You think?" Dallas's sarcasm slipped out before he could pull it back.

She stormed away, and he shook his head, more confused than ever.

He explored the cabinets, and when he found a glass mixing bowl, he had to rinse off the dust. If this was her kitchen, she had not used anything in it for a while.

He wasn't sure how much of what Gwen had told him was fact, or something she'd made up to distract him. In the past, he'd had other targets baffle him to keep him from getting too close. But with this woman, everything felt different. Her facts didn't add up, and that frustrated him. Dallas hated being frustrated by anyone, especially a woman.

❦

Cold water trickled over his hands as he scrubbed the pan he'd used to make his omelet. The mundane chore allowed him time to think without being under Gwen's constant glare. Her resistance created concerns. She also wasn't the shy, reserved, homebody. He'd expected someone he would have to coax out of her shell, not a ballsy spitfire.

The floorboards in the living room creaked. He dried his hands with a towel and crept to the kitchen doorway, hoping to observe her. She had a receipt in her hand as she paced the living room.

He eased around the doorway. "Everything okay?"

A few lines deepened on her brow. "Just checking over a feed order."

He walked into the room, keeping his eye on her.

"You haven't gone paperless?" He stopped at the stone hearth and caressed the smooth wood beam mantle, the wheels turning in his head. "Wouldn't that make things easier?"

"Are you encouraging me to get on the computer?" She chuckled behind him. "My father would have your hide and mine. He ordered me not to use my cell or computer for the duration of the trial. I'm only to use the landline for emergencies. He believes the feds are monitoring my activity."

Her father's forethought, or perhaps Carl's paranoia, impressed him. Either way, it meant he wouldn't get any useful information listening in to her communications.

The floorboards groaned as she headed to the sunroom.

Dallas fondled the box of matches he'd found on the mantle as he searched for a way to look into her office without being obvious. A pile of books on the coffee table close by gave him an idea.

He went to the sofa and appraised the line of sight to her office. He could see her perfectly from this vantage point.

Dallas sifted through the books, intent on pretending to read. But when he discovered a familiar green cover in his hand, he froze and read the title—*Unfinished Business.*

It was the novel he'd watched Nicci write during their year together. Her tale of the search for a killer in post-Katrina New Orleans. She had based the main character, August Daniels, on him and wove how they'd met and fallen in love into the story.

His loss ricocheted through him like a bullet.

"Good book?"

Dallas shrank into the sofa. He hadn't realized she'd left the office.

Sloppy. Get it together.

He set the book down and willed his shaking hands to still. "I, ah, read it a while ago."

Gwen came around and leaned over the coffee table, perusing the book cover.

"Hard to think you would be interested in something like that. Figured you to be more of a true-crime man."

"I knew the author," he admitted.

Gwen crossed her arms, observing him. "Former client?"

A whirlwind of trepidation sprouted in Dallas. He needed to be careful.

"Yes."

She slid onto the sofa next to him. "How did you meet her?"

He waved to the books on the coffee table, formulating a story as close to the truth as possible. "In New York, when she was promoting her first book, *Painting Jenny.*"

"From the look on your face, I'd say you and Nicci Beauvoir were pretty close."

He tried not to laugh at her attempt to pump him for information, but a slight snicker escaped his lips.

"We weren't close. I helped her out of a tight spot and then she went on with her life."

"Shame you weren't around to save her during that Greg Caston mess in New Orleans last summer. It was horrible what happened to her." She eased back on the sofa. "I've heard Nicci had a lot of secrets—things she kept from those closest to her. Many believed that's why she died. If you don't share your secrets, they can kill you."

He took in her profile, his inner bullshit alarm blaring. "Perhaps not kill you, but they do have a price. Secrets should be shared, if anything, to relieve the pain they might cause."

"I agree," she said in a measured tone. "You keep something bottled up inside you long enough, and eventually it takes a toll. You're a man who keeps a lot locked away. By the looks of it, I'd say you're paying a hell of a price."

He got to his feet, and his voice turned dark. "You've got a lot locked away too, Gwen. Your mother's death, your husband's sexuality, should I go on?"

"Good boy. You did your homework. Sorry to disappoint, but my mother's death didn't leave me irrevocably damaged. She was a sick woman."

"I find it hard to believe that witnessing such an act didn't scar you. You were six when she shot herself. I don't care how self-assured you may pretend to be, somewhere inside you there's a lot of trauma associated with such a horrible memory."

She came right under his nose. "What are you going to do? Use my past to worm your way into my trust?"

"But you don't trust anybody." A smidge of admiration for her spirit arose in him. "I doubt you ever have."

"How are you any different from me?"

"I'm not." The flush on her cheeks let him know he'd gotten to her, even if she wouldn't admit it. "But in my business, not trusting people is the only way to stay alive."

"Your business? I'm still not convinced that you're just a bodyguard. I sense you have an ulterior motive for being here."

She's quite the interrogator.

He relaxed his stance, exuding calm. "Do you think all men have ulterior motives? Like your ex-husband, Doug? Why did you marry a man you knew could never be a real husband to you?"

Her eyes burned into him.

The thrill of finding a chink in her armor sent a blast of heated excitement pouring though his system.

"Where did you learn that little technique? Quantico?" she demanded. "Don't be quick to judge people you haven't taken the time to get to know."

She was so close, and he ached to discover if her velvety skin was as tempting as it appeared, but discipline kept him from reaching out.

"And how can I get to know you?" He motioned to the living room wall. "Is that why you took down your pictures? To keep me from learning more about you, or are you trying to hide something else from me?"

She eased in front of him and rested her hand on his chest, making him shiver.

"That's another secret you're going to have to pry out of me."

He wanted to recoil from her touch, but couldn't let her see how much it had affected him.

"Why am I the enemy? I've told you, I'm here to help and I can't do that if you fight me every step of the way."

She removed her hand. "I'm not the one who needs rescuing."

The chill left by the loss of her warmth reminded him of his job. He had to do more than participate in the constant back and forth. It afforded him little headway with her. He needed to figure out an approach to get through her thick armor plating.

She moved toward the stairs, but Dallas didn't want to let her walk away, not yet—not until he had put her on edge. He was the one in charge, and her life was in his hands.

He held out his arm, blocking her from getting by. "I've locked all the doors and windows downstairs. You're not to go outside unless I'm with you." He lowered his arm. "We can figure out who is rescuing whom in the morning."

He enjoyed her cold, hard stare. He surmised she didn't care for him being so thorough.

"I'm up before sunrise," she said in a low grumble.

"So am I." Dallas leaned into her and caught a hint of jasmine on her skin. "I'll come back down and do a sweep before I turn out the lights."

He headed for the stairs, eager to get away from her alluring aroma.

"I usually have a nightcap before turning in," Gwen called behind him. "I've got a bottle of Stolichnaya Vodka under the sink."

Dallas halted midway up the stairs. Had Lance offered her the tip about his favorite vodka? Probably. Still, it showed it wasn't utterly hopeless between them.

He turned and leaned against the railing. "I pegged you for a Johnny Walker Red girl."

"I am." She approached the steps with her shoulders set like she was ready to face a firing squad. "Just wanted to let you know it's there if you need it."

He tapped the railing, sizing up her intentions. "Lance tell you anything else about me?"

"Oh, I learned plenty, and not just from Lance." She passed him, heading up the stairs. "Goodnight. I hope Lawrence's snoring doesn't keep you awake."

She slowly climbed the steps as if taking her time to entice him with the sway of her hips. It was a bold move, but also pretty amateurish.

Gwen rounded the second-floor landing, and he slumped against the railing as if he had just run a marathon. She was more than a handful. He'd expected a wilting flower, avoiding him at every turn. This woman was a thorn bush, jabbing at him whenever she could.

He started up the stairs, vowing the next time he saw Lance, he would give him an earful.

CHAPTER EIGHT

Dallas lay in his bed, twisted up in his covers, unable to sleep. The intermittent chirp of night birds outside his windows occasionally drowned out Lawrence's snoring. The animal sounded more human than feline as it reclined on the pillow next to his head. He'd attempted to push it off the bed, but the cat went back to his spot, ignoring Dallas. He tried a pillow over his ears to block out the noise, but that didn't work. Eventually, he ended up counting off the gurgles, snorts, and varying degrees of sighs rambling around the room. And when he couldn't take it anymore, Dallas took his pillow, phone, and gun, and relocated downstairs.

With a blanket around his shoulders, he maneuvered the stairs in the dim light. On the first floor, he checked the lock on the front door once more before heading to the sofa.

But his new accommodations did little to help him sleep. Without the distraction of Lawrence's snoring, Gwen's comments haunted him. He reached for his phone and scanned his emails, eager for a diversion. Most were from Stokes, updating him on new clients, and a few specialists. One was from Keen, anxious to begin his case.

He debated calling Stokes to give him instructions regarding Keen, but Dallas couldn't chance getting caught. Instead, he headed to the kitchen, looking for something to soothe his restlessness.

He flipped on the lights and browsed the pot rack, the bread maker on the counter, and the expensive knife set by the sink. A kitchen usually reflected the personality of the cook who ran it, but the cozy room gave him no sense of the real Gwen.

One by one, Dallas went through the cabinets, searching for a clue about her odd habits. She had a fancy eggbeater, some intricate molds for cakes, cookie cutters, several cookie sheets, and a wide array of other culinary devices shoved into drawers or placed on shelves. For someone who preferred frozen dinners, Gwen Marsh sure had a lot of paraphernalia for baking.

He went back to the sofa, stumped. Perhaps she was attempting to hide her true nature. It wouldn't be the first time a target tried to distract him with false clues.

Dallas glimpsed Gwen's study, and a determination to outsmart her sent him hurrying into the room.

He flipped on the lights and found row after row of equine veterinary books neatly arranged on a set of bookcases. On top of the desk were invoices for feed and hay. Dallas got the locked file cabinet open with a paperclip and went through it. All the paperwork he found went along with running a small horse farm.

He shut the cabinet and sat in the desk chair, staring at her laptop. He lifted the closed lid and started the computer. The request for a password made him slap the top closed and spin around to the window. In the distance, the full moon illuminated the barn and storage shed. He toyed with the idea of going through them, but it would be too risky. He would have to bide his time.

Below the window, Harley lay stretched out on the grass, looking dead to the world.

Great guard dog.

Within seconds, Harley jumped to attention. Dallas scrutinized the darkness for what had spooked him.

A car had pulled up at the gate. The headlights were off, but the interior lights still streamed through the windows. Harley trotted toward it but didn't bark.

Dallas dashed back to the sofa for his gun, his muscles quivering with the thrill of the chase.

He made his way to the front door and stopped at the bottom of the stairs, listening for Gwen. Not a sound came from the second floor.

He eased the lock open and winced as the door creaked. Once out on the porch, the brisk night air hit his naked chest, sending a shiver through him.

Next time you go after intruders, put on more than pajama bottoms.

His senses came alive, taking in every trace of sound and flicker of movement as he climbed down the porch steps. He got a better view of the car, and his first thought was it was the night crew from the FBI sent to cover Gwen's house, but he had to make sure. His job was to protect her, and that's what he intended to do.

Dallas moved slowly and stuck to the shadows next to the house so as not to give the visitors any chance of discovering him.

The rays of the half-moon shone down on Harley as he waited by the passenger door, wagging his tail. Dallas listened for voices, and when he didn't detect anything, he eased off the safety on his gun. A slight breeze rustled the limbs of the oak tree next to the house, scratching the wood exterior. Dallas used the noise to cover his tracks. He became so attuned to the car, he forgot about the cold.

He snuck across a bit of open land between the house and the gate. Then, once safely in the shadows of the three-railed fence surrounding Gwen's property, he studied the occupants of the car and debated his next move.

They were only a few feet away. Dallas could rush the car, but then he could be picked off by anyone inside, leaving Gwen defenseless. He needed to act smart and surprise the visitors. He closed his grip around his gun, ready to aim for the head and chest—the fastest way to take out any threat.

Then movement made him hunker lower. Two men got out of the car. One walked over to Harley, carrying something.

Dallas took advantage of their preoccupation with the dog. He darted along the fence, heading to the car, his gun raised and his finger on the trigger.

With sweat gathering on his brow, Dallas slipped out from the cover of the fence, stuck to the grass to muffle the sound of his advance. He came up behind the men with his aim locked on the head of the closest intruder.

"What are you doing here?"

They spun around, hands already inside their suit jackets, going for their weapons.

A chicken wing landed on the ground. Harley snatched it up and trotted off to the side.

"Take it easy, buddy?" The man standing closest to the car kept reaching inside his jacket.

Dallas raised his gun. "I wouldn't do that. I'm the one asking the questions. Why are you here?"

"I'm Agent Taylor," the man by the car said, raising his hands. "And that's my partner, Agent Hickman. We're assigned to protect Ms. Marsh."

"I wouldn't call what you're doing protecting." The raw, animal survival instinct pumping through him slowed. "Who's the officer in charge of this case?"

Both men appeared surprised by his question.

Dallas corrected his aim. "Just give me a name."

Taylor lowered his hands. "Dan Wilbur out of the Washington Bureau is running this case."

"Dan Wilbur?" Dallas chuckled at the mention of his old friend. "Is he still over the Internal Affairs Division?"

"Organized Crime," Taylor replied.

Hickman walked around the car. "You asked for the officer in charge of the case and not our ID's, which means you're familiar with protocol." His friendly Southern drawl clashed with his cautious gate. "How long were you with The Bureau?"

Dallas lowered his gun. "Seven years. I also knew Dan is over Organized Crime. I just had to make sure you did."

Taylor took a step closer. "Who exactly are you?"

"Dallas August." He clicked on his gun's safety. "A friend of the family."

Taylor nodded to the house. "You the owner of that Mercedes?"

Dallas observed as Harley finished his chicken wing. "Does Gwen know you feed her dog?"

Hickman wiped his hands together. "I always bring the big guy a treat. Keeps him quiet."

These two men were nothing more than surveillance. Anyone charged with protecting Gwen would have shot Dallas without asking questions. The FBI wasn't there for her, but to see who had come to get her.

Harley went to Hickman, sitting at his feet and licking his lips, begging for more chicken.

"I'll call Dan in the morning to let him know I'm here." Dallas gestured to Harley. "In the meantime, don't feed the dog. I know you're here as a courtesy to Gwen's father, but she will have a fit if she finds out you guys have been bribing her guard dog with chicken wings."

He marched toward the gate, keeping to the grass and avoiding the sharp rocks on the driveway.

"If you used to be one of us, why are you doing private duty, August?" Taylor called.

Dallas showed the men his profile. "Like I said, I'm a friend of the family."

He walked through the gate, letting the moonlight guide his way across the grass. Dallas kept his focus on the darkened porch while indignation swirled in his belly. He'd participated in many stakeouts, but the lax attitude of the agents was the worst breach of protocol he'd seen. They didn't give a shit about Gwen and it showed.

Despite his irritation, the introduction had served a purpose. With the agents keeping her at arm's length, Dallas could live under her roof and not raise any suspicions.

That leaves me one less problem to worry about.

He climbed the porch steps, and the light went on over his head. Gwen must have been watching his conversation.

Dallas pushed the door open and found her casually leaning against the newel post, wearing a long blue robe. Her gaze scoured his bare chest. He expected her to blush or voice some protest about his half-naked body, but she never looked away.

"I see you met the boys," she said as he shut the door. "Taylor and Hickman work the night shift."

He flipped the deadbolt. "You could have told me that before

I went out there waving this around." He held up his gun.

"You didn't ask."

She turned to head back upstairs, but he grasped for her forearm as she reached the first step.

"This attitude of yours is starting to piss me off."

He yanked her back to him, and she stumbled on the step, tumbling into his chest.

"I didn't come here to get my ass shot off, and I sure as shit don't want any trouble with the feds." He tightened his grip on her. "Now, either you can start helping me by telling me everything I need to know, or I'm going to make your life a real hell."

She placed her lips temptingly close to his. "I'm not the one who wanted you here. If your ass gets shot off, why should I give a damn?"

"I've had just about enough of this, Gwen."

She lifted her mouth to his ear, letting her breath graze his cheek. "What are you going to do about it?"

The sweet perfume of her skin sent a tickle racing through his groin. He hadn't expected that reaction. She was meant to be a target and nothing more.

Dallas let her go and then pushed her back onto the steps. "Get back upstairs. I'll stay down here for the rest of the night."

Gwen motioned to the goosebumps on his shoulders and arms. "You might want to wear something a little warmer next time you go out at night. You'll catch your death."

Sweat beaded his upper lip as he watched her climb each step.

After she closed her bedroom door, he wiped his hand over his mouth and peered down at his pajama bottoms. The cold night air surrounded him, chasing away the warmth she'd created.

He marched back to the sofa, plotting how to overcome her infuriating obstinacy, but more disappointed with his physical reaction to her manipulation. That wasn't supposed to happen, not with a woman who aggravated the living shit out of him.

Dallas tossed his blanket around his shoulders and punched his pillow.

This is all I need.

CHAPTER NINE

Something wet traced the shell of his ear, and a strong, musky odor rose in his nostrils while damp fur brushed his cheek. Dallas bolted upright, disoriented and reaching for his gun. Then Harley licked his hand. The dog sat next to the sofa, looking as if he couldn't figure out why Dallas wasn't up yet. The dark still covering the windows and the ungodly hour on his watch—a little before five—brought a groan to Dallas's lips. Fully awake thanks to Harley, he threw off the blanket and put his feet on the cold floor. His duty done, Harley went clamoring into the kitchen.

Bastard.

Freshly brewed coffee coaxed him to stand. A twinge in his back almost dropped him to the sofa. He attempted to work out the stiff muscle, but to no avail, so with his hand supporting his aching back, Dallas shuffled toward the kitchen.

Gwen, wrapped in her long robe, sat on a stool at the island with a mug in her hand. The shine of her hair cascading down her back made him think of a river of black water glimmering in the moonlight.

He took a moment to admire her profile, her slender neck, and her exquisitely curved jaw-line. The heat from her touch the night before returned.

It might be better if I keep my thoughts limited to Harley's cold nose.

"Good morning," she said, sounding unusually chipper.

Dallas squinted at her, bewildered by her upbeat mood.

Instead of commenting, he made his way to the coffee pot.

"Not a morning person, eh?"

He retrieved a mug from the cabinet and faced her. "What did you do? Take a happy pill?"

"I just like mornings. Unlike some people."

Dallas poured the steaming liquid into his mug. "Try sleeping on your sofa and see how you feel the next day."

"Told you Lawrence snored."

He ignored her and sipped his coffee, enjoying the rich, bitter flavor.

She eased off her stool, holding her mug. "I'm going to change before heading to the barn to feed everyone."

He set his drink down. "I'll throw on some clothes and join you."

"I hope you packed some old jeans along with that gun of yours because you're going to help me this morning." She made her way out of the kitchen. "Might as well put that fine ass of yours to work around here helping out."

He raised his eyebrows. "I got the impression you weren't interested in having a man in your life."

She stopped at the doorway and slowly faced him. "I'm not, but that doesn't mean I can't look. I'm reclusive, not dead. Now don't get cocky."

She strolled across the living room, leaving Dallas perplexed.

He leaned against the kitchen counter and took another sip of his coffee. Yesterday, she was ready to cut out his heart and feed it to Lawrence. Today, she commented on his ass.

What had changed?

Harley whined from the other side of the kitchen.

The imposing mastiff standing in front of his empty food bowl implored Dallas with his sad brown eyes.

"Don't feed Harley," Gwen shouted from the stairs. "He got enough chicken wings last night from the feds."

Dallas pointed at the dog. "Busted."

Harley lay on the floor next to his bowl, and his heavy sigh filled the kitchen.

"Yeah, I know how you feel."

Dallas took one more strong pull of the coffee before leaving the kitchen to change. He had a sneaky suspicion it was going to be a very long day.

Sunlight crept across the barn floor, shining on Dallas's dusty shoes as he carried a bale of hay. He fought back a sneeze, not wanting to drop the bundle that he'd carted from the back of the barn. His every step labored, he maneuvered down the aisle between the stalls, peeking over the top of the flakes to find the stall door of a horse named Whippadu.

He made it to the bay's door and then had to struggle to shove the hay into the tangled web of netting. It took several attempts, and after more than a few curse words, he got the jumble of hay situated by the door. The itchy sensation on his hands, face, and arms became unbearable.

The magnificent bay watched his dance as he patted down his shirt and jeans, wiping off every last scrap of hay. Then, the gentle creature stuck his nose in Dallas's hair and retrieved a few stems that he'd missed.

He petted the horse's thick nose while it munched on the hay, enamored with his beauty and grace. He spotted Gwen pushing a wheelbarrow filled with feed, and for a moment, he envied her life. There was a peaceful rhythm to it—something he'd forgotten could exist.

"How did you get started in all of this?"

Gwen set the wheelbarrow down. "I always loved animals, especially horses. I began riding when I was a kid. It was the one thing I could be better at than my brothers." She scooped up a bucket of feed and came toward the stall. "So I worked my butt off, and trained morning, noon, and night. Within a few years, I became one of the top riders in the state. That's when I started learning about racehorse rescue. I found my first racehorse soon after I won my first state championship. By the time I was fourteen, I had four horses. At eighteen, I had homed those four and found eight more."

Her features softened as she petted the bay's neck and spoke softly to him. He liked seeing her tenderness.

"And after that?"

Gwen poured the feed into Whippadu's bucket, and the sweet aroma of molasses and oats rose in the air. "After that, I went off to college. In nursing school, I got out of riding completely. When I married Doug, I began riding again."

The obstinacy had melted from her voice, and with it, the iceberg between them shrank. He enjoyed this side of her—the caring and tender Gwen she kept hidden from the world.

"How did you and Doug meet?"

Gwen took in a shallow breath, and a faraway look crowded her eyes. "I was in nursing school. Doug was doing his residency in cardiology when I was in ICU. We started talking, and then he asked me out."

Dallas leaned against the stall door. "When did you find out he was gay?"

Gwen held the scoop against her chest. "On our first date. He said he wanted to be friends and that being with a woman ... Well, he'd tried it once, but it wasn't his thing."

"That would have been enough for most women to walk away." Dallas studied her face, searching. "Why did you stay with him?"

"That first night, after our pseudo-date, he walked me to my front door. My brother, Jackson, was waiting up. He was always the overprotective type and never liked Doug. When Jackson and Doug started shouting at each other, I grabbed my brother's arm and tried to push him back inside the house. Jackson shoved me away, and I fell hard to the sidewalk. Doug went ballistic and punched my brother in the face, breaking his nose." She raised her eyes to Dallas. "All my life I'd been fighting with my brothers, competing with them for every scrap of attention. For the first time, someone watched out for me. Doug started checking in on me, taking me out to dinner, and coming over to my house. We became the best of friends. I knew he never wanted anyone to find out about his lifestyle, but when he proposed marriage, at first, I was against it."

Dallas moved closer, relaxing his shoulders as he listened to her tale, hoping to encourage her to tell him more.

"What changed your mind?"

A *clunk* resonated beneath the rafters as she hurled the scoop back into the wheelbarrow. "I figured, why not? It got me out of the house and away from my brothers. Doug promised to take care of me. Raising a father and two brothers most of my life, I was ready to be taken care of."

He kept close to her. "What did your father think about Doug after he found out he was gay?"

"He always knew. So did my brothers." She crossed her arms and sighed. "My father isn't someone who readily accepts people into the family. He wasn't keen on Doug, made a lot of horrible references to his sexuality when we were first engaged, even tried to talk me out of the wedding, but he ended up liking him. Probably because he knew Doug could never hurt me."

He wiped his face. "What does your father know about me?"

Her gaze shifted to him. The light changed, and her coldness returned.

"Ed Pioth knows everything. He always knows everything."

Her voice had lost all vestiges of the softness he'd admired when she'd spoken of her horses. It reminded him of the iciness in his voice when he brought up Simon La Roy.

"The way you say his name, it's obvious you don't care for the man."

"Stop trying to pick me apart." Her jaw muscles quivered as she grabbed the wheelbarrow's handles. "You got seven more stalls to hay and water. Get to it."

The sawdust on the ground flew up around her feet as Gwen trudged the heavy wheelbarrow to the next stall. A dapple gray with a black nose stuck out his head in greeting and tried to stretch for the feed without success.

The moment between them had passed, and he was sorry to have lost it. It was as if she'd reached the threshold of what she could share with him, and like a door slamming closed, she shut down.

Dallas peered ahead to the stalls where empty hay nets waited for him.

He shook his head, preferring the biting New York cold to being covered in more itchy hay.

I need to give myself a raise.

CHAPTER TEN

Dallas sat by his open window in her pickup, enjoying the winding country back roads as they headed for the local grocery store. The rising sun shone on the pastures dotted with towering trees and occasionally broken up by swampy ponds. Herds of grazing cattle stayed behind wire fences with a few newborn calves nursing from their mothers. He also spotted paddocks of horses, their heads pointed at the road, munching on hay. The area had all the country charm a woman like Gwen would cherish, but to Dallas, the lack of cement and high-rise buildings remained disconcerting.

She hadn't been thrilled at leaving the farm, but Dallas had insisted. He had to get her out of her element to make her uncomfortable. Targets on edge usually turned to someone for comfort. That's where the specialist came in, offering support and building trust. Well, that was the theory, but like most tactics Dallas had attempted with Gwen, he questioned if it would work.

Her FBI team in their Black Crown Victoria remained at a discreet distance, assuring him that if anyone got too close, they would be there for backup. In case things got heated, he'd stashed his gun in his jacket pocket.

A small store with green awnings cropped up on the side of the road. Stands with fruit and vegetables had been set up out front, and a few cars dotted the parking lot. Dallas spied the sign— *Earl's Grocery.* The truck passed, and he questioned why she hadn't stopped there, but didn't bring it up. Maybe she preferred another place.

But when they drove by a bigger shop with a tall glass front and several cars in the parking lot, he confronted her.

"Why didn't you stop at those stores back there?"

Gwen kept her eyes on the road. "How am I going to explain you, Brewster, and Crawford to the people I know in those stores? Better to go somewhere no one knows me."

"Brewster and Crawford?"

"The day shift," she clarified, glancing in the rearview mirror.

Dallas pulled his brown leather jacket closer. "I hate to admit it, but your reasoning does make sense."

"There's a compliment hidden in there somewhere."

Her smile was slight, but it lifted her face.

Dallas raised his head to the dreary gray sky. "Don't get cocky."

The road expanded from one lane to three, and the traffic around them increased. She weaved through the cars, and Dallas noticed as the pickup trucks dwindled and the number of minivans and SUVs increased. They had left the country behind, and the tightly packed rooflines of subdivisions appeared over the treetops marking the outskirts of the city of Covington. Businesses popped up along the side of the road, first the smaller, local shops selling everything from tires to saddles. Then large chain stores crowded the landscape.

Dallas analyzed the packed parking lots around them. "We should go back to one of those smaller stores closer to your home. There are too many people here. You're vulnerable."

Gwen turned off the highway and into the entrance of a supermarket. "My truck, my choice of store."

Dallas adjusted the side rearview mirror to track the black car behind them.

"What if I insisted?"

Gwen kept on driving along one of the aisles, seeking a place to park. "I seriously doubt anyone is going to off me in the middle of a grocery store." She found a spot and pulled in.

Dallas observed as their tail eased into a spot right next to them. He patted the gun under his jacket.

"You're going to be the death of me."

He climbed from the truck and monitored for anyone coming toward them, someone staring, or anyone acting in any way that would raise his suspicions.

They walked across the blacktop, and Dallas stuck close to her side. Cameras set in the signposts around them offered some security, and he was thankful for the extra set of eyes.

He took her elbow, steering her clear of any people. His other hand, he kept inside his jacket on his gun.

She turned to him, her mouth set in a semi-pout, but she didn't fight.

He noticed the agents remained inside their black car instead of sticking close to their assignment.

I bet they were ordered to stay back. Assholes.

He'd give them an earful when they returned to the farm and demand an explanation. From now on, he would choose the destination and not leave anything to her discretion.

They walked through the automatic glass doors and a blast of warm air greeted them. Gwen seemed unfazed by the crowds, the overhead music, and the activity around them. Dallas stayed right with her as she selected a grocery cart. While she pushed the cart across the sleek white floors, he scanned their surroundings.

"It's just a store," she muttered next to him.

"I sometimes wonder if you realize the risks you're taking."

"My father and others have reminded me more than once, but I'm not going to let it run my life."

She browsed the selection of fresh produce, and when she zeroed in on the mound of pineapples, his inner chef shuddered.

She'd picked the prettiest piece of fruit. Classic mistake.

"Always smell a pineapple on the bottom to see if it's ripe." He selected two pineapples for her to test. "A ripe pineapple will have a sweet smell."

There was no argument, no flurry of caustic remarks. She put her nose to the base of each pineapple.

Gwen pointed to the dark one. "It's sweeter."

He set it in their cart. "You should learn the finer points of how to select produce."

She put her pineapple back. "Did you pick this up when you worked in your mother's restaurant?"

Dallas nodded as he perused an assortment of oranges. "She was a chef. She taught me about cooking, preparing food, and how using the best produce, meats, fish, and chicken, can add to the flavor of a meal."

Gwen pushed their cart along the produce aisle. "What do you mean she *was* a chef? What does she do now?"

He hadn't noticed the slip but was thankful he'd said it. Perhaps his past could help him with her.

"She died a long time ago," he told her without any emotion in his voice.

He made a point to stay by her side and not look at the other women shopping. It was another of the finer points of being a specialist—give your target a hundred and ten percent of you.

93

"What about your father? What does he do?" she asked.

He went to a bin of russet potatoes, deciding to stick with the truth. "He used to build yachts before he died." Dallas selected two brown potatoes. "My family has a yacht building business in Connecticut."

"Why didn't you go into the family business?"

"Who's to say I didn't?" Dallas bagged the potatoes and set them in the basket. "Perhaps I'm a boat builder, moonlighting as a bodyguard."

"You, a boat builder?" Gwen's light laughter floated in the air. "Look at you." She waved her hand down his figure. "Everything about you, from the way you look, to the way you move, screams intrigue and adventure. Some men are made for a quiet life of running a business and providing for a family. I could never see you settling for anything ordinary."

"I'm no different from any other person in here." He lowered his voice; her comments had touched a nerve. "Everyone wants an ordinary life, a safe life, a life filled with family. How can you think I don't want that?"

"I can spot the signs a mile away when someone is pretending to be something they aren't." She left the cart and came up to him. "The sooner you embrace what you are, the happier you'll be."

Dallas turned away and went to a box of mushrooms, keeping his face slack to discourage any further dissection of his character.

Gwen came alongside him. "Did I say something wrong?"

Dallas picked at the mushrooms. "No."

She leaned in front of him, demanding his attention. "For a man who doesn't say much, you sure do speak volumes with your body. You don't have to express pain for it to be evident in everything you do."

He would have turned the other cheek and ignored her if he hadn't felt like she'd smacked both already. "What makes you think I'm in pain?"

"The long moments of silence, your restlessness, and the way you sigh, like every breath is an overbearing weight." The right side of her mouth rose in a half-smile. "I'm a nurse, Dallas. I may not be able to tell a broken heart from a happy one with my stethoscope, but when I look into someone's eyes, I can see the difference."

For someone not in his line of work, he had to hand it to the woman—she could break through a well-planned cover faster than his best specialist.

He shoved a few mushrooms in a plastic bag, not even checking their freshness, and returned to their cart.

"Analyzing me isn't going to keep you from getting killed."

"I'm not trying to analyze you." She stepped back behind their cart. "I'm simply saying I'm here if you need to talk."

"That's not part of my job," he smoothly replied. "Besides, when this is over, you'll forget all about me."

Dallas stepped away, but she pushed the cart forward, keeping up with him.

"I never forget a fine-looking ass," she whispered.

"You sure are unusually flirty."

"Flirty?" She snickered, sounding coy. "Is it flirty for a woman to notice the attributes of a man?"

Gwen was far from a typical woman. But perhaps that was how he needed to be handled—like the rule and not the exception.

He took in another couple shopping close by while debating the ripeness of the avocados. "Can I ask you a personal question?"

Gwen eyed him suspiciously then nodded.

"When exactly was the last time you were with a man?"

At first, she didn't react, but then something in her changed, and her expression became a steely-eyed mask of irritation.

"I don't think that's relevant."

"No, it's relevant. Answer the question."

"I'm not going to answer that question. Not everything is about sex." Her fingers turned white as they gripped the shopping cart handle. "I take that back. For a man, everything is about sex. For a woman, not so much."

"You're a woman who tries to confirm her disappointment in others by seeking out relationships that will only hurt you in the end. You married a gay man to punish yourself, not to save yourself."

The sound of air rushing through her flaring nostrils gave him a brief thrill of satisfaction.

"Don't tear down my reasons for marrying Doug to help satisfy your smug condescension. What's your excuse for not being married, or could you not find a woman to love you?"

His smugness receded. "Now you're getting defensive."

"People who have something to hide get defensive. People who know that what they are hearing is the truth get angry." She got within inches of his ear. "Which one are you right now?"

He stopped and faced her, keeping his voice low. "I'm neither. I'm here to guard that lovely ass of yours."

"My lovely ass?" Her pinched features smoothed, and her wicked grin returned. "Any other parts of my anatomy you would like to critique?"

"When I find something, I'll be sure to let you know." He hooked his hand around the front of the cart, pulling it away from her. "Let's get this shopping done. And if you play nice, I'll show you how to pick out a great chicken."

CHAPTER ELEVEN

The sun already passed the point of midday, and a hint of warmth traveled through the pickup. The grocery bags rolled around in the back seat when Gwen made the turn off the main highway toward her house. The rocking motion relaxed Dallas during the last few miles. His eyelids grew heavy, but he fought to keep his focus on the side mirror and the black car following them. Perhaps Gwen's games had worn him down, or his sleepless night on the sofa had hindered his sharpness, but he couldn't give in to his weariness—not when the FBI team assigned to her was doing such a shitty job.

"I don't know why you couldn't let me get my frozen dinners," Gwen said as the dust from the dirt road rose around the truck. "I just don't see the point of cooking for just me."

Her voice roused him. "Why anyone who likes to cook would want to eat such tasteless food is beyond me."

Gwen pulled up to her gate. "Have you ever tried them?"

The black car followed them right up to the property entrance. He studied the sedan, anxious to get a glimpse of the agents inside.

"What did you say their names were again?"

"Brewster and Crawford," she said, stopping the truck in front of the gate.

He opened the door. "I want to have a word with them." He got out and looked back at Gwen. "Go to the house. I'll be along shortly to help you unload the groceries."

"I thought you said you didn't want any trouble with the feds."

He adjusted his gun and zipped up his leather jacket, hiding his concern. "I don't. I'm just going to introduce myself and make sure we're all on the same page."

He opened the gate and waited for Gwen to drive through before he returned his attention to the black car. Dallas strolled toward the car, taking his time. He was real damned interested in finding out why they had broken with protocol.

Two men in sunglasses, and wearing matching scowls, exited the vehicle. With muscles bulging under their gray suits, they were a lot more intimidating than the night crew. The slight breeze billowed their knotted black ties, awakening memories of days when he too had worn such constrictive attire. Their short-cropped hair mirrored his—it was the one practice he'd not given up since leaving The Bureau.

I'll bet these guys are the senior officers. Seniors always get the day jobs.

The man who had exited from the driver's side came up to him. Taller and teeming with attitude, he removed his sunglasses and held out his hand.

"I'm Mark Crawford. Dan Wilbur told us to extend you every courtesy."

Agent Crawford's round face and engaging green eyes lifted when he smiled, but his hesitant handshake came across as shrinking. Perhaps the jagged scar running the length of his right cheek had something to do with his reserved manner.

The other agent came around the car and offered a hand manicured to perfection. Unlike his partner, he oozed confidence as he flashed his flawless smile. He shook Dallas's hand with the ideal squeeze and eye contact. Dallas reciprocated, but would never trust someone who tried so hard to be perfect. The more practiced the image, the greater the violence underneath. Everyone had flaws, like Crawford, but this man had polished his out of existence.

"Brewster, Al Brewster. Senior agent in charge of this case." Brewster placed his sunglasses inside his jacket pocket. "Dan spoke very highly of you. He said you were one of the best when you were with The Bureau."

"That was a long time ago." The back of Dallas's neck tensed as he analyzed the man. "Is Dan the one who told you to hang back? I noticed you didn't stick with us in the store."

Brewster swept his gaze down Dallas's jacket and jeans in a manner resembling a disapproving parent. "Dan said not to crowd you. He figures you're here for more than the girl. Care to tell us why you ended up taking this job?"

Dallas's anger balled in his chest, and he drew in a sharp breath. "I'm just a family friend volunteering my time."

"You're in pretty tight with associates of Carl Bordonaro." Brewster kept a close eye on Dallas's reaction. "Any idea where we can find Bordonaro?"

"Not a clue." Dallas relaxed his shoulders, and a semblance of a smile, just enough to show that he enjoyed their curiosity, snaked across his lips. "How long have you two been assigned to Gwen?"

"Little over a week now," Crawford admitted. "Dan sent us down here from Washington right before the trial. We were told to keep an eye on her until the verdict is read."

"Then what? Are you taking her and her old man into witness protection? That's standard procedure after such a high-profile case."

Brewster looked at his shoes, hiding his reaction. "Her father has refused witness protection for both of them. We figure he's cutting a deal with Bordonaro."

He had not considered that variable. And if it were the case, it would put her life at greater risk.

Brewster reached into his jacket pocket. He pulled out a white business card and handed it to Dallas.

"Dan instructed me to give you this. He wants you to call the number on the back at your earliest convenience."

Dallas flipped the card over and looked at the slanted handwriting. Yeah, he'd be sure to call him. They had a lot to discuss.

"If you need us …" Brewster removed his sunglasses from his pocket. "You know where we'll be."

Dallas eased back toward the gate, keeping his eye on the two men. The business card added to the pile of bullshit he'd received about the entire operation. The slack FBI presence and Gwen's laissez-faire attitude came across as a game between two tentative contenders. Whatever their ulterior motives, he needed to figure out something before the bullets started flying.

With a determined stride, Dallas headed through the gate. He saw her waiting on the porch, and by the looks of her smirk and raised eyebrows, he guessed she'd expected a tense exchange.

"Interesting conversation?" she asked when he reached the porch.

"We chatted about the weather." Dallas motioned to the truck. "Let's get the groceries inside before we say anything else. They'll probably try to listen in."

She climbed down the steps. "Do you have any idea what they're after?"

He opened the passenger door. "Who they're after, not what."

He dropped his voice and leaned in closer. "They want Carl Bordonaro. Protecting you is just an excuse to get closer to him."

She stopped at the truck, and her color faded. "So I'm the bait."

"That's one way of putting it." He lifted a few bags from the truck. "If they were trying to protect you, they wouldn't be doing such a half-assed job."

"It would explain why Carl sent you." She pulled a few grocery bags from the truck, keeping her head down. "What about the trial?"

He handed her a plastic bag. "They don't care about the trial. They want Bordonaro. This trial is a golden opportunity to flush him out." Dallas nodded to the house. "When we climb those steps, I want you to laugh. Look like I said something funny. You're way too serious right now. They might suspect something."

She hid her smirk. "I'll do my best."

Halfway up the porch steps, she tilted back her head and gave out a loud, bellowing laugh.

"How was that?" she asked with a wicked gleam in her eyes.

Her audaciousness surprised him. "That should be enough to set them at ease."

"Best not to overdo it, though." She trekked across the porch. "They would get suspicious if I did it again. You're not that funny."

His confidence bristled. "I can be funny."

She waited inside the door. "I don't see it. You're more the brooding and quiet type. You know, shoot first and tell a joke later."

Dallas brushed past her on his way to the kitchen, irked by her appraisal. "There's a lot you don't know about me, Gwen."

"You'd be amazed by what I know about you, Mr. August."

101

Her snicker rose behind him.

He gritted his teeth and headed into the kitchen.

☙❧

The midday sun sent rays across the porch floorboards as Dallas relaxed in a wicker chair, keeping his eye on Gwen. She sat atop the horse named Whippadu, working him in a circle in front of the house. The proud animal arched his head, bulging the muscles in his sleek neck and kicked out his front legs in an elegant ballet of equine agility. Horse and rider appeared melded together, working as one. Their fluid movements entranced him.

Gwen was a different person on a horse. Graceful and almost serene, she seemed so at ease. She had him completely mesmerized, drawing his gaze like a stream running through a rocky glen.

Shame she doesn't share that connection with people.

He sat back, and the white card Agent Brewster had given him fell out of his jacket pocket. Dallas picked it up and read the number, debating.

Eventually, he dialed the number, and the muscles in his back became taut as if bracing for the tornado about to engulf him.

It took three rings for Dan Wilbur to answer, and when his deep, melodious voice came over the speaker, the indelible stain of his past with the FBI resonated through him like icy rain.

"Hello, Dan. It's Dallas August."

"Well, well … Dallas. How are you? It's been a long time."

How was he? He didn't even know. But Dan wasn't interested in Dallas's emotional state—why he was screwing up his assignment would be his primary concern.

"I, ah, got your message," Dallas said with an apprehensive

hitch in his voice. "I was rather surprised you wanted to talk to me."

The painful eerie silence that came through the speaker added to Dallas's misgivings.

"I never blamed you for Carol's death." Dan's voice tumbled out softly. "It was a stupid car accident caused by the perp you were chasing. I wanted you to stay on with The Bureau."

Dallas pictured their car rolling over and smelled the coppery odor of blood mixed with the pungent tang of gasoline. The bitter taste of fear returned when he saw Carol's pale hand cooling in his, knowing there was nothing he could do to save her.

"I couldn't stay. I didn't want to spend every day on the job thinking of Carol. I don't know how you were able to endure it."

"Hey, she was my sister, and I loved her, but she knew what she was signing on for when she joined the FBI. So did you." Dan's assertiveness dwindled. "I know how much you loved her, but I don't think she would have wanted you to leave because of her. And she certainly would have been disappointed you walked away to join that little cretin, Simon La Roy. When I got word that you'd signed on with that son of a bitch, I damn near shot my secretary."

"I'm sure you already know what happened to Simon." Dallas's irritation came through in his blunt tone. "News got around pretty fast about his death."

"Yeah, he ended up in some swamp outside New Orleans. Then a nasty rumor started circulating that you picked up the reins of his organization. Any truth to that?"

Dallas didn't bother to answer. Dan's fingers dipped into a lot of pies, and his sources would have filled him in on the transition.

"Would it surprise you to know I wasn't crazy about taking

the job?"

Dan's throaty laugh filled the air. "I know you, and I know a lot more about the events from last summer than you think."

Dallas warily glimpsed at the agents sitting in their car. "I'm listening, Dan."

"Your association with the whole Greg Caston murder-suicide set up was well-documented by my people. I know about your former fiancée, Nicci Beauvoir, and her new husband, David Alexander, and how they're living happily outside of the small town of Hammond under new identities. Identities you arranged."

That Dan had figured the entire situation out didn't bother him. He was thorough, and he would want something to use against Dallas later—that's what smart federal agents did. But Dan had been sitting on this information for months; bringing it to light now meant he needed something from Dallas.

"I know nothing about all the stuff you just mentioned."

"And La Roy?" Dan paused, and the sound of a neighing horse carried from the stables. "Hey, not that I'm complaining. One less asshole in the world is just fine by me. But now you're tangling with associates of Carl Bordonaro. I can only turn a blind eye for so long, Dallas. When you show up muddying the waters on my case, we need to chat."

"And Bordonaro is your bottom line—not Gwen or her father."

Dallas waited for Dan to break out in a rash of rapid-fire grunting sounds—something he usually did when cornered—but instead, he remained composed. Too composed.

"The case against Devon Robertson is pretty cut and dry thanks to old man Pioth's testimony," Dan admitted. "But that was the bone he threw us to put us off Bordonaro's scent. That was the man we originally wanted, not Robertson."

Dan's clipped tone told Dallas he wasn't pleased with the situation. He rubbed his chin as he put the pieces together. The only thing that made Dan unhappy was when his superiors were breathing down his neck.

"One bad guy is just as good as another." Dallas tapped the arm of the chair while the grip of mistrust squeezed his chest. "That's what you taught me."

"Except when the bad guy is Carl Bordonaro. This man is a big, big fish in the underworld ocean. To catch him would be a coup for my department and me. I would be able to pay back a lot of favors after that. Maybe even turn the other way when specialists in your organization perform certain felonies in the name of business."

Smugness, smoother than the best vodka, slithered through Dallas. It all made sense.

"Agent Dan Wilbur, is that a bribe?"

"For you, it's a piece of advice." Dan's tone became short and efficient. "Help me nail Bordonaro and I will make it worth your while."

"What if I like being alive?" Dallas pictured Dan's round cheeks reddening. "You know what kind of man Bordonaro is and what he's capable of."

"Call it a vocational hazard. If you want to go on with your little business venture without any interference from my boys, I would suggest you consider helping me out."

Dallas raised his gaze to Gwen. Dust billowed around the horse's hooves as she slowed the gentle giant to a stop. She swung her leg over the saddle with ease and then landed on the ground. The sound of her patting the gelding's thick neck echoed across the field.

The idea of telling Dan to shove his offer appealed to Dallas, but then what would happen to Gwen? He had to tread a fine line between keeping Dan happy and honoring his promise to Carl. And in the center of that tightrope teetered Gwen's future.

"What would I have to do?"

"Give me a time and a place where I can nail Carl Bordonaro. All I need is to find the slippery asshole, and then I can hand him over to the Justice Department. That's all I ask. Think about it."

Gwen walked back to the barn while Whippadu kept his head eased into the small of her back, affectionately nipping at her shirt as he followed.

Dallas's gaze stayed on her until she disappeared into the shadows of the barn. The slight jab of anxiety about keeping her in his sights urged him to his feet. The woman's safety was his duty now more than ever. He was all she had.

"I'll think about it." He moved to the porch steps. "But I make no guarantees."

"Don't take too long. And for what it's worth, I was looking forward to having you for a brother-in-law."

The line went dead, and Dallas stared at his phone. That had been unexpected. Carol had been the first woman he'd loved. When he'd slipped the diamond ring on her finger and asked her to be his wife, he'd pictured a modest house not far from Quantico, a desk job like Dan's, and a family he went home to every night. But fate had taken away those dreams and left him to find his way out of grief.

Dallas heard Carol's sweet voice in his head. *Dan's an ass-kissing toad.*

He chuckled to himself. Carol had been right.

106

Dallas hurried down the porch steps, eager to get to the barn and check on Gwen.

Along the way, he waved at the agents in their car, wanting to get a rise out of them. They didn't wave back, but he didn't care. Now Dallas knew where he stood in the food chain, and he was damned if he'd listen to Dan or his lackeys.

CHAPTER TWELVE

The chilly water from the tap trickled over his hands, sending a shiver up his back. Dallas had almost finished dicing the carrots on the cutting board in the kitchen sink, but his mind kept rehashing Dan's ultimatum. The more Dan's voice rolled through his head, the faster his knife hacked into the carrots, almost turning them to a pulp. No one threatened his people or his organization. He had shit on several higher-ups in The Bureau—secrets collected by specialists hired to topple men with powerful egos and fat wallets. He'd never divulged what he had but perhaps—

"Whatcha cooking?"

He spun away from the sink and halted, captivated by her. Her damp black hair tossed around her shoulders, and her jasmine scent eclipsed the stew he had simmering on the cooktop. The rosy hue on her cheeks accentuated their delicate curve. She licked her lips, deepening their pinkness.

The stillness between them seemed to go on and on. His throat grew thick as Dallas struggled to find his voice. Gwen dropped her gaze and turned to the cooktop.

He wiped his hands, coming out of his daze. "Ah, I'm making chicken stew."

Gwen moved as soon as he stopped next to her and went to the freezer. "Smells good, but I'll stick with my frozen dinners."

He slumped his shoulders, genuinely disappointed. "I was hoping you would want to join me for dinner. That's why I cooked."

Her brow scrunched as if debating the issue.

He retrieved a wooden spoon and handed it to her, wanting to sway her. "At least try it."

Dallas waited as she tentatively took a spoonful of stew, tinier than what you'd feed a baby, and dabbed her tongue into it.

He hung on her every facial expression. He might have existed in a world of peril and intrigue, but he fell apart when anyone disapproved of his cooking.

"It's good." She handed him the spoon. "Okay. I'll try a bowl of your stew instead of my usual frozen dinner."

"I bet it just killed you to say that." He hid his grin as he set the spoon on the counter. "You're the kind of woman who never likes to admit she's wrong."

"Oh, and I suppose you're the kind of man who admits when he's wrong?"

He picked up his knife by the cutting board. "Only when I'm wrong about people, which is most of the time."

"Who have you ever been wrong about?"

The list was longer than he cared to admit.

He returned to his chopping. "I've been wrong about damn near everyone I've ever met." He hovered the knife above the cutting board and took a few seconds to change the topic. "How about you? I know your marriage to Doug Marsh was difficult, but why haven't you found someone else to share your life with?"

Gwen reached across the cutting board and snatched a slice of carrot. "What makes you think I want to settle down with anyone? Maybe I don't need a man in my life."

He turned to her and frowned while she munched. "Being with your animals is a fulfilling life, and you don't need anyone. Is that what you're saying?"

She stole another piece of carrot. "People tend to fill up your life, not fulfill it."

"Explain that concept to me." He set the knife aside.

She scooted onto the counter, settling next to him. "People clutter your life. They bring all their drama, problems, and opinions with them. Soon, you don't know where your life begins and theirs ends."

"That's called sharing your life with someone."

She shook her head, and her voice hardened. "No, that's called marriage, and I don't recommend it."

"Your marriage wasn't real, so how can you be an expert?" He noted how her eyes darted around the kitchen. "Resenting Doug or even hating him isn't a sin."

She jumped from the counter. "Let me know when that stew is ready."

He stepped in front of her, not about to let her walk away. "Do you resent him for not being a real husband?"

Silence loomed between them. The drip of the faucet on the cutting board reverberated around the room like a car horn.

Gwen squared her shoulders. "You seem awfully interested in dissecting me like some frog in a laboratory. Why?"

He turned back to his cutting board, curtailing his eagerness. "You're getting defensive again. I was trying to be helpful."

"No, you're not. You're trying to get something out of me. Why don't you ask me what it is you want to know?"

He stabbed the knife into the cutting board, giving an outlet to his frustration. "I want to know why you live shut away in this world of yours, afraid to let anyone in."

"I thought your job was to protect me, not figure me out."

Her rapid breathing filled the kitchen, amusing him. She was anxious for an answer.

Slowly he faced her, formulating another lie—one he hoped would make some headway.

"I can't protect someone who keeps things from me."

Her arms fell to her sides as if too heavy to lift. "That street runs both ways, Dallas."

Gwen lowered her head and walked out of the kitchen.

Dallas returned to the sink and snapped up the knife, pissed his plan had backfired. He was about to return to his carrots when the blade slipped and sliced into his index finger.

Deep red ribbons of blood poured down his left hand and stained the cutting board and carrots.

"Fuck!"

Gwen stuck her head in the kitchen doorway. "What is it?"

Dallas grabbed some paper towels next to the sink, wanting to hide the blood. "Nothing."

When Gwen saw the red on the cutting board, she rushed to his side and pulled his hand to the sink. A gush of cold water came from the tap, and she deftly put his hand under the stream.

Dallas scrambled for a way to diffuse the situation. She was too close, smelled too good, and he wasn't the one who needed rescuing.

"I got it," he told her, pulling back his hand.

She never let go. "You did a good job on yourself." She examined the wound as the water ran over it, draining away the blood. "You're going to need stitches."

Dallas shook his head, a bead of sweat forming on his upper lip. "I don't need stitches."

She unwound more paper towels from the roll, appearing

uninterested in his refusal. "I'm a nurse, and I'm telling you, this cut needs stitches."

He slanted away from her. "No. I need some gauze and tape. Then it will be—"

She held the paper towels against his finger and looked him in the eye while she spoke in a steady, low-pitched voice.

"You're going to be working in a barn for the next two weeks. That cut could easily get infected, and then you would have a whole lot more to deal with than a few stitches."

A heaviness settled over him. She was right, and he would have to submit to medical attention if he wanted to avoid problems down the road. But letting her take the lead was difficult. He wasn't someone who allowed others to care for him. It made him vulnerable.

He slowly nodded, but his clenched jaw never relaxed.

"I've got sutures and a medical supply cabinet in my bedroom." She gave his shoulder a light squeeze. "Keep pressure on it while I grab the vodka."

Dallas clutched his finger. "What do you need vodka for?"

She ducked below the sink. "Painkiller."

Gwen held the vodka, and her probing gaze disappeared, her stiff posture relaxed, and the wariness deepening the lines of her face evaporated. Something had changed between them.

Dallas followed her upstairs, and when he arrived at her bedroom doorway, the first thing he detected was the smell of lavender, and then he wanted to laugh. The cerulean and white décor, complete with lace windows and a homey quilt-like patterned bedspread wasn't what he'd expected. The azure-tinted bulbs in the ceiling fan cast a dismal pall over the room.

"This doesn't look at all like you."

Gwen thumped the bottle on the nightstand, and proceeded to an antique oak armoire.

"I was in one of my experimental decorating phases." She opened the armoire. "Don't judge me by the décor."

He walked up behind her and perused the shelves of medical bandages, medications, surgical instruments, gloves, IV fluid bags, and syringes.

"Where did you get all that?"

She retrieved a bottle of hydrogen peroxide, hemostats, and a pack of black nylon suture.

"I collect it from different clinics. I have sick horses on my farm and get a lot of sick wildlife. Cuts back on having to call the vet out." She took the supplies to the bed.

Dallas clutched his finger as his gaze darted to the bed. "When was the last time you sewed up a human?"

"Two months ago." She rolled up her sleeve to reveal a scar along the outside of her wrist. "I caught my arm on a nail in the barn. I gave myself a shot of antibiotics and put in ten stitches."

Dallas ventured into the room and inspected her scar. "That looks more like a knife wound than a tear from a nail."

"How would you know the difference?"

He sat on the bed. "I've seen enough knife wounds in my day."

"Quite a profession you have there." Gwen eased the paper towels away from his finger, and a trickle of blood ran down his palm. "Guess I wouldn't be the first to tell you maybe you should consider a career change."

Dallas winced as Gwen probed his gash. "No, you wouldn't."

She reached for the bottle of vodka and unscrewed the cap. "You had a tetanus shot recently?"

"A few years back."

"Take a couple of swigs from this." She held out the bottle. "It will help ease the pain."

The last thing he needed was to lose his edge. "I'm fine. I won't need it."

Gwen picked up his right hand and placed the bottle in it. "I know you would like me to think you're tough, but I don't need any of your macho shit right now. Just drink the goddamned vodka."

Not wanting to argue with a woman about to jab him with a sharp needle, Dallas took two quick gulps while Gwen cleaned his wound. The burn of the vodka in his throat settled him. He took another big swig as she put on a pair of sterile rubber gloves.

She retrieved the black suture, placed the scissors on the bed, and reached for her hemostats. When Gwen kneeled next to the bed, she pulled his left hand under the lamp.

"This isn't exactly sterile, but I can give you a shot of antibiotics to make sure it doesn't get infected. Are you allergic to anything?"

Dallas shook his head, suddenly queasy. He didn't know what unnerved him more—the fact that she wanted to attempt to sew him up or that he was letting her.

Gwen set the suture needle in the teeth of the hemostats and the heat drained from his cheeks.

He slammed his jaw closed as she took his injured finger and pressed the edges of the cut together.

"This is going to hurt." Gwen pushed the needle through the flesh.

The pain wasn't sharp like a needle point or a knife. It burned better than a branding iron, and everything she touched felt scalded. His queasiness spiked as she worked the needle through his skin for the second stitch.

"Three more to go after this one."

Gwen's black hair shimmered in the lamplight, taking his mind off the torment.

"Where did you learn to do this?"

"Doug taught me. He wanted me to know how to suture properly in case he ever needed me to sew him up. He was always accident-prone."

"What else did Doug teach you?"

She stuck him for the third stitch. "He taught me about art, how to fly planes, how to select the best wines, to appreciate opera, and to be a little more patient with people."

He swallowed hard as his finger stung, but the change in her, the tenderness of her touch, encouraged him.

"Sounds like quite a guy. So why did you leave him?"

Gwen tied off the third stitch. "I was tired of pretending." She pressed the edges of the laceration together as she drove the needle into his finger once more. "I couldn't live with the lies anymore. I was tired of people asking when we were going to have children, knowing we'd never ..." Her voice faded.

He'd never noticed the refined quality she exuded. She'd hidden it behind her rigid bearing and menacing scowls. Her luminous skin and pink cheeks would tempt any man, but her stubbornness and quick mind would chase many away.

He banged the vodka bottle on the nightstand. "Why haven't you found someone you can have a real relationship with?"

Gwen tied off the fourth stitch. "You don't need any more stitches."

"You didn't answer my question."

Gwen sat back on the floor as her sigh echoed across the cozy bedroom. "I'm no good with people. Haven't you figured that out by now? I married a gay man because I thought I would be safe from getting hurt, but in the end, we both got hurt. I fell in love with him, and when I realized it, I walked away." She gathered her equipment. "I was stupid to marry a man I knew I could never have."

He held her wrist with his good hand. "You weren't stupid for marrying Doug. No more than I was when I fell in love with a woman who loved another man. But I thought, like you, I could make her love me. I couldn't like you couldn't change Doug."

Her gaze met his, and for a moment her lower lip trembled

It was the most emotion he'd gotten from her since arriving.

She wrenched free of his grip and grumbled, "We need to dress that finger."

After tossing her gloves into the trashcan by the bed, she returned to the armoire.

Dallas stood and walked up to her, getting close enough to touch her shoulder with his.

"Talk to me, Gwen. Tell me what you're thinking."

She kept her attention on the tube of ointment in her hand, measuring out a dollop on a square swath of gauze.

"I've said too much already." She dropped the gauze on his finger. "I should have never told you that."

She took the clear tape from the shelf and worked methodically, bandaging his finger.

He didn't like not being able to see her face. Dallas lifted her chin, bringing her gaze to meet his.

"I'm glad you told me."

She pushed his hand away. "What good would it serve for us to learn anything more about each other? Soon, you'll be gone. You said it before—I'm just a job."

He cupped her cheek and whispered, "You're not a job now. Far from it."

When he grazed her cheek with his thumb, her limbs turned to lead. She dropped her hands to her side and became like wood against him.

He debated every second as he drew closer to her lips. The moment he kissed her, a wave of tension passed through her body.

Then as fast as it had risen, the rigidity left her limbs, and she melted into him. He waited for her to pull away and slap him, but she didn't. She gave into him, parted her lips, and the sweetness of her invitation railroaded his senses. He lost himself in her, basking in their undeclared ceasefire. He knew it was stupid, a breach of his rules, and it could threaten the outcome of his assignment, but still, he kept kissing her.

This wasn't him—a man overpowered by a kiss. He was the one who called the shots and was well-versed in how to make her want him. But Gwen had turned the tables and shattered his confidence, upending his principles.

She tempted him to sink deeper into her trap by teasing his lips with her tongue. He gripped her hair, wanting to bend her to his will. Her head tilted back as his kisses nipped her neck, triggering his desire to give in to her.

What are you doing?

His inner voice pulled him back from the brink. He searched her face, her feverish bright eyes never blinked, never strayed from his.

A tingle, slight and slithering, eased up from his gut.

She broke away from their heated gaze and tossed the tape into the armoire.

"What was that for?"

Her voice came out flat as if she were attempting to hide her excitement.

He ran his hand through his hair, stifling his arousal. "Something changed between us. For the first time, you let me see the woman you keep locked away."

She straightened her back, and the last vestiges of softness disappeared.

"Why don't I believe that?" She took a step back from him. "I think you craft every action with intent. Sort of like a snake cornering a mouse."

His aggravation flared, and he raised his voice. "Who's the snake here? I wasn't the only person enjoying that kiss."

She wrung her hands and gravitated toward the open door. "Why don't we go downstairs and have some of your stew?"

Before he could stop her, she scurried out of the bedroom.

He punched the air. *That turned to shit real quick.*

Heady lavender closed in around him, chasing away her enticing fragrance, and leaving Dallas questioning why she'd walked out on him. The swirl of desire still burned in his gut. He needed something to chase it away. On the night table, the vodka in the bottle glinted in the strange blue light. He snapped it up with his injured hand, no longer thinking about his assignment, and took another long sip. The action set off the throbbing in his finger, but the alcohol easing through him cleared his head.

He sat on the edge of the bed. The kiss had not been what he'd expected. She'd responded to him, but he'd also been swept away by her. That wasn't part of the job. His emotions were never to come into play, but they had.

Now what?

Dallas leaned back on the bed, wishing he could close his eyes. But as he sank into the bedspread, his back hit something hard beneath the sheets.

He sat up and set the bottle aside. When he pulled back the bedspread, he discovered a Glock 17 semi-automatic pistol sticking out from under her pillow.

"That sneaky little …"

He replaced the bedspread and collected the vodka, hatching a new plan of attack. From now on, he needed to be tougher. He had to push her hard, and never let up until he got her to reveal everything Carl Bordonaro wanted. Then he could put her and this shitty assignment behind him and retreat to the safety of his penthouse for good.

CHAPTER THIRTEEN

Night had darkened the living room windows when an angry Dallas marched down the stairs and into the kitchen. The tang of his chicken stew greeted him as he walked up to Gwen. Seated at the island and hunched over a bowl of his stew, she didn't hear him come in. He had to act quickly while her guard was down.

He stopped, folded his arms, and leveled his cold stare on her. "When did you get the Glock?"

She set her spoon aside and arched her back, but never looked at him. "Were you snooping in my room?"

"No. I leaned back on your bed and found it. I thought you hated guns."

Her gaze wandered the kitchen. "My father gave it to me when I moved out here. He wanted me to have something for protection."

It sounded reasonable, but that nudge of disbelief continued. "Did your father ever serve in the military or with law enforcement?"

"My father?" She snickered. "Hell no. He spent his life ducking the police."

"Glock 17 is the gun of choice for a lot of law enforcement agencies. Seems odd he picked that particular gun." He took the next stool and sat facing her. "What else are you hiding from me?"

She pushed away her half-eaten bowl of stew. "Don't start that again."

He held her hand, gentled his voice, but remained adamant. "It's time you told me what's going on."

Gwen attempted to shake off his hand. "Nothing is going on."

Dallas squeezed her hand. "If you don't start talking, I can't protect you."

Gwen cocked back her free arm, and before he could stop it, her fist rammed into his shoulder, knocking him back.

He recovered quickly and wrapped Gwen in his arms to keep her from throwing another punch. She crushed against him, and her scent brought back the memory of their kiss.

He set his lips next to her cheek, and murmured, "You better start talking, Gwen. Tell me everything I need to know before one of us gets killed."

"You son of a bitch." She grabbed his bandaged finger. "Don't ever do that again."

He let her go when searing pain surged up his arm. It bent him over, triggering tears.

She'd gone for his most vulnerable spot. Any well-trained police officer, federal agent, or hired thug knew that to overcome an opponent, you always went for a debilitated or injured body part.

Gwen let go. Dallas grabbed his sore finger.

"Where did you learn to do that?"

"My father insisted I take self-defense classes growing up—a lot of them. Having two older brothers in the military helps. They're always showing me moves I could use to protect myself from men." She rubbed her hand across her brow. "I'm not keeping anything from you, Dallas. You know what I know."

He rested against the counter and stared at her. "I can't figure you out. One minute you're soft and vulnerable and the next you're using moves I haven't seen since my days at the FBI."

Her eyes rounded. "You're a former FBI agent?"

He wiped a trickle of sweat from his brow. "A long time ago, before I got into private security."

She rushed up and poked him in the chest. "And you accuse me of keeping things from you?"

"I didn't think it was necessary to tell you about my past," he argued.

"How can you kiss me and then tell me something like that?"

Dallas hunched his shoulders, unable to contain his smirk. "I was wondering when you were going to bring that up."

Her gaze darted around the kitchen as if looking for what to say. "Is kissing me part of your job?"

"You know better than that," he scoffed. "It just happened."

Shooting pain from his finger made him look down. A blossom of red stained the white bandage and appeared to be spreading. He shook his hand, attempting to soothe the throb, but it only made his discomfort worse.

She came up to him and inspected his dressing. "You shouldn't have grabbed me like that."

Dallas refused to look at her. Instead, he grabbed a towel from the counter. "Don't worry. I won't do it again."

She took his bandaged finger in her hand and touched the spreading patch of red. "I'm sorry. You and I have been at odds since we met. I don't want to keep fighting with you. It's not getting us anywhere."

Warmth radiated through his chest. It was the first sign he'd peeled back her thick layers of defense and gotten through to the woman underneath.

"Fighting with you isn't the problem." He admired her

delicate hands as she held his finger. "Getting you to trust me is."

She let go of him and took a step backward. "Perhaps you should get to know me first."

The comment released a sudden avalanche of doubt. The advice he'd received from others about getting to know Gwen revolved in his head. He wondered if all his counselors had been right all along.

"What would you suggest?"

She raised her chin, exposing her smooth neck, and then leaned back, seeming more at ease.

"A truce. We've spent more time attacking each other than actually getting to know one another. Perhaps you could stop trying to pick me apart like I'm a slide under a microscope."

Intrigued, he set the towel aside and folded his arms, waiting to hear more.

She went back to the island and picked up her bowl. "And I promise to try and trust you, a little."

He followed her to the sink and leaned against the counter, attempting to gauge her sincerity.

"If you're serious about me learning more about you, perhaps we should have a visit with your father. I could ask him about what he taught you about self-defense and guns."

She dropped the bowl in the sink. The *clang* reverberated throughout the kitchen. "That wouldn't be wise considering he's in the middle of the trial."

He smugly rested his back against the counter, having no intention of bringing her to the city, but remaining interested in her reaction to the possibility.

"Yes, but he probably has more agents around his house than you. We'll be perfectly safe."

She let out an exasperated sigh. "My father is one of those Neanderthal throwbacks who believe men should be men, and a woman's job is in the kitchen. So, unless you want to be grilled about why you like to cook, and what you like to shoot and kill, I would prefer to avoid him."

Dallas ignored the pain in his finger and concentrated on the information about her father. "But he taught you to take care of yourself, gave you a gun, self-defense lessons, so he can't be all that against women."

"Ed didn't know what to do with a daughter. He figured he would find me a womanly sport. Every hour of my life that wasn't devoted to school, my father expected me to spend at the stables."

"What did your mother say?"

"I don't know," she admitted. "He never talks about her. After she died, he took down every picture of her in the house, except for one. Then he never spoke of her again."

"Is that what happened to your pictures?" He motioned to the living room. "I noticed the empty walls when I first walked into your house."

She sagged against the sink. "Do you ever stop being suspicious?"

He pushed away from the counter. "No."

Gwen gripped the edge of the sink and squeezed. "We'll never get anywhere if you keep going on like this. And if you must know, I took down the pictures because I'm getting them all reframed and preserved." She glared at him. "Happy?"

He studied her—the slight color in her cheeks and the way she bit her lower lip. He wasn't convinced, but if he kept pushing, it could undermine her trust.

Dallas flipped the faucet in the sink and ran the water into her bowl. "Thank you for telling me."

She examined his bloody bandage. "I'll put some gauze and tape on your bed so you can change your dressing. Think you can do that before you run my picture through Interpol?"

He retreated from the counter. "Yeah, I'll be fine."

Without giving him another glance, she left the kitchen.

Well, that got me nowhere.

He went to the island and lifted the lid on the pot of stew. Suddenly, he wasn't hungry. His muddied sense of direction for the assignment had taken away his appetite. He carried the pot to the counter by the sink, replaying their conversation. She'd opened up and given him more, but things still didn't add up.

The vibration of his phone in his back pocket roused him from his thoughts. When he saw the number for his New York office, Dallas quickly took the call.

"What's up?"

"Can you talk?" Stokes's voice deepened.

Dallas peeked out the kitchen doorway. Gwen moving around in her bedroom caused creaks and the occasional groan in the living room ceiling.

"Make it fast."

"One of our specialists has gone missing," Stokes announced. "Lennox Hill was due to check in yesterday, and he isn't taking calls."

Lennox Hill. Dallas instantly knew who the specialist was. One of his men, and a genius at extracting data from computers, he'd been assigned to get close to a prominent industrial analyst stealing from hedge funds.

"Shit." Dallas rubbed his left hand across his brow and then winced when he hit his sore finger. "Have you checked emails?"

"Emails, voicemails, I even had the ox, Charleston, go over to his cover place, faking a UPS delivery. No sign of him."

"Where's his target?"

"He's due at The Met in an hour. Then has reservations for four at Marley's in the Upper West Side."

"Put a tail on him," Dallas ordered. "Then put a tap on his cell. Get a call into Wilson. If you get any word on where he is, send Wilson in. He's the best muscle we have for hostile extractions."

"You think it will get hostile?" Stokes demanded.

Dallas leaned against the kitchen counter, hating to use his extraction man before any specialist called for it. "Might just. Email me with any updates. And try any family members of his. When he gets in trouble, he goes to a sister's place in Philadelphia. The number is in his file."

"I'm on it."

There was a brief sound of papers shuffling.

"I've also got a few messages for you," Stokes added. "Mostly clients wanting to schedule meetings. There was one from an attorney, insisting you call him back."

"Send that one to our civil attorney, Ed McComb. He can take care of it. Anything else?"

"Yes, Visa called." Stokes softly chuckled. "They want to upgrade you to a black card."

Dallas shook his head. "Not interested." He listened as Gwen walked around on the floor above him. "I've been saddled with more debts than I can handle right now."

CHAPTER FOURTEEN

T he sun crept higher in the morning sky when Dallas settled beneath the shade of the porch, covered in sawdust and filthy from taking care of the horses. He slid into a chair, still processing what had happened the night before. The strange turn of events with Gwen had shaken his confidence. She was far more complicated than the spirited woman he'd continuously debated.

Harley came on the porch wagging his tail, probably ready for his breakfast.

Dallas rubbed the dog's neck, and then his attention veered to the black car by the gate.

I wonder if Dan has them watching me now.

Gwen came out of the barn on the back of a red roan. Her jeans and T-shirt boasted mucky stains from their morning rounds, and her hair remained pinned in a messy ponytail.

He eased back in his chair so he could watch her from the house. Harley settled at his feet, and then Dallas reached into his back pocket for his phone, ready to contact Stokes for an update.

"I couldn't call earlier. I was with the woman," he said after Stokes picked up. "Any news on Lennox Hill?"

"I found him at Presbyterian Hospital early this morning. He's been pretty badly beaten up."

Shit! Guilt pressed on his chest. "Any idea by who?"

"He was jumped from behind," Stokes told him. "He thinks his target got wise to him. The thugs who beat him were pros. They didn't take his wallet, keys, or phone, and said nothing while they broke two ribs and busted his right arm."

Dallas wished he could get back to New York to handle this, but he couldn't risk it.

"You got security on him at the hospital?"

"I've got one of our guys on it. He's staying low profile to see if the attackers show up to finish the job."

"Call Ed Jordan, the administrator at Presbyterian," he suggested. "He's a former client. Tell him I'm calling in a favor. I want our man looked after."

"Will do, but I need you back here." Stokes sounded uncharacteristically worried. "The clients are piling up, and some are getting antsy."

Dallas didn't need to hear that. He was sick enough about not being around to help.

"I'm working as fast as I can."

"How's the woman?" Stokes's playful curiosity came through the speaker. "Tougher than you anticipated?"

"Unfortunately, yes." Dallas raised his gaze to Gwen. "She's going to take some extra work."

She trotted the horse right by the porch. The scowl that cut across her lips was probably for him.

He wondered what he'd done to merit such a hostile glare—and if she planned on taking it out on him later.

"Extra work? I know what that means." Stokes's voice pulled him back. "Any woman that requires that much time to crack usually ends up in bed with you."

It had crossed his mind more than once. "That was the old me."

"I find that hard to believe," Stokes said with a snicker.

"Despite everything that happened with the Beauvoir woman, you're still the same old August." A phone rang in the background. "Fuck her and get out of there. I need your ass back in New York." Stokes hung up.

Dallas stretched out the cramp in his leg. "I knew I shouldn't have taken this gig."

The plight of his specialists and the ever-increasing list of things he needed to see to in New York churned in his stomach. He couldn't walk away from Gwen to take care of his business until he got the information Carl Bordonaro wanted from her. And if he did leave her before the assignment had proven successful, Carl would make sure his organization, and the people associated with it, suffered. He gritted his teeth, mystified at how his world hinged on the whims of a stubborn woman.

But then the softness of her lips when she'd kissed him came back in a heated rush. There was more to her, and he wanted to uncover that part she kept skillfully hidden, at least once more, before he had to walk away.

❧

After the long shadows of the afternoon sun cut across the field, she dismounted the last of five horses she'd ridden that day without taking a break. She rested for a moment against the horse and then led the palomino to the barn.

He didn't want her riding into the evening when the darkness would make her hard to see, so he descended the porch steps to tell her it was time to call it a day—even if she didn't want to.

"You should try punching a pillow," he suggested, entering the barn.

Gwen placed her English saddle on a stall door next to her. She didn't look at him but picked up a brush from a bale of hay.

"I don't know what you're talking about."

"You're angry. Try punching a pillow next time your emotions get the best of you."

Gwen ran the brush over the horse's golden coat. "Is that what you do?" She pitched the brush to the ground.

Simon La Roy had taught Dallas to find a target's weakness and exploit it, much like the tactics used by the skilled interrogators. Once a target felt supported, then they would reveal their secrets. All Gwen required was encouragement, and then he would have her right where he wanted her.

Dallas shoved his hands into his pockets. "What's bothering you?"

She picked up the brush, hiding her gaze. "You know what's bothering me."

"Me? Or are you still thinking about the kiss we shared?"

She sighed and rested her head against the neck of the horse. "How can you be so arrogant to think that one kiss bothered me?"

He chuckled. "Then it must be me."

A horsefly buzzed past. Dallas frantically waved at it, but stopped when he caught Gwen staring at him with her lips twisted into a wry grin.

His embarrassment was worth it to see her smile again.

"What's with you? Every time something flies by, you damn near have a seizure."

"I told you, I don't like bugs."

"But you probably hurt people, or even kill them, and you're bothered by a fly?"

He rolled his shoulders, uncomfortable with the leading

question. "I don't kill people."

The weight of her gaze turned his discomfort into an unbearable urge to get away.

"Are you in trouble?"

The question gave him pause. "Ah, no. What makes you ask that?"

"I saw you talking on your phone while I was working one of the horses. I saw you doing that yesterday, too. Just wondering if everything is okay?"

He cleared his throat. "I had to make some business calls."

"You don't text?"

He fixed his stare on her, counting off the seconds before he spoke. Then Gwen's eyes lost their daggers, giving him an opportunity.

"What about you?" He motioned to his phone. "How are you coping with not having one of these?"

She clutched the brush to her chest. "I manage. But, unlike you, I don't have a lot of people to call."

"What about friends?" he asked in a lackluster tone. "They might want to check on you."

"And what if they showed up here?" She faced the horse and brushed its neck. "What would you do? Think they're out to kill me and shoot them?"

"People coming here could put you in jeopardy. I don't want any surprises."

She stepped back from the horse and ran her hand over the brush's bristles.

"I bet you like surprises. Once you have someone figured out, they become boring and predictable. You like the rush the unexpected brings, don't you? Any man who prefers the boring and predictable wouldn't be doing what you do for a living. Is that why you've never married?"

The twinge in his back flared along with his exasperation. "Why I'm not married isn't important."

"You think you can interrogate me about my life, but I can't ask you the same questions? Guess again, buddy."

He groaned, a little louder than he'd intended. "I'm not married because what I do doesn't mesh with marriage."

"Then do something else."

He ran his hand over his hair, knowing he would get nowhere with her like this. He'd never met someone who turned everything into a war of words.

Yes, you have. She's just like you.

Dallas ducked his chin as the realization sent a chill through him.

His need to challenge her faded—even though the rush of blood in his veins longed for gratification. He had to calm down. Perhaps hacking into vegetables would soothe him.

"I'm going to start dinner." He turned for the barn doors. "And I'll be staying on the sofa from now on to make sure you don't go sneaking outside without me."

"Lawrence not working out as a bunkmate?"

He halted and debated what to say. Dallas needed to create the same unease in her as she generated in him, and there was only one way to do that.

"Let's just say he's not the one I'm hoping to share my bed with."

He waited for a few beats before he faced her, eager to see her expression.

Apprehension darkened her features. She dropped her head

and hurried to her saddle.

"I'm just a job, remember?"

He cocked his head. "You weren't a job last night when I kissed you."

Gwen lifted the saddle and, without glancing back at him, walked with a purposeful clip down the aisle, heading toward the tack room.

Dallas relaxed against the barn door, pleased. He'd found a way to break through her well-guarded walls by using her attraction to him. He pushed away from the door and shut down the pang of guilt gnawing at his gut. He'd done what was needed. It was the only way to get him back to New York before any more of his specialists got hurt.

CHAPTER FIFTEEN

The sun had dipped below the horizon as Dallas sat on the porch nursing his fourth cup of coffee while keeping an eye on the brightly lit barn where Gwen settled the horses for the night. His nervous instincts had him heading to the barn more than once to check on her. Every time he did, he found her putting a blanket on another horse. She'd refused his help, acting almost nervous around him. With nothing to do, he stuck close to the house.

Dallas tapped the side of his red mug, fighting the need for a nap—he made a mental note to dispatch Lawrence from his bedroom by any means necessary.

He stole glimpses of the black Ford at the gate. Crawford and Brewster had left a few minutes before the night shift arrived, leaving the farm unattended for longer than he liked. If he noted the gaps in surveillance, someone else might, too.

The shrill ring of his phone sent him back to the leather jacket draped over the chair arm. When he saw the number on the screen, he sucked in a fortifying breath.

"Hello, Lance."

"Just thought I would check-in and see how it's going with Gwen," his old friend told him. "Are you making any headway with our girl?"

Dallas smirked at Lance's usual candor. "You were right. She's a tough nut to crack."

"I hope you're getting some good food out of the deal." Lance chuckled. "Gwen may not be a lot of things, but she's a great cook."

Dallas slid his cold hand into the pocket of his jeans. "I wouldn't know. She won't cook for me."

"That doesn't sound like Gwen," Lance's voice became tinged with disbelief. "She'd cook for her horses if she could."

His mind immediately jumped to a rash of explanations about why she didn't sound like the woman Lance described. His nerves vibrated with a growing sense of distrust.

"Doesn't sound like the woman I know."

"Maybe she's distracted by the trial."

Dallas glanced at the gate—the black car sat poised like a snake about to strike. "The feds have got their tag team out here, but I'm convinced they're not here because of the trial."

"So our mutual friend told me." Lance cleared his throat. "He's been keeping an eye on you two. Making sure you're safe."

Carl keeping tabs on them alarmed Dallas. He'd been vigilant about checking for intruders. He would go through the house for cameras or bugs after Gwen went to bed.

"I've got something else you may want to pass on to our mutual friend," he said, his gaze still on the black car. "I've been asked to accommodate the feds with times and places our friend might appear. Otherwise, I might have certain problems come up in my business."

"I'll pass it on." Lance went quiet for a moment. "Watch your back out there."

"I'm keeping my eyes open."

Lance chuckled. "I was talking about Gwen."

Lance's laughter still rang in his ear as Dallas hung up.

The time had come to make his move and get the information he needed. He shifted his gaze to Gwen, who was still moving about in the barn.

There are a lot of things not adding up here.

☙❦❧

The tangy piquant of green peppers rose around him as the *chomp* of his knife echoed across the kitchen. The peppers Dallas diced were for the garden salad he'd prepare to go with dinner. With every stroke of his knife, his desire to call Gwen out on the discrepancies he'd encountered swelled.

The secrets she kept locked away meant a great deal to many, but mostly to him. His organization and the people he protected needed her to come clean.

Gwen sauntered into the kitchen, smelling of jasmine and having left her damp hair down. Her skin glowed, her jeans clung to her slim figure, and her ever-present smirk drove him insane.

"You sure you should be wielding a knife?" She pointed to his bandaged finger.

"Would you like to do it?"

Gwen raised her hands, acquiescing. "No, it's your dinner."

Her response flexed the muscles in his neck. He set the knife aside and watched her, appearing perfectly at ease as she lifted the cover of the skillet on the cooktop. The subtle hint of the chicken breast cooking in a white wine reduction wafted by.

He folded his arms as he sized up the best way to make her squirm.

"You could make biscuits to go with our meal. Since you're the baker, you'd be better at them than me."

Her face paled as she set the cover back on the skillet. "If my biscuits don't measure up to your standards, I'll be embarrassed.

136

Besides, there's plenty of food."

He didn't budge from the counter, but kept his focus on her, searching for any indications that she wasn't the woman she pretended to be.

"I don't see what the big deal is." Dallas pushed away from the counter and closed in on her. "Or perhaps you don't know how to make biscuits, is that it? Would you be more comfortable making the dressing for the salad?"

Her hooded eyes cast a dark cloud over her features. "You seem to be keen to try my cooking. You ever think the more you push, the less willing I'll be to prepare anything."

Dallas slinked closer, closing the distance between them, looking for any slip, any fault in her performance. He needed something to silence the damned doubt eating at him.

"Is there something you need to tell me?"

She jutted out her chin and arched her back, appearing as headstrong as ever.

The hum of the appliances around them sounded like thunder as he waited for her to crack.

A torrent of barking came from the barn and blasted across the kitchen. The dog's angry tirade took Dallas's focus off Gwen. He dashed into the living room and grabbed his gun from where he'd left it on the sofa.

"Harley!" Gwen darted for the kitchen entrance.

"Gwen, wait!" Dallas rushed after her, Lance's warning about being watched quickening his steps.

He reached her just as she touched the front doorknob.

The barking stopped. A yelp followed. Then there was silence.

Gwen pulled against his hand. "Something has got Harley."

"Or someone," Dallas countered. "And they're using him to

lure you to the barn."

Gwen took in a shaky breath. "What do we do?"

"We go together. You stay behind me."

Dallas let her go and flipped the safety off his gun. He debated about sending her back to the kitchen for his phone to call for back up. Then he remembered the agents stationed at the gate. If he and Gwen had heard Harley, they must have, too.

He opened the door and put his arm out to keep Gwen back. He stopped to listen for more noise coming from the barn. The moonless night was alive with the sounds of crickets, the hoot of an owl, and the far-off chug of a car racing down the nearby highway.

He stepped onto the porch and peered across the field at the barn. It was dark without a speck of light peeking through the closed doors.

Behind him came the stomp of footsteps on the porch floorboards. A rush of cold air brushed against his right cheek. A blur of a white T-shirt bolted past him.

Before he could stop her, Gwen bounded down the porch steps.

The air left his lungs. *Goddamn it!*

The woman's propensity for running into danger's arms would end up getting both of them killed.

His teeth locked together as he tore down the steps, determined to stop her before she reached the barn.

The faint light from the house illuminated her silhouette as she raced across the clearing. Damn, she was fast. Dallas hauled ass to catch up with her, wanting to get her back inside the house and lock her in a closet to keep her safe.

The black car remained hidden in the darkness next to the

gate. He considered letting off a warning shot to get the agents involved but feared the noise would only let whoever might be in the barn know they were coming.

She was ahead of him, running flat out with her arms pumping hard.

He had to push himself to catch up with her. He'd not expected that. She was in better shape than he'd figured.

They were almost to the barn doors. Dallas had to stop Gwen before she went running inside and got nailed by gunfire. He reached out, kicking hard to catch her, and right before she reached the barn doors, he snagged the sleeve of her T-shirt and yanked her back, sending her to the ground.

She remained stunned for a moment, but before she could lay into him with her usual verbal ferocity, he covered her mouth.

"Shh," he murmured in her ear. "Listen."

Gwen stilled. Her pounding heart lashed against his chest.

Muffled voices came from inside the barn.

A hush settled over him and he let his training take over. He reviewed the layout of the barn in his head, eager to find a way to sneak inside and assess the situation while keeping Gwen safe.

Dallas helped her from the ground and whispered, "Stay here. I'll go around back."

"I'm coming with you," she softly insisted, not letting go of his arm.

Dallas shook his head and pointed adamantly at the ground with his gun.

With a defiant scowl, Gwen let go of him and made a move toward the barn doors.

Dallas jumped in front of her and then waved her behind him. She nodded and thankfully followed his direction.

The damn woman is like a rhinoceros.

He didn't register the chill in the air, only the tickle of the high grass against his hand as they crept closer to the barn doors. When he reached the red-painted boards, Dallas made sure Gwen remained behind him. She kept low and hurried up to the side of the barn to meet him.

He pointed to the corner on the right, waiting to see if she understood his signal to follow the outline of the barn to the rear.

She stayed with him, keeping quiet as they made their way around to the corner. Dallas got a look at the side of the barn, heading to the rear doors. There was no one there.

He raised his finger to his lips, encouraging Gwen to be as quiet as possible.

The snuck along, staying low and hugging the shadows. Through the open windows above them, horses stuck their heads out as they passed. The animals sniffed their hair, one or two nuzzled Dallas's cheek, but none of them made a sound.

He arrived at the rear doors to find them left slightly ajar. He waited for Gwen to come to his side before putting his ear to the opening.

The raised voices of two arguing men came from inside.

"You find anything?" one disgruntled deep voice asked.

"Nuttin'. We need to go to the house," the other said with a slight lisp.

All he could hear was the two men. He didn't know if there were others hidden throughout the barn. Dallas silently cursed his stupidity for not alerting the feds. With two men or more, all probably armed, and only one of him and Gwen, he needed back up.

He put his lips to Gwen's ear.

"Get the feds. Tell them someone is here."

"You get the feds," she whispered. "I'm going to find my dog."

He wanted to throttle her. He couldn't leave her to get the agents because she'd probably try to rush the intruders alone.

Think. What can you do with what you have?

It was one of the first lessons he'd learned at Quantico—how to survive without any help from other agents. He'd been in similar situations before, and as a specialist, he'd always worked alone, but now he had to find a way to keep Gwen out of harm's way and himself from getting shot.

Footfalls from inside the barn alerted him that his intruders were on the move. He needed to have a closer look—assess the number of men, their weapons, and positions before he could figure out how to proceed.

Dallas turned to Gwen just as more voices came from the crack in the barn doors.

"We should check the upstairs, too." It sounded like the same man from before.

"I heard ya's the first time," the man with the lisp called out.

She leaned against the doors, listening.

He put his hand on her shoulder and pulled her back. He put himself between her and the opening in the doors to keep her from running inside.

The voices faded, and he peered through the doors.

He didn't see anyone but rustling came from the aisle that led to the tack room. Dallas debated what to do with Gwen. He couldn't leave her alone, so he pointed at the ground behind him, directing her to stick close.

They slipped through the narrow opening, making sure not to push on the doors and create any noise. A single lightbulb on a chain lit up the rear of the barn. Dallas searched for where they could take cover. To the side, a pile of hay bales offered the perfect refuge. He reached for Gwen while the sawdust kicked up around their feet, but as soon as he caught her elbow, she froze. He followed her gaze to the faint outline of the large dog lying in the shadows on the other side of the back entrance.

He shifted his weight, moving toward her, knowing what she would do. He went to put his arm around Gwen, but she shot out from his grasp and ran toward Harley.

Of all the stupid, fucking …

Three successive gunshots erupted. Dallas hit the ground, frantic to locate Gwen. The horses neighed, kicking at their stall doors. He crawled toward the hay bales, hugging the barn floor.

Dallas got down behind the bales and then peeked around the side, looking for Gwen. He found her, crouched against one of the stall doors a few feet away with her arm around Harley's motionless body.

He wiped his sweaty brow on his sleeve, but never took his gaze off her. He kept watch over her while the stench of manure added to the dryness in his mouth.

Then, stomping came from the back of the barn. The two men were coming back, and if he didn't do something soon, they would stumble on Gwen. He pointed the gun into the shadows at the back of the barn.

They came into the light from the single bulb. One man was heavyset with a wide girth and a .9mm in his hand. The man next to him was stocky, with a thick neck and a revolver carried loosely in his grip.

"I told you there'd be nuttin' there," the stocky man with the lisp announced. "It was probably a rat."

142

Dallas's heart hammered as they approached Gwen's spot.

She had tucked into a ball, attempting to hide behind Harley's body.

He would have to shoot one or both of the men before they found Gwen. It was the only way to give her cover to get away from her vulnerable position.

The men were almost right on her, so he had to act fast. Dallas eased out from behind the hay bales and crawled toward the back of the barn, placing himself between Gwen and the armed men.

He snuck into a darkened corner near the last stall, taking advantage of the shadowy hiding spot.

"You ready to hit the house?" the round man asked.

"Yeah, let's get what we came for," his friend replied.

Dallas aimed for the fat man's head. He calculated the amount of time he had to get off one shot before his companion came after him.

Make it count.

His finger on the trigger, he let out his breath to steady his hand, and squeezed.

Beams of bright light penetrated the darkness, bouncing around the aisle and revealing Dallas's hiding place and Gwen's.

"FBI, drop your weapons," a man's voice called out.

Dallas leaped into the open stall next to him, getting out of the way. He had just tumbled into the muck and manure when gunfire roared like thunder beneath the rafters of the barn.

Panicked horses screeched, rushed their stall doors, and kicked at their enclosures. Desperate to keep Gwen in his sights, Dallas stayed low to the ground and hovered close to the stall door. He found her across from him, covering her head and hiding behind the dead dog.

The agents ran past his stall, pursuing the men to the back of the barn and firing their weapons.

Dallas seized his chance. He launched headfirst from inside the stall and landed on his stomach a few feet from Gwen. He crawled toward her as the last crack of gunfire echoed throughout the structure. When he reached her, he threw himself on top of her, keeping her head and chest covered.

He stayed on her, his chest frantically rising and falling, but then the gunfire ceased. The only noise around them was the restless pawing, snorting, and kicking of the horses.

The acrid smell of gunpowder drifted past. He stayed on her as he counted the seconds. She never moved beneath him, her hands covering her ears.

"Ms. Marsh, are you all right? It's Agent Taylor."

The familiar voice carrying throughout the barn sent Dallas sinking to the ground next to Gwen as he rolled off her. The stampede of adrenaline in his system eased, cooling the fire in his blood, and expanding the world from the tunnel vision brought on by his fight or flight instinct.

Gwen moved out from her huddled position and immediately grabbed her left arm. She wobbled over to her side, and a flurry of expletives poured from her lips.

He hastily examined her arm. A patch of red spread quickly over the sleeve of her long-sleeved T-shirt. Blood stained his fingers.

The high of surviving the shootout evaporated.

"Taylor," Dallas shouted. "Get over here! Gwen's been shot!"

CHAPTER SIXTEEN

The metallic smack of blood mixed with manure assailed Dallas's senses. He tightened the tourniquet he'd made with his shirt to stop Gwen's bleeding. The sweat on his chest accentuated the cold air blowing through the open barn doors, but he didn't leave her side or take the jacket offered by agent Taylor. He kept his focus on the red staining her shirt, sickened by the gash on the left upper arm.

"You're damn lucky it didn't hit the bone." Dallas checked the wound once more, satisfied that the bleeding had ceased. "How in the hell am I supposed to protect you when you run into harm's way like that?"

The horses had settled, and the fluorescent lights lit up every corner of the barn. The only sign of the confrontation was Gwen's blood splattered on the sawdust.

Agent Taylor came up to their bale of hay in his lumbering gate, his lips pinched and deep lines, accentuated by dust, covered his forehead. His sweat-stained shirt and hollow rugged face reflected the severity of the chaos that had transpired.

"There's no sign of the two men. We found some bloodstains over there." Taylor gestured to several bales of hay stacked next to the tack room. "We combed the grounds, but they must have hauled ass out of here." He nodded at Gwen. "Ma'am, we should take you to the hospital."

Dallas admired the lanky man's attempt to talk Gwen into something he'd already brought up half a dozen times.

"No thanks." Gwen shook her head. "I've got everything I need at the house to see to it."

She removed Dallas's hand from the tourniquet and attempted to rise to her feet, but never made it.

The color drained from her cheeks, and she wobbled, perilously close to teetering over. Dallas was at her side, slipping his arm around her before she passed out. He set her back down on the bale, intent on making her see reason.

"We're going to the hospital."

She held his forearm while the pink slowly came back to her cheeks. "I'm fine."

His jaw ached from clenching, but short of dragging her to the emergency room, he saw little chance of convincing her.

Taylor knelt by the hay bale. "Ms. Marsh, please reconsider. You might need stitches."

She waved away his concern. "I can take care of that. I got up too fast." Her pained gaze wandered to the back of the barn. "I need to see to Harley."

Dallas had not been able to look at the corner where the dog remained with a single gunshot wound to his head. The sight of him made Dallas feel lower than dirt. Without the loyal companion's warning, the intruders might have surprised him and Gwen, and possibly killed them.

Dallas patted her hand, wishing he could think of something to say to ease her sorrow.

"I'll see to him later. Let's get you out of here."

The smaller of the two men, Agent Hickman, came around from the back of the barn, still carrying his sidearm at the ready. Broader and more muscular than Taylor, Hickman moved with a precision in his step that hinted at his wariness for their safety. He scanned the barn as he approached, and when he arrived at Gwen's side, he didn't acknowledge the blood on her arm. His cool detachment reminded Dallas of how he'd once been when he worked with The Bureau—blood was something you got used to.

Hickman holstered his gun on his hip, and his mouth spread into a strained line. "If you don't mind, ma'am," Hickman said with a smooth drawl, "I'd like to take care of Harley for you. We were friends."

Dallas's indifference for the agent melted. He'd forgotten about the late-night treats Hickman had shared with the gentle giant.

Gwen's lower lip trembled. "Thank you."

"You two need to consider relocating," Taylor advised.

Dallas gazed out the barn doors toward the lights of the house, agreeing with the agent. The farm wasn't safe.

"I'm not leaving my horses," Gwen sliced a willful hand through the air. "If they had no qualms about killing my dog, what will they do with my horses when I'm not here?"

Taylor ran his hand over his short-cropped hair. "Ms. Marsh, please. I can't guarantee your safety if you stay."

Dallas furrowed his brow at the agent. "Why don't you let me get her back to the house and fix up her arm? Then we can talk about this."

Taylor gave a reluctant nod. "But don't put this off. You're running out of time."

Dallas was well aware of the risks, but he needed to convince Gwen. He knew as long as her horses remained on the farm, she would never leave.

He put his arm around Gwen's waist and lifted her from the hay. "Let's see to that wound."

She leaned into him, and he helped her walk out of the barn and into the field. The glaring lights from the barn momentarily blinded him, obstructing his view of the surrounding land. He kept his hand on the gun in his waistband. Whoever had arrived at the farm was sure to come back.

The glare from the barn escorted them across the field, fading as they got closer to the house. The cold seeped under his skin, and he shivered as the glow of her windows appeared ahead.

"You sure you don't want me to carry you," he whispered halfway across the field.

"I'm a lot tougher than you think."

He reached the porch and allowed Gwen to hobble up the steps. He noticed she leaned on him less and less, growing stronger with every passing minute.

He got the door open, stuck his head inside, and did a quick appraisal while keeping his hand on his gun.

After a visual sweep of the living room, he quickly guided Gwen to the stairs, wanting her off her feet and in bed. But on the steps, she hesitated, swaying slightly against his shoulder—her pink complexion waned to a dusty gray.

Dallas didn't take any chances and scooped her into his arms. She nestled her head against his chest, the silkiness of her hair teasing his skin. He pulled her closer and headed up the stairs, taking two at a time, the small swell of panic getting the better of him.

Once on the second-floor landing, he went to her bedroom door and nudged it open with his foot.

"Let's get you into bed before you pass out."

❧

The stench of antiseptic and blood-soaked gauze in his hands prompted Dallas to hurry down the stairs. The fresh shirt he'd put

148

on did little to offset the lingering chill. He stepped onto the first floor, and the stillness of the house disturbed him. It was always tough for him to quiet the rush after any aggressive action, but after watching Gwen clean and bind her wound, the weight of uncertainty in his chest didn't ease, it intensified.

He took a step toward the kitchen, eager to dump the bandages in the trash and get the vodka to help ease Gwen's pain. Then a man's shadow moved out from the side of the porch. He couldn't make out who it was through the curtains covering the windows.

The nervous butterflies in his head buzzed with a number of possibilities—all of them bad. He tossed the smelly gauze to the bottom step and then reached for the gun still tucked into his jeans.

Agent Taylor stepped into the light and peeked in the glass of the front door. He saw Dallas and crooked his finger.

Dallas lowered his gun and opened the door. Before going outside, he peered up the stairs to make sure Gwen had stayed in her room.

He walked onto the porch. It had gotten colder, or perhaps it was him. Why couldn't he shake the chill haunting him?

He shut the front door before he spoke. "This was Robertson's doing. He wanted to put pressure on Ed Pioth for testifying."

Agent Taylor scratched his head, the gun holstered at his side, gleaming in the porch light.

"We can't be sure of that."

Dallas went to the door window, monitoring for any sign of Gwen. "Do you have a place we can go?"

"We're not here in an official capacity. This is a courtesy. I can't offer you a safe house unless Dan Wilbur clears it."

Dallas tucked his gun into his waistband, imagining Dan's

explosive reaction to the request. "And knowing Dan, he won't clear it."

Taylor rubbed his chin, appearing lost in thought. "Maybe I can come up with an alternative. There might be—"

The front door flew open. Both men reached for their guns.

Gwen came into the light, a fresh bandage on her injured arm and her head held high.

Her color had returned, and she seemed pretty solid on her feet. Even her twinkle of defiance had reappeared.

"We'll stay at my father's until all of this blows over." Gwen came out onto the porch. "I called him on the landline. He's making arrangements for my horses and the farm while we're away."

Agent Taylor set his hands on his hips. "Ms. Marsh, you can't go there. Your father's a bigger target than you."

Dallas touched her shoulder, hoping to gentle his advice. "Taylor has a point. We need to protect you, not put you in the line of fire."

Taylor shook his head. "Ma'am, you have to find another place. We promised your father we would keep you safe, and we can't—"

"Your deal is with my father, not me," she argued in a firm tone. "So, I am free to do as I please."

"Gwen, you need to think about this." Dallas inched closer. "The FBI can—"

She glared at Agent Taylor. "Would you like to call my father and tell him that we won't be staying at his house?"

Taylor backed away. "No, ma'am. I can't get involved."

She turned to Dallas, her cheeks glowing with a rosy hue. "My father will be expecting us in the morning."

She stormed back inside, leaving the door open.

Dallas showed Taylor a troubled frown. He waited until she climbed the stairs and then muttered, "Let me talk to her. I'll work something out."

Taylor chuckled. "Good luck with that."

Dallas secured the front door and went upstairs to check on Gwen. When he peeked in her bedroom, she wasn't there.

He stepped into the hall, his footfalls eliciting moans from the old floorboards. Then he noticed the light beneath his bedroom door.

He put his hand on the brass knob and hesitated. Perhaps she'd gone to his room wanting comfort. If so, it was an opportunity he couldn't ignore.

The door creaked open, and he found her curled up on the yellow bedspread with Lawrence in her arms. The cat's loud purring carried across the room, mystifying Dallas. All the time he'd spent with Lawrence and the creature had never shown him one iota of affection.

He walked into the room, scrutinizing her red eyes. "You should have mentioned you planned to call your father."

"As soon as I told him what happened, he demanded I go home."

He settled on the bedspread next to her. "You do realize he's probably at the top of Robertson's hit list."

Gwen pushed up still holding the fat cat to her chest. "Yeah, but they didn't go after him tonight. They came after me."

"What if I found us another safe house? Maybe in the city, not far from your father's home."

"I don't want to be locked up. I can't live like that." She buried her chin in Lawrence's gray fur.

He let out a long sigh. "Who's going to care for the horses?"

"Brett Guidry, a horse breeder I know in Folsom." She set the cat aside and stroked his back. "Brett will send two of his grooms in the morning. They can bunk in the apartment above the barn. His people have covered for me before."

Dallas searched for something to alleviate her concerns, but nothing came to mind. He patted her leg, ready to leave her alone.

"You could have dumped me on the feds," she said in a sulky voice. "Then your job would be over."

Guilt made him pull away. "I promised Carl I would stay until the trial was over. So, I'll be around a while longer."

"How much longer?"

He lost himself in the delicate curve of her cheeks, and the promise of her soft skin. Her disarming blend of toughness and sensitivity captivated him. Unable to resist, he lowered his mouth to hers.

He stopped inches from her parted lips, the tug of the gun in his waistband reminding him of his job. He gazed into her eyes, seeing her hunger amid the liquid specks of hazel, and then he sat back on the bed, craving some distance. He could have used that moment to get what he wanted—but it felt wrong.

"We're both tired and stressed. There's still lots to do."

"Yes, you're right." She scooted off the bed, ducking her chin as she brushed past him. "I'd better pack."

He glared at the open door she'd walked through and chastised his moment of weakness. He needed to be objective.

Dallas reclined on the bed, suddenly exhausted. His cell in the back pocket of his jeans rang. When he saw the number, the weight of his assignment returned, sinking him into the bed.

"What's up, Lance?"

"Heard there was a little gunfight at the OK Corral. Everyone alive?"

He wiped his face, pushing his fatigue aside. "Gwen got shot in the arm … nothing major. How did you find out about it?"

"Gwen called her father. Her father called our mutual friend, and then our mutual friend called me. I've been instructed to get you two out of there and settled in the city."

Dallas scratched his head, amazed at how fast the news had gotten around. "Where are we going?"

Lance lowered his voice slightly. "Right outside of the Quarter. It's a big house, well protected, and I can guarantee nobody will touch you there."

"How can you be so sure?"

Lance laughed, sounding like his usual overly confident self. "I'll call in the morning with the alarm code and instructions for the security system. It's on Esplanade Avenue at Burgundy. Can't miss it—the house stands out like a boil on a beautiful woman's creamy white ass."

Dallas hung up and stared at his phone. It may not have been an ideal solution, but anything was better than heading to Ed's.

Gwen appeared in the open doorway, holding her bandaged arm.

"What did Lance say?"

He held up his phone. "He has another house for us in the French Quarter. He says he can guarantee our safety there."

"Guarantee?" She stepped into the room. "Does my father know?"

Dallas dropped his phone on the bedspread. "He knows."

Gwen cast her gaze to the floor. "Look, about before …" She ran her hand along her forehead. "I don't want you to think that

I'm looking for anything with a man. I mean it's been a while." She rolled her eyes. "It's been a long time since … I don't know if I'm ready."

"I'm not expecting anything from you." He kept his voice indifferent, adding an icy quality to it. "We have more important things to worry about."

She twisted her lips into a half-pout. "Yeah, I know. I'm worried about my animals, too."

CHAPTER SEVENTEEN

The sunlight crept through the tall, shady oaks along Esplanade Avenue, creating a lacework pattern of shadows on the road in front of Dallas's car. Stately homes looked out over the median, or neutral ground as the locals called it. He kept his eye in the rearview mirror for the black sedan on their tail. His fingers fidgeted with the steering wheel, unable to still his restlessness. They were close to the house Lance had set up, and Dallas wanted to get Gwen safely inside before he could relax. On the road they were vulnerable, but at least they were in a city he knew well, surrounded by people, police, and lots of places to hide.

He spotted the address Lance had given him. His mouth slipped open as he pulled in front of an opulent French Quarter mansion. The towering three-story home cast a long shadow on the street, blocking the sun and the view of the houses behind it. With round columns supporting a second-floor balcony wrapped in a decorative railing, it boasted french windows throughout, an impressive glass transom above the entrance, and intricately carved statues of women draped in togas topping a brick wall that ran along the sides of the house. The bright red plaster on the exterior stood out like a sore thumb amid the rest of the sedately decorated homes on the block. There were gardens trimmed in white azalea and gardenia bushes, a round cupola painted white atop the red-shingled roof, and throughout the structure—etched into the leaded glass front doors, welded into the balcony railing, and spelled out in the shingles—were the letters *C* and *B*.

Gwen stepped from the car, carrying her purse and two overnight bags over her right shoulder, still favoring her injured arm. She peered up at the three chimneys rising from the sloping roof.

"Who in the hell owns this monstrosity?"

He shut his car door and walked around to the trunk. "Knowing Lance, I'm afraid to ask."

The black car pulled up, and Brewster climbed out. He discreetly pulled Dallas a few feet away from the back of the Mercedes.

"Is this a joke?"

A flush of heat rose to Dallas's cheeks. "What are you talking about?"

"This is Carl Bordonaro's home." Brewster pointed to the leaded glass front door displaying a familiar *C* and *B*. "His initials are all over the place. He even wanted to put them in the roof shingles, but the Port Authority said it would only confuse helicopter pilots making tours of the riverfront."

Dallas wanted to strangle Lance. "What do you want me to do? Go somewhere else? Where would you suggest?"

Brewster leaned in closer. "I don't know. Just find another place to stay. If something happens, we can't go inside the house without a damned warrant."

Suddenly, the house sounded ideal. He needed time alone with Gwen to learn her secrets without the ever-present scrutiny of her minders interfering.

"I would be an idiot to refuse Carl's hospitality. I doubt there's a safer place for Gwen right now. Robertson's men wouldn't be stupid enough to break blatantly into Carl's home and try to hurt us. You and I know that would be tantamount to declaring war in the underworld."

"Dan Wilbur said you were going to help us, not pull shit like this."

Dallas's patience with the man had grown thin.

He went back to his car, curtailing his desire to punch Brewster square in the nose. "I am helping you." He lifted his suitcase from the trunk. "I'm protecting Gwen for you. Anything other than that was strictly Dan's imagination."

Brewster lowered his voice. "I don't know what kind of crap you have on Dan Wilbur, but I don't like it. I would love to bust your ass for interfering with a federal investigation."

"Are you threatening me, Agent Brewster?"

"I don't like you. I don't like the way you talk to me, or think you're better than me." His voice dripped with spite. "Thugs like you give The Bureau a bad name."

Dallas smirked. "I'm glad we cleared that up. Now if you don't mind, I'm going to get Gwen settled in the notorious Mafia kingpin's home."

Brewster sneered at Dallas and then returned to his car.

Gwen came up to his side, tilting her head at Brewster. "What was that about?"

"I think Brewster doesn't like me."

She repositioned her overnight bags. "He reminds me of every self-righteous asshole I've ever met. Why was he upset about us staying here?"

Dallas lifted his overnight bag from the trunk. "This is Carl Bordonaro's house. You've never come here before?"

She browsed the home's façade. "No. I never knew where Carl lived. He always visited us when I was little."

Dallas scanned the street, checking every car and pedestrian. He wanted to get her inside before anyone discovered they were there.

He hurried her along, carrying his bags up the bricked walkway to the leaded glass front doors. A myriad of questions about doors, windows, security features, and vulnerable points rushed through his head. Without the FBI backup, he would be Gwen's only hope of survival.

"How do you feel about staying here?" Gwen traced the initials in the leaded glass doors.

He climbed the front steps and an empty sensation settled in the pit of his stomach. He pulled the notes Lance had given him about the security system from his jacket pocket.

"I know one thing—no one would be foolish enough to trespass on Carl's property."

He punched a code into the keypad next to the doors.

Gwen raised her eyebrows. "Or we could be huge targets because it is Carl's property."

A loud *click* came from the front doors. Dallas recoiled when the doors popped open. A current of warm air hit his face as he inched closer and peeked into the darkness.

The scent of pine floated by, and then the glistening of something catching the morning sun caught his eye.

"Well, at least here we'll be out from under the thumb of the self-righteous Brewster." He pushed the doors all the way open. "Feds won't set foot in Carl's house with anything less than an edict from the Pope."

They stepped inside, and their footsteps reverberated around them. The light from the open doors splashed across white marble floors and offered a glimpse of the massive foyer.

Dallas set down his bags and hurriedly shut the front doors. The cold *thud* echoed through the room.

He entered the same code on an interior keypad and waited until a green light flashed on the console.

"We're locked in." He picked up his suitcase. "Don't open the garage door or these front doors. Otherwise, you'll set off the alarm and the half of the NOPD that's on Carl's payroll will show up."

He found a switch close to the alarm panel and flipped it.

Warm yellow light streamed from a twelve-tier brass chandelier set into the arched-white plaster ceiling decorated with running rose vines. Every few feet, a perfectly formed plaster rose interrupted the molding.

Flecks of gold in the burgundy wallpaper glistened and brought his attention to the paintings situated beneath small spotlights.

"Is that a Remington?" Gwen asked.

On the walls, Dallas found more than a few artists he recognized—John Frederick Peto, and Fitz Henry Lane.

He went to a small drawing in an ornate gold frame of a woman shaped like a puzzle box.

"I think this is a Picasso."

The world spun around him as his focus locked on the portrait of a slender, familiar woman, with creamy skin. His throat closed as he stared at her graceful figure, peering into a golden sunset. Her long green dress appeared caught up in a gentle breeze as her auburn hair flowed behind her, brushing her shoulders. The artist had captured her oval face, high cheekbones, straight nose, and full lips to perfection. Their time together inundated his mind. The agony of her loss zapped his strength and that familiar sting cut across his chest.

Will I ever be free of her?

"That's stunning," Gwen spoke up beside him. "I know this painter, but I can't recall his name."

"David Alexander," Dallas said, keeping the emotion from his voice.

"Ah, yes, his Jenny." She admired the portrait. "Nicci Beauvoir was a beautiful woman."

He swallowed hard, pushing his past with Nicci to the back of his mind. "Yes, she was."

Dallas led her through the massive foyer, checking around corners and inspecting shadowy recesses while she admired the modern art collection. Carl's interests seemed to spread across several movements, from impressionists to expressionism.

At the end of the room was a curved mahogany staircase with a banister carved to resemble intertwined rose vines, complete with a burgundy runner. Along the walls next to the stairs were more paintings of western scenes and vast landscapes by American artists whose names eluded him.

Dallas set his suitcase and overnight bag on the floor, deciding he could cover more ground without his luggage weighing him down. He felt for the gun in his jacket, still anticipating trouble at every turn.

"Let's check out the rest of the first floor before heading upstairs. I want to get the layout."

Gwen put her overnight bags and purse down on the first step. "Sounds good to me."

Off to the side of the staircase was a short hallway done in alternating shades of gold and green with sconces that resembled flickering candles. It led to an arched doorway made of red brick. Beyond, he could see the glint of stainless appliances.

160

"This must lead to the kitchen."

Dallas ushered her through the archway and reached for a switch. It took him a second or two, but when the lights came on, he grinned.

A built-in refrigerator and matching freezer, done in the same dark wood as the kitchen cabinets, took up most of the wall on the right. An eight-burner gas cooktop set in an island made of dark wood cabinets filled the center of the room and sat below a wagon-wheel copper chandelier. Next to a double sink were four built-in electric ovens with stainless doors. The countertops, decorated with a sandy-colored Italian tile, had an array of appliances—a brass espresso machine, a juicer, and a wine station. There was even a wood-fired pizza oven set up at the far end of the room, with a fresh basket of logs below it.

Gwen caressed the imported coffeemaker. "I guess we know where you'll be sleeping."

He opened the fridge doors and found an array of fresh fruits, vegetables, fish, meat, chicken, eggs, milk, cream, and a variety of cheeses.

"I always wanted a kitchen like this—the kind you could get lost in."

Gwen stepped behind him and peered into the fridge. "A gift from our host?"

"Probably Lance," he suggested. "He made the arrangements."

Dallas indulged his curiosity and explored the pantry, his imagination running wild with the dishes he could create. He sifted through drawers and perused an array of culinary tools from rolling pins, spatulas, tongs, vegetable peelers, cake decorating tools, coffee bean grinders, pastry brushes, and even a small chef's torch.

He was deep inside a cabinet to the side of the gourmet oven, inspecting the array of sauté pans, when Gwen leaned in behind him.

"Why didn't you become a chef instead of a bodyguard?"

Dallas cleared his throat and shut the cabinet door. "After my parents died, I tried my best to forget about cooking. I graduated from college, joined the FBI and … Cooking has only become something of a hobby in the past few years. I would never be any good as a chef."

"It would be a hell of a lot safer than your current profession."

He rubbed the middle of his forehead, questioning her concern. He couldn't put his finger on why, but there was something about her that didn't ring true.

"Let's see what else we can find." He pushed past her to get to the kitchen entrance.

Agitation fueled his need to finish doing a sweep before he could settle down. He followed the short hallway to a pair of closed oak double doors with elaborate *S*-shaped brass door handles. Dallas stopped, his heartbeat creeping upward before he peeked inside.

He gently eased the door open, his hand on his gun. The only light came from a long, rectangular stained-glass window sending an intertwined *C* and *B* shining into the center of the room.

Dallas crept inside, attuned to every creak and groan in the old home. He felt along the wall, groping for the light switch.

He touched the plate, flipped the switch, and a brass chandelier with lotus-shaped sconces came to life. With every inch of the room aglow, he eased his hand off his gun. A rectangular mahogany table sat directly before him, capable of sitting twenty-five. The chairs around it had gold velvet upholstered cushions and lion faces carved into their backs. Three silver candelabras graced the table while a gold and white tapestry rug covered the shiny hardwood floor.

"Very nice." Gwen leaned over his shoulder. "He must have great dinner parties."

Dallas let out a haggard breath while eyeing the artwork on the walls. "Carl doesn't strike me as the dinner party type."

Gwen had her nose pressed against a lighted china cabinet with extensive decorative scroll details, oversized claw feet, and carved inlay veneers.

"This stuff looks very expensive."

He turned from the room. "Only the best for Carl."

Dallas followed the hallway and found himself back in the foyer at the base of the staircase. He relaxed against the newel post while Gwen came up to his side.

She pointed at a panel of the wall covered in burgundy wallpaper but with white wainscoting.

"What's that?"

Dallas's hand wrapped around the pummel of his gun as he examined the wallpaper. "What am I missing?"

She set out across the foyer to the panel. He rushed to stick close to her.

"It's different from the rest of the wall." She pushed on it. "There's an outline around it, like a doorway."

He was about to tell her to stop when the panel gave way. Behind it lay a hidden door.

"What sharp little eyes you have."

She glanced back at Dallas, beaming with pride. Her peculiar smile washed away when she saw the gun in his hand.

"Why do you have that?"

He ran his hand along the door, checking for wires. "Because until we've gone through every room, I won't feel safe."

With no wires discovered, he gently pushed Gwen aside.

He pressed on the door. It clicked and then eased all the way open.

"Old houses like these used to have hidden doorways hiding studies and libraries," she said next to him.

"I'd love to know where you picked up that piece of information."

"Just one of my secrets."

Dallas held his gun at the ready and slinked through the door. He waited, his finger on the trigger, as Gwen fumbled for the light switch.

A flash blinded him. His eyes adjusted, and the octagonal room came into focus. The musty odor curled Dallas's nose, but then he became lost in the walls of walnut bookcases rising from floor to ceiling. Leather-bound books, in all shapes and colors, covered every shelf. A rolling ladder on a brass rail system shimmered beneath the brass chandelier. In the center, two red-leather armchairs shared an oak table. Two brass reading lamps sat on top of the table, along with a few books.

"Wow." Gwen appeared at his side. "This is magnificent."

It reminded him of something seen in the home of a professor, or famous writer, not a nefarious man who had barely made it out of high school.

She walked to the table and selected one of the books.

"This is a first printing from 1901," she said, leafing through the pages.

Dallas casually surveyed the shelves. There were no paperbacks anywhere. His guess was all the books in the library were antiques or rare additions.

"Did you know about Carl's love of books?"

"Of course not." She set the book back on the table. "I wasn't aware he knew how to read."

Dallas chuckled.

His nerves settled as they returned to the foyer. He kept the gun in his hand as he scanned the other walls for any similar indentations, eager to find more hidden rooms.

They came across another hallway right off the main entrance, and the muscles in his arms tensed. He raised his gun, keeping it level with both hands as he swept the corridor, checking every cranny.

"Stay behind me."

She did as he asked but seemed more enthralled by their adventure than afraid of it. It wouldn't be the first time he'd seen a target suffer a delayed response to fear. Sometimes those who never crossed paths with his world didn't comprehend how diabolical people could be.

The hallway wasn't as tall as the one leading to the kitchen. The walls had no art work and there was only one arched doorway at the end.

More fancy brass door handles decorated dark wooden doors shaped to fit the archway. He made sure Gwen remained behind him before he nudged the doors open with his foot.

Blue light engulfed them. It came from a one-hundred-and-fifty-gallon saltwater aquarium. Tropical fish with neon colors in their fins and tails dashed about in the water. On the stone floor next to the aquarium were a treadmill, elliptical machine, free weights, and a stationary bike. The room glistened with metal trim around the ceiling and a mirror on one wall.

Dallas lowered his guard as he got a closer look at the

treadmill. He inspected the console, debating if he should give it a spin.

"You run?" she asked.

"When I can."

Before he could stop her, Gwen headed across the room and pushed open a pair of pocket doors behind the aquarium.

"Dammit, Gwen."

He rushed to catch up with her, but by the time he stumbled into the room, she'd turned on the lights.

Four widescreen televisions set into the wall stared back at him. A large sectional sofa made of black leather faced the TVs. An old-fashioned circus popcorn machine set on wheels and painted red waited in one corner while a fully stocked glass bar, with a black granite countertop, sat in another.

"You need to let me go first," he said, walking up to her.

She ventured to a plain wooden door leading from the media room. Not as ornate as the others, it was set off by an alcove decorated with alternating shades of light and dark wood.

Gwen put her hand on the brass knob. "Why? We're all alone here."

He removed her hand from the knob. Dallas held up his gun, tensed, and then gently pushed open the door.

Light glowed from a single lamp atop a modern desk, done in walnut and curved like a crescent moon.

Dallas stood inside a windowless mahogany-paneled room with no other point of entry. He went to the fireplace trimmed with green marble and closed the damper. Satisfied, he put his gun to the side.

Gwen walked in and raised her head to the portrait above the fireplace. A pasty, flat-faced, chubby man in a double-breasted suit sat in a wing-back chair, staring ahead at the artist through his thick black glasses.

"All that fabulous art in this house and he puts this painting here. Why?"

Dallas stared at the beady brown eyes of the man who had brought him to the odd home. "Who knows why Carl does anything."

Gwen turned to him. "Aren't you curious why he gave us this place?"

"Your father." Dallas went to the desk. "He owes him."

Gwen shook her head. "If that were the case, we would be at my father's with a lot more men protecting us. Not here. This is about you." She squinted at him. "What have you got on Carl Bordonaro?"

He scowled at her. "Not a goddamned thing."

She slowly approached the desk, never breaking eye contact. "One day I'm going to shock you with how much I know about you, Dallas. But until then, keep your secrets. It won't make any difference."

He set the safety on his gun. "I have no secrets. I'm the guy who was sent to protect you. Anything else you think you know about me is strictly your imagination."

CHAPTER EIGHTEEN

T he crisp scent of pine grew stronger as Dallas rounded the second-floor landing. The twitchy apprehension plaguing him had eased since going through the downstairs, but as he set his bags on the plush white carpeting, he frowned. The walls were white, the benches and tables around the landing were white, and a single hall leading away from the stairs appeared stark in contrast to the opulence of the first floor.

"Well, this is a letdown," Gwen said next to him.

She went to a bench covered with a white silk cushion. She set her overnight bags down and inspected a charcoal drawing of the city on the wall.

Six doors faced the hall, all done in cypress and rather plain. He moved deeper into the corridor, wanting to get a better look, and then the faint whiff of cleaning products stopped him. He cocked his head, attuned to any sounds coming from the rooms on either side.

It's too damned quiet.

The tomblike silence would make detecting any intruder easier, but could also let someone anywhere in the home know where to locate either one of them.

He pointed to the bench where Gwen waited. "Stay there while I check the rooms."

She flopped down and winced, holding her bandaged arm.

He pulled his gun and went to the first door in the hall, closest to the stairs. It was already half-open, and Dallas cautiously tipped it with his toe.

Bright sunlight streamed into the room from the french windows overlooking the balcony. The steel blue curtains matched the rug beneath a king-sized, four-poster bed topped with a royal blue comforter. Even the paintings on the wall displayed various shades of blue. He went to a Georgian dresser set with the same carved pillars in the bedposts and opened the drawers. They were all empty and smelled of cedar.

At the nightstand, he flipped on the lamp—with its cornflower-tinted shade—and opened the single drawer. He found a deck of playing cards.

Dallas sat on the bed and decided he liked the room—blue was his favorite color.

"That's a lot of blue," Gwen said, standing in the doorway.

"I told you to wait while I checked the rooms."

She strolled inside. "I didn't hear any gunfire and figured it was safe."

"Please do as I say." He pointed at her injured arm. "Otherwise, you might get shot again."

He rubbed the stiffness from his neck as he left the room and went to collect his bags.

At the top of the staircase, he paused and listened for any movement in the house—nothing.

"I'll take this one," he told her, heading back into the room. "It's closest to the stairs and better positioned to fend-off anyone coming after us."

Gwen stepped closer to the open bathroom door. "I hope they're all like this. Otherwise, I might have to fight you for it."

Next door, they found the same bright light from the balcony windows flooding the room, but the décor was all in green. The mahogany furniture, four-poster bed, and private bathroom were identical to Dallas's.

He set her two overnight bags on the comforter. "Maybe you should have packed more than that. We may be here a while."

"I don't need much, just my clothes and a few medical supplies."

Dallas's eyebrows went up. "We're on the run, and you haul along medical supplies?"

"With your knife skills, I figured I'd better plan ahead." She unzipped one of the bags. "I can get more when we head back to the farm."

A hitch caught in his chest. "What if you can't go back home?"

She lifted a handful of gauze from her bag. "What do you mean?"

He sat on the bed, not sure of how to tell her of his concerns. "Your father refused to go into the Witness Protection Program after the trial. He refused for both of you." Dallas took the bandages from her hands and dropped them on the bedspread. "Don't you understand? You're going to be just as vulnerable after the trial as you are now. Even if Robertson gets convicted, he could still order someone to kill you."

She twisted her hands together, her lower lip quivering. "I told my father I wouldn't live in hiding. He promised Carl would make arrangements for our safety, and he will."

"You have a lot of faith in him."

She reached into her bag, avoiding his gaze. "I don't have any other choice, do I?"

He studied her while she unpacked tape, scissors, and assorted ointments, concocting a plan to get her to reveal more.

"What made you want to become a nurse?"

Gwen collected the medical supplies in her arms. "It seemed like a good fit for me."

Dallas stayed with her as she marched into a bathroom done in green and white tile. He followed her to the vanity and leaned against the shelves stuffed with green towels by the door.

"Did you like being a nurse?"

Gwen deposited the supplies on the vanity counter. "I liked my patients."

Dallas traced his finger along the shower curtain next to him. "I bet you liked talking to your patients. You seem like someone who cares."

Gwen swept the medical supplies into an empty drawer and softly smiled. "Yeah, I liked talking to my patients. Heard a hell of a lot of great stories."

"What about secrets? Did any of your patients ever tell you things you wished they hadn't?"

Gwen shut the drawer. "Yeah, some told me secrets, mostly people at death's doorstep. There were things I wished they had never told me, but my job was to listen."

Dallas stepped closer to the vanity. "That sounds dangerous."

Her voice softened. "Listening to the last confessions of the dying isn't dangerous."

"It is when you learn things that others may want to know."

She tilted her head and deepened the lines on her brow. "What kinds of things?"

"Did anyone you took care of ever tell you things that could hurt others?" Dallas blocked her way out of the bathroom. "Information, perhaps. About their business, or something they knew about another person. Something that others would kill for."

"And if they had, why would I tell you?" She hurried from the counter, almost running into him. "You're here as my protector; not my priest."

She rushed past him. He reached out to stop her, wanting to push her harder, but all the lies and manipulation suddenly lost their appeal, and he let her go. He had to get what Carl wanted, but it didn't feel right. Dallas believed he could step into the field and pick up where he'd left off, but he didn't have the stomach for hurting people anymore.

The slam of the bedroom door twisted the knife of regret deeper into his belly.

When had he changed? He couldn't pinpoint a time or place, all he knew was that he wasn't the cold-blooded specialist he'd attempted to resurrect. That Dallas August was dead.

He still had days ahead locked away with Gwen in the enormous house. The prospect terrified him, but then he remembered her skin, her gentle kiss, her eyes, and the daunting task ebbed. Perhaps what had changed wasn't so much Dallas, but how he felt about Gwen.

Enough of this bullshit. Do the job and walk away.

His frustration needed venting before he did something stupid. If he didn't extract Carl's information soon, he feared losing himself in her and never returning to New York.

His lungs burned for air, and his muscles screamed to take a break. Dallas ran flat out on the treadmill, immersed in the blue light from the aquarium, pushing himself harder with every mile. He needed this. He had to eradicate Gwen from his head and get back in the game. The only way to do that was with a hard run.

Simon La Roy had taught him to sever himself from his emotions, and he'd been very good at it until Nicci. He couldn't afford to repeat that mistake. Dallas had people counting on him to be cold and professional. He had a business to run that she would never understand.

A ping alerted him to an incoming text.

He slowed the treadmill and snapped up his phone from the console.

> Coming by tomorrow after lunch with fish food. Our friend wondered if you and Gwen wouldn't mind seeing to his herd of future sushi rolls.

Lance's message made Dallas chuckle. He hit pause on the treadmill and typed his reply.

> See you then.

Dallas pressed the resume button on the treadmill, letting the speed climb higher as he jogged and then ran to keep up. His fatigue helped him to focus on his situation.

Lance coming by might be the perfect opportunity to find another means to get through to Gwen. His old friend could also clear up some of the misinformation—either Lance was a terrible judge of women, or he didn't know Gwen as well as he professed.

He had just hit his stride again when the blaring ring of his phone broke his concentration. He saw Stokes's number and took the call, refusing to stop his run.

"Yeah," he snapped over the whirring of the machine.

"Still in hell?" Stokes's brisk voice came over the speaker.

"I've relocated away from the farm to a house in the city. We had visitors. The woman was shot. Nothing serious, but I had to get her out of there."

"Are you safe, or do you want me to find you another place?" Stokes asked, sounding alarmed.

"We're very safe. At Carl Bordonaro's home."

"Talk about skating on thin ice." Stokes chuckled. "What's that noise?"

"I'm on the treadmill. Just wanted to get a few miles in before bed."

"Is there a problem?"

Getting a little winded, Dallas dropped his speed. "Nothing I can't handle."

"I know you. You run when you're restless and you drink when you're upset."

"Wrong." A few darting fish in the aquarium drew his attention. "I run to stay in shape and I drink to stay sane."

"You drink a lot when you're thinking about a certain woman in New Orleans. I've seen the bottles of vodka Corpus Christi has been buying."

Dallas hit the stop button on the treadmill. "Damn it, Stokes, it's Cleveland. And what I drink is none of your business."

Stokes sighed. "Ah, there it is—that famous Dallas August short fuse. It only appears when you're frustrated with a target. What's the problem?"

Dallas clutched the towel on the rail of the treadmill. "There is no problem. She's coming around."

"Or maybe you're just rusty. You've not been on an assignment in over a year."

Dallas wiped his face, getting irritated. "Is there a reason for calling and not putting this in a text? Or did you intend to piss me off?"

"I got files from Sugar Hill today. I downloaded them onto our server. The client already has all the requested information."

Dallas shook his head, upset he hadn't bothered to ask about his people in the field. "Did she get out clean?"

"She's laying low."

"Did you transfer her payment?"

"Already done." Stokes paused for a moment. "There's just one other thing. She sent her resignation with her files."

He rubbed the center of his forehead, juggling the concerns of his business. He didn't want to lose any specialists. It created problems with paranoid clients obsessed with keeping their secrets safe. It also produced a sense of failure in him as if he'd let them down.

"Do you want me to send it to you?" Stokes asked, breaking his train of thought.

"No." His edginess returned. "I don't need to see it." He turned up the speed on the treadmill. "Remove her name and contact info from the files."

"Just like that?" Stokes sounded surprised. "You're not going to call her?"

Dallas hit his stride, anger giving him his second wind. "There's nothing to say. She wants out, then cut her loose."

"If you say so, Mr. August. You're the boss."

☙❦❧

The dim light coming from the candlestick sconces set into the foyer showed him the way across the marble floor. Dallas tossed the towel over his shoulder and set out toward the kitchen, searching the shadows along the way. He stopped at the staircase, listening for any sounds from her bedroom—nothing. A chill enveloped him as the darkness made the subjects in the paintings along the grand staircase look like ghostly observers. When a creak came from the shifting house, he peered at the alarm pad by the front doors. The green light still shined.

He made his way down the short hall to the kitchen and halted at the arched entrance when he spotted the open doors of the fridge. With her back to him, hunched over, and only in her nightshirt, Gwen rummaged through the shelves. Her lean, toned legs, and the way she swayed from side to side, as if dancing to a tune in her head, brought a surge of heat to his body, chasing away the cold.

"Can't sleep?"

She spun around, her hand on her chest, gasping.

"You shouldn't sneak up on people like that." She settled down and gestured to his running shorts. "What have you been up to?"

Dallas admired the silhouette the refrigerator's light created. "I was running." He strolled into the room. "What are you looking for?"

She tucked a lock of hair behind her ear. "Earlier, I smelled something delicious filling the house. I figured you were cooking."

He'd seen her reading when he had stuck his head into the library but hadn't disturbed her. "Why didn't you join me for dinner?"

She shrugged. "I wasn't hungry, but …"

"Now you are," he said, filling in her words.

He gripped her shoulders to move her out of the way.

"Is there any particular reason you spent the day in the library reading?"

She tugged on the hem of her nightshirt. "Were you checking up on me?"

"Yes. I always know where you are."

Dallas reached into the refrigerator and noticed the way her gaze drifted over his broad chest.

He handed her a container. "Here. It's chicken cacciatore."

An electric jolt blasted through his fingers when he touched her.

Her cheeks reddened, and she dropped her head. "Ah, thank you." She clutched the container against her chest.

Dallas folded his arms, waiting for her reaction to change. "So why were you hiding from me?"

She retreated, putting some distance between them. "I wasn't hiding. I was avoiding you." From a drawer next to the sink, Gwen retrieved a fork. "I didn't want to go through another interrogation." She pulled out a chair from a breakfast table in the corner.

"I wasn't interrogating you." His lie deepened his husky voice. "I wanted to see if there was anything that might make you, us, vulnerable." He plucked a bottle of water from the fridge. "Something that might get us killed."

She wrestled the top off the container and stabbed her fork into the leftovers. "I don't know anything."

The silence between them became a gaping chasm, or at least it did to him.

"Why couldn't you sleep?"

"I don't know." She chased a piece of chicken around in the container with her fork. "I've been thinking about everything that's happened—worrying about my horses, poor Harley, and then there's …" She pointed her fork at him.

"Me?" He hadn't expected that. "I'm glad to know I'm on your mind, even if I do come behind your animals." He took a sip of water. "I just wish you could trust me."

She set her fork in the container, and her expression softened. "Perhaps if I knew more about you. You know everything about me."

A flicker of interest stirred in him. "What would you like to know?"

Gwen watched him for a few seconds, and his curiosity ticked higher.

"Where do you live?"

He squeezed his bottle. "New York City."

"Any brothers or sisters?" She shoved a forkful of chicken into her mouth.

"No brothers or sisters. I do have an Uncle Elliot who lives in Connecticut. He runs the family yacht building business."

He stuck with the truth. It made it easier to look natural.

"Why aren't you running the family business?" She wound a stubborn noodle around her fork. "Do you not like boats?"

Dallas took a seat next to her at the table, wanting to get closer. "No, I love boats, but running the business wasn't for me. I don't have the patience." He ran his fingers over the tabletop, uncomfortable with his honesty. "I got frustrated with the customers and sitting around doing the books drove me crazy."

She pushed her bowl away and rested her head on her hand. "So that's why you protect people—because it's not like a nine to five?"

"Yes, and it's profitable. But that's not why I do it. I like the adventure, and sometimes the danger keeps me on my toes."

He hated to admit it, but the urge to fight to survive was hard to replace with anything, or anyone, else.

She studied him, deepening the creases in her brow. "But you can't do this forever. What will you do instead?"

He picked up her fork. "I'll go back to the boatyard, or sail around the world. I'm not sure which." He lifted a piece of chicken from the container. "I'll figure it out when the time comes."

Gwen held his gaze while he chewed his chicken as if sizing him up, a lioness about to strike.

He picked up the container, and the *snap* of the lid brought her out of her spell.

"I hope you figure that out sooner than later." She got up from the table. "Experiencing life from the shadows is no way to live. If you keep doing what you do, you'll eventually find that out."

"How different will my life be from yours when this trial is over? You'll be living looking over your shoulder. Last night was just a sample of what's ahead for you."

"What do you suggest? I would rather die living my life my way than on the run."

He leaned across the table, his hand almost touching hers. "What if I could help you avoid all that? I could make it so you wouldn't have to hide anymore."

"How would you do that?" Her hand cut through the air. "Forget it. I don't want to sleep with you."

Dallas took her hand and held it. "I'm not talking about sex. Since the moment we met, I've sensed there's something you're fighting to keep hidden. It's like you're carrying around some great burden." He squeezed her hand, hoping to assuage her. "If you let me, I would like to help you."

She frowned and yanked her hand away. The sincerity between them dissolved and the obstinate woman with the discerning gaze stared him down. But the seconds of honesty he'd shared intensified his craving for her.

Careful, August.

"Thanks for the chicken cacciatore." She grabbed the container. "I'm going to head to bed."

He took in her jerky movements as she hurried to return the dish to the refrigerator and get out of the room. He fought to keep the smug grin from his face, glad he'd gotten to her.

"Think about what I said," he told her right as she reached the entrance.

Once outside, he leaned against the table, suddenly aware of the chill her departure had created. It was getting harder to see her as a target and not a beautiful woman. He had to hold out until he'd completed his job and then make sure he never saw Gwen Marsh again.

CHAPTER NINETEEN

The rolling chime of the doorbell echoed throughout the home. Dallas emerged from the kitchen with his gun in his hand. Light coming from the crack in the library door filtered into the foyer. She was in there with her nose in a book. He'd looked in on her a few times since breakfast—the last time only five minutes ago. He wondered if she planned on coming out to greet their guest.

Dallas peered through the leaded glass doors and recognized Lance's broad shoulders, thrust out chest, and smirk. He flipped off the safety, turned off the alarm, and eased one of the heavy doors open.

Lance held up his hands when he saw the gun. He waved a small brown bag in surrender.

"I bring food for starving fish."

Dallas didn't lower the gun but searched the street for the black sedan.

It was there, at the end of the bricked walkway leading to the house, sitting beneath the shade of a tall oak.

He kept the gun raised and nodded Lance inside.

Dallas examined every car and person on the street for any suspicious movement. The world seemed so normal, but the constant burn like gasoline in his stomach hinted that all was not what it seemed.

He didn't lower the gun until the door closed. At the keypad,

Dallas punched in the code. It wasn't until he saw the green light flash that he relaxed and engaged the gun's safety.

Lance shoved the bag into his chest. "Nice to see you, too." He pointed to the bandage on his finger. "Is that from the shoot out?"

Dallas shook his head. "No. I just cut myself chopping vegetables."

"Glad to see your cooking skills haven't improved."

Dallas clasped the bag and inspected Lance's black suit and gray silk tie. "Kind of a fancy outfit for delivering fish food."

Lance examined the brass chandelier. "You have any contact with the Hardy Boys out there?"

Dallas took another look at the black car through the glass in the doors. "Not since we arrived yesterday. Why?"

Lance's gaze traveled from the marble foyer floor to the detailed plaster ceiling, "Where is she?"

Dallas put his gun in his waistband, worried by Lance's dour mood. "Library. She's been holed up there all morning. I think she misses her horses. A friendly face might help her."

"I doubt what I'm about to tell you will cheer her up." Lance moved in closer and dropped his voice. "The jury was handed the Robertson case today. It's all over the news."

Dallas rubbed the back of his neck, that sickening sense of time running out intensified.

"I thought we had at least another week to get her ready."

"The defense didn't present much of a case." Lance shoved his hands into his pants' pockets. "They either didn't have a defense or …"

"They got to the jury," Dallas said, finishing the sentence for him. "I thought this was a done deal."

Lance left his side, shaking his head. He walked up to one of the paintings in the foyer, directing his attention to the subject—a young woman in a slinky red dress.

"Maybe Devon Robertson has one more ace up his sleeve. If he gets off, Gwen and her father might have to leave town for a while."

Dallas knew how Gwen would take that news. "Any idea where they will go if the verdict is not guilty?"

"I'll leave that detail to Carl. He's the master puppeteer of this situation."

Master puppeteer? Dallas's hands shook as he recalled the day Carl had arrived at his office, insisting he take the assignment. "It would explain why he sent me here to babysit, practically blackmailing me into guarding Gwen. He probably hoped I'd take the heat off him."

Lance cocked an eyebrow at him. "No, he wanted you here because he trusts you. And he knows you can get what he needs from the woman without killing her."

The sense of betrayal warming Dallas's gut didn't diminish. "Then explain why my contact in The Bureau was aware of David and Nicci's new identities. There were only a few of us there that night privy to what happened. Carl was one of them."

Deep lines cut across Lance's tanned forehead. "The feds have been keeping tabs on all of us. I'm sure they put the pieces together after Greg Caston and Simon La Roy showed up dead, but they've never approached us. With you in charge of Simon's operations, they're probably making sure you're aware of what they know. Careful. They'll be playing those cards soon, and you'll have to find a way to appease them."

"Yeah, that's what bothers me. How many more people are we

going to have to pay off or kill to keep David and Nicci safe?"

"As many as it takes." Lance placed his hand on Dallas's shoulder, giving it a friendly squeeze. "Now, take me to Gwen. I'm sure she'll be thrilled to see me."

His mounting dread for what lay ahead sucked the strength out of Dallas, but he never let it show. Instead, he motioned to the library entrance, ready to break the news to Gwen.

"This way."

With ferocity in his step, Dallas headed deeper into the foyer. He shoved the hidden door out of the way, ready to deal with Gwen. The musty library had only the light from a single reading lamp to guide him.

He reached the center table, but when he turned to the chair, there was no Gwen, only an open book sitting in her place. He set the fish food on the library table and touched the chair. It was still warm.

"Nice room," Lance said behind him. "Never knew this was here."

Dallas went up to him, a prickling sensation climbing his spine. "Gwen was just in here."

Lance gave a dismissive nod. "Maybe she went to the kitchen to get a bite to eat?"

Dallas guided him out of the library, urging him to hurry. "Let's find out."

He scoured the shadows of the foyer for Gwen. Dallas turned down the short hall to the kitchen, and when he shot through the archway, she wasn't there.

He even went to the small laundry room to the side.

"Whatcha do? Piss her off?" Lance asked with a sly grin.

Every groan of the house, every creak came alive as Dallas tried to pick up any trace of her.

"Maybe something happened to her."

"Would you relax." Lance waved a hand around the kitchen. "The house is a fortress. No one can get in or out."

Dallas wiped his sweaty palms together. "Someone could have snuck in when we were talking."

Lance came up to him and put his hand on his shoulder. "She's probably upstairs in the bathroom or taking a nap. That's all. Stop being so … you."

"We should check and make sure."

Dallas bolted out of the room.

He followed the short hallway and stopped right before entering the foyer to look out the pair of glass doors that led to the patio.

He tugged hard on the doors. They remained locked just as they had been when he'd done his rounds earlier. He peered through the window at the ivy-covered pergola above the entrance to the patio. The empty white wicker chairs resting beneath the arbor's shade raised his simmering blood to a rolling boil.

Lance sauntered up to his side. "Everything okay between you two?"

Dallas swallowed the lump of uncertainty in his throat. "Do you know any reason she would hide from you?"

"Several. But this isn't about me." Lance turned to the foyer. "I've got to get back to the courthouse. Show me out."

He stared at Lance's back, dismayed by his lack of concern. "Don't you want to find Gwen? See if she's like you remembered?"

"Not particularly. I didn't come here for her." Lance raised his voice as he kept walking. "Have you always been this much of a hard ass?"

The reply barreling up from his chest faltered at his lips. There was no point in telling Lance of his suspicions. The man would probably laugh and suggest either sex or alcohol to quiet his overactive imagination.

In the foyer, Dallas raised his gaze to the staircase, expecting to see her on the second-floor landing, but she didn't show. Perhaps Lance's visit had spooked her, or her absence might have hinted at something more profound—the strain between them.

The sunlight coming through the doors warmed the pantlegs of Dallas's jeans as he tapped in the code for the alarm.

Lance inched closer, his voice oozing with blustering smugness. "Sleep with Gwen. The woman is getting to you. It's written all over your face."

And there it is.

Dallas opened the doors but didn't bother to enlighten him about why that plan wouldn't solve anything.

"Keep me posted on the trial."

Lance stepped outside and sucked in the fresh air. "I'll text as soon as I have the verdict." He looked back at Dallas over his shoulder. "Have fun with Gwen."

He strolled along the walkway, appearing as if he hadn't a care in the world.

Dallas shut the doors, and rested his head against the glass, taking a second to focus.

Enough games. It's time for answers.

CHAPTER TWENTY

Dallas marched up the grand staircase after going through every room in the first floor, the dead quiet adding to his barbed rage. He walked toward Gwen's partially opened bedroom, formulating what to say. He set his hand on the crystal doorknob, hoping not to find her inside. Hiding in her bedroom seemed too coincidental, and if she were there, it would confirm his darkest suspicions.

Dallas pushed open the door and sagged into the doorframe when he found her on the green comforter, her long hair spread out on her pillow. She appeared deep in slumber, but he didn't buy it.

He'd always prided himself on his ability to read people, find their weaknesses, and get what he needed out of them. But Gwen was different. It was as if she were able to pick up his thoughts and then cut him off at the knees. She outmaneuvered him when he interrogated her, used his weaknesses to her advantage. Gwen always seemed to be one step ahead at every turn.

"Have a nice nap."

She opened her eyes and immediately sat up.

"What is it? What's wrong?"

Gwen didn't sound groggy or flustered like someone awakening from a deep sleep.

He stepped into the room, an icy chill in his voice. "You missed Lance. We went looking for you, but then he had to get back to the trial."

She shook her head and swung her legs over the side. "I got tired of reading and decided to come up here for a nap."

He pointed at her tennis shoes. "Do you usually sleep with your shoes on?"

She pressed her fists into the comforter. "What difference does that make?"

He took another step toward the bed, warily sizing up her menacing pose. "Someone wanting to sleep would take off their shoes, but someone wanting to pretend to sleep might not have the time."

Gwen's gaze flicked around the bedroom. "So now you're accusing me of faking my nap to avoid Lance?"

He folded his arms. "You tell me."

Her bottom lip briefly disappeared between her teeth. "I fell asleep, but I'm glad I did. Seeing Lance would have been unpleasant for me."

The tension in his chest became like a vise. "And why is that?"

She went to the Georgian dresser and rested against it, letting her fingers curl around the brass pulls.

"Every time we meet, he hits on me."

He nodded, but his doubts persisted. "Sounds like Lance."

"Doug threatened to have Lance neutered if he keeps asking me out."

Dallas rubbed his right eye, suppressing his chuckle. "Lance is a notorious playboy, I will grant you that, but I can trust what he tells me."

Gwen put her hand on her hip and glared at him. "And what did he tell you?"

"The jury got the Robertson case after closing arguments

today."

Her shoulders drooped, bringing an end to her aggressive stance. "So soon? I thought it would take at least another week for the defense—"

"There was no defense." Dallas stood. "The defense barely presented a case."

"What happens next?"

He shook his head. "That's not up to me, but if Robertson gets off, you and your father will have to consider your next move carefully."

The wrinkle between her brows became more pronounced. "I guess you're happy about the early reprieve."

He dipped his chin, unable to look at her. "As are you."

"What will you do next?"

He turned for the door. "I have other jobs waiting."

She maneuvered in front of him. "Any of them like me?"

The breathlessness of her tone escalated his discomfort.

He walked past her to the bedroom door. "No. They won't be as ... complicated."

"I'm complicated?"

He stopped at the door and faced her. "You and all the business around you has made this job different from most." He ran his hand over his short-cropped hair, stumbling for something to say. "You're hard to get a handle on."

She walked in a slow, purposeful way toward the door. "I could say the same about you, but I'm sure it's not been easy hanging around with me. I make you work in stables and torture you with stitches." She tapped the white bandage on his finger. "How are they looking?"

The hint of jasmine coming from her forced him to take a step backward. "They're healing."

She reached for him. "I should take a look."

The tingle her touch created was getting harder to ignore.

"I said I'm fine, Gwen." He brushed her hand away. "I don't need you to take care of me."

"Do you push everyone away or is it just me?"

He put his face in front of hers. "Only the people who tell me one thing but do another."

Her brows tipped up. "You think I'm lying to you? About what?"

The rolling doorbell chimes echoed throughout the house.

"Sounds like Lance has come back," Gwen said, sounding smug. "That should make you happy."

A wave of acid welled from his belly. Dallas retrieved his phone from his back pocket, not convinced Lance would be so careless.

He sent off a quick text.

Are you at the front door?

His fingers tingled as he waited for a reply.

"Who are you texting?" she asked, pointing at his phone.

No!

Dallas held up the phone to her. "It's not Lance."

The doorbell chimes rang again.

He put his phone back in his pocket and considered his options. His mind reviewed every way in and out of the house, coming up with a back-up plan for Gwen.

"Lock your bedroom door and don't come out until I come and get you. If I don't return, if you hear gunfire, climb onto the balcony and get away. Do you understand?"

"You're scaring me." Her hand went to her throat. "Who do you think it is?"

He took the gun from his jeans and clicked off the safety. "I'm going to find out."

Dallas waited for the *click* of the lock on Gwen's bedroom door. He shook the knob to verify she was secure. Gripping his gun, he headed to the stairs, the cold in his belly spreading to his limbs.

He arrived at the doors and stepped to the side before peering through the glass. Movement revealed a man wearing a dark suit and black tie, but his face remained obscured.

The alarm keypad was right next to him. He could set off the alarm and send for help or at least alert the feds outside. But if the men in the black sedan were out there, how had this person approached the doors?

The foyer closed in around him as he ran through escape scenarios to get Gwen out of the house.

"August, it's Brewster. Open up," came from outside.

Then a meaty fist pounded on the glass.

Dallas bowed his head, and the icy rush in his arms and legs faded.

He punched in the code and waited until he saw the red light. Before he reached for the doors, he put the gun back in his waistband and tucked it under his shirt.

A sweaty faced Agent Brewster, greeted him.

Something's up.

He raised his head to look over Brewster's sizable shoulder. All appeared calm on the street. The black sedan remained parked under the tree like before, but there was no sign of Crawford inside.

Brewster peered over Dallas's shoulder to the foyer. "We saw Lance Beauvoir leaving earlier. I expect he told you about the trial."

Dallas reflexively put his hand over the gun under his shirt. "Lance also brought fish food. But I guess you already knew that."

"We've been ordered to pull out. Our observation of Ms. Marsh ceased the moment the case went to the jury."

Dallas tensed. "But the trial isn't over."

"We promised to look after Ed Pioth's daughter until the case went to the jury, not until the verdict was read. I hope you're prepared for the consequences if the verdict is not guilty."

Brewster's flushed cheeks and slight sway didn't present as the assertive, stiff-necked man Dallas had dealt with in the past. He appeared fatigued, frazzled, and not as in control.

"You didn't risk coming to Carl Bordonaro's doorstep to tell me that. Why are you here?"

He held up his phone. "Dan wanted a word before we go."

Brewster went to hand him the phone, but it slipped and dropped to the floor.

Dallas bent over to catch the phone, but froze when he heard the familiar rub of a gun slipping out of a holster.

He rose slowly, holding his breath, as he assessed Brewster's wide-leg stance, the empty holster beneath his jacket, and the barrel of the .9mm Sig pointed directly at him.

"Step back," Brewster ordered. "You know the rules, always keep a safe distance."

Dallas took one step back and then another while his many hours of close quarters combat training ran through his head.

"I was wondering who Robertson would send."

Brewster stepped inside with the gun secured in both his hands. He kicked the phone aside and then tipped the front doors closed with his foot.

Dallas became acutely aware of the cold foyer closing in around him. His senses went into hyperdrive as he listened to every nuance in the house, praying Gwen had complied with his orders.

Brewster removed his handcuffs from his jacket pocket and then slid them across the floor to Dallas.

"Put them on. Hands behind your back. You remember how it's done."

Dallas eyed the flashing red light on the alarm keypad. He slowly dipped for the cuffs and took his time standing. He kept his attention on the light, counting off the seconds since the door had closed. The cold steal clasped around one wrist, and by the time he'd reached twenty seconds in his head, he hesitated before clasping his other wrist, waiting for the peel of the alarm to go off.

He cinched the last cuff into place.

Twenty-five, twenty-six … Where is the alarm?

He raised his head. Brewster stepped away from the alarm console. The red light had turned to green.

His muscles screamed to run, to fight his way out of the situation, but Dallas quieted the energy building in him. He had to sort through the runaway carousel of ideas feeding his panic and find a way to think clearly and stay in control.

"I've been tapped into your friend Lance Beauvoir's phone for some time now." Hate peppered Brewster's voice. "He never suspected a thing. Neither did you. When he gave you the passcode for the alarm, I got it, too." He cautiously approached, keeping the gun aimed at Dallas's head. "Move, and I'll kill you."

Dallas became a warm statue, straining not to move as

Brewster lifted his shirt, exposing the gun tucked into his jeans.

A dozen ways to overtake the man even in handcuffs came and went, but he couldn't risk it.

Wait. You'll get your chance.

"What does Robertson want?"

Brewster backed away and secured Dallas's pistol in his jacket. "Insurance to turn the trial his way. I take the girl and her old man recants his testimony. Then the verdict gets thrown out, no matter what the jury decides."

Dallas noticed how their voices carried in the darkened house, echoing through the high ceilings of the foyer and up the staircase.

He raised his voice and asked, "How long have you been working for Robertson?"

"Since I discovered that retiring on a government pension wasn't going to be quite enough for me."

"I assume Crawford is dead." He nodded at his disheveled clothes. "And by the looks of you, he put up a fight."

Brewster searched the foyer and then directed his attention to the staircase. "I need Crawford. Once I have the girl, I'll bring his body inside and leave it next to yours. That should give the local police something to investigate for a few days."

"Dan Wilbur will hunt you down."

Brewster waved the gun into the foyer, directing him toward the staircase. "Dan Wilbur hasn't stepped out of his office in ten years." The contempt in his voice bounced around the vast room. "He has no idea what half his agents are into."

Dallas moved, keeping his gait slow and steady while Brewster followed him, maintaining his distance.

"You're not the only one on Robertson's payroll then."

"Your buddy Bordonaro has his people, too. But he doesn't

pay as well." He came out from behind Dallas and glimpsed the stairs and then the hallway behind it. "Protocol is to secure the subject of surveillance before investigating any threat." He smirked at Dallas. "And I know you were a by-the-book guy in your day, so where's Gwen?"

Dallas worked his hands in the cuffs while on the lookout for a weapon he could use to stop Brewster.

"I'm not an agent anymore."

"Old habits die hard no matter what line of work you're in." He went to the mahogany banister carved to resemble entwined rose vines. "I would have locked her in a bedroom. Easy access to the balcony and street if you needed an escape route." He pointed the gun at Dallas. "Move."

The cold steel on his wrists pinched his skin. Dallas raised his head to the steps, his throat constricting, and the maelstrom of outrage blotting out his rational thought. Plotting his way through every action, weighing Brewster's reaction, was the way to stay ahead of the game of cat and mouse. He had to keep his wits together. If he didn't, Gwen was as good as dead.

CHAPTER TWENTY-ONE

The faces in the portraits hugging the walls along the curved staircase stared back at Dallas, generating a sense of foreboding. He raised his foot onto the first step, wondering if Carl's collection of captivating canvases would witness his demise. He stiffly climbed, sizing up the heavy wooden frames, and debating if he could get to one while in handcuffs. It didn't seem likely. He'd have to try another tactic to stop Brewster.

"Carl Bordonaro will come after you if you hurt Gwen."

"Bordonaro isn't my concern." Brewster stayed well behind him, and his voice reverberated throughout the foyer. "Robertson will take care of him soon enough."

Dallas took another step and stared ahead to the landing. "That's Robertson's ultimate goal? Getting rid of Carl? What about Robertson turning on you? Any way you write this, you're going to die in the end."

"They'll have to find me first."

Dallas's muscles quivered, starved for action. With each step, he judged the distance to Gwen's bedroom door, counting off how long he had before making his move.

He trudged slowly, aware of the creak of their weight on the old staircase, and Brewster's heavy breathing as they reached the top.

Is he tired or injured? Use that.

At the landing, Dallas stepped onto the white carpeting, and the silence reassured him. Not wanting to tip off Brewster, he used his peripheral vision to check Gwen's closed door.

Brewster came around in front of him, surveying the long corridor.

"Which bedroom is Gwen's?"

Dallas dipped his head to the first door on the right. "We share that room."

"We? Didn't expect you to fall for one of your targets. Isn't that what you people call them?" Brewster shoved him toward the door.

Dallas's shoulder connected with the wood, sending a loud *thud* into the hall. He winced and sucked in a breath.

"Who told you about me?"

"Everyone knows. Nothing worse than an ex-agent getting caught up in your dirty business."

Brewster stayed a few feet back, aiming the gun at Dallas's chest. "Ease it open, nice and slow."

Dallas honed in on the door and not his desire to beat the shit out of Brewster. He shifted around to work the handle with his cuffed hands.

It took a little jockeying to get one hand settled around the crystal doorknob. Dallas turned it, keeping an eye on Brewster and how he held the gun. In a bedroom crowded with bulky furniture, there wouldn't be much opportunity to get off an accurate shot. He would have to risk going after Brewster once they got inside.

Dallas opened the door, and then a kick to his back catapulted him into the room.

He tripped, almost heading headfirst into the carpet. When he regained his footing, Brewster cruised inside, eagerly examining the blue bedroom.

"Where is she?"

Sweat trickled down Dallas's cheek. He remained in the center of the room, waiting for Brewster to come closer.

"It's a big house."

Brewster checked under the bed and stuck his head in the bathroom, glancing back at Dallas once or twice while keeping the gun on him.

Dallas fixed his attention on the wall between his room and Gwen's. Another drop of sweat rolled down his back.

Make your move.

Brewster rummaged through the night table and pulled out the deck of cards. He tossed them across the bed, sending them fanning out over the comforter.

"Looks too clean. No makeup, perfume, and only one toothbrush in the bathroom." He went around Dallas, keeping his distance. "Women are messy. A whole lot messier than this."

Dallas gauged the distance between them. "Gwen isn't like most women."

Brewster rested his hip against the dresser, relaxing the gun a little. "I will give you that."

Dallas wiped the sweat dripping into his eye on his shoulder. He used the gesture to get a good look at the distance between Brewster and the open bedroom door.

The *whump* of a drawer opening made Dallas look back at Brewster.

He had the top drawer of the dresser open. His brow furrowed as his hand reached inside.

Dallas arched his back, getting ready.

Brewster raised his hand, holding up a pair of men's white briefs.

The veins in his neck popped as he threw the underwear to the floor. "I always knew you were a lying sack of shit."

Brewster lifted the gun and brought it down hard on the right side of Dallas's face.

The blow sent him flying back while shards of pain exploded in his head. He dropped to his knees, dazed. His vision blurred and then went black. Dallas fought to stay upright, but the dizziness overtaking him was too intense. He flopped to his side, hitting the soft rug with his shoulder while a metallic taste filled his mouth.

Dallas lay stunned, scrambling to think, to plot, to keep conscious. His vision came back, first as a blur of light, then colors appeared. He concentrated on everything he could make out, adamant about locating Brewster.

"That must have hurt."

The low voice rumbled in his head, setting off agonizing blasts of pain.

He attempted to push up from the floor, but the handcuffs and his wooziness compounded his efforts.

Something came down on the side of Dallas's neck, pressing on his windpipe.

He fought for air like sucking each breath through a straw. His hunger for oxygen escalated his panic.

Stay focused.

The words repeating in his head helped bring his body back under control. He concentrated on staying calm, and then his vision cleared.

Brewster stood over him with the sole of his shoe rammed into Dallas's throat, and his gun gripped loosely in one hand. He lowered his head to Dallas, showing his white teeth through his sneer.

"I told you not to do anything stupid."

Dallas clenched his fists and summoned his strength.

He rolled his shoulder, getting Brewster's shoe off his neck, and tipping him off balance. He gasped, gulping in air. Dallas's stamina returned and he used his legs to push up from the floor and throw his weight into Brewster.

The hit sent his opponent into the dresser. The *thump* echoed around the room.

It bought Dallas time to get to his feet. The dizziness came back with a vengeance, but he swallowed the bitter taste of vomit and faced Brewster, keeping his back to the wall. He planted his feet and tensed, waiting.

Brewster was off the dresser and lunging at him.

His shoulder connected with Dallas's gut and sent him hurtling into the wall.

His back slammed against the hard surface, and the impact sent a shockwave through his system. It knocked the air from his lungs, shot a sharp jolt up his back and a fiery stab across his left shoulder.

Dallas crumbled to the floor. He tried to breathe, but couldn't. It was like stone blocks crushing him, making it impossible to expand his chest. He lay caught up in his anguish. He couldn't see Brewster with the blackness crowding his blurry vision.

Then a rush of cool air entered his mouth, and his lungs expanded. The tears and spots retreated from his eyes. He glimpsed the wall next to him—the one connected to Gwen's bedroom.

I bet she heard that.

"You're one dumb son of a bitch." Brewster sauntered up to him, shaking his head. "I'm in charge. I've got the gun."

200

Dallas spat out the taste of blood and chemically carpet fibers from his mouth. "A gun doesn't put you in charge. That's one of the first things they teach you at the academy. Never assume that because you have a weapon, you have the advantage."

He attempted to rise from the floor, but a jabbing pain spread from his left shoulder and down his side like a thousand hot needles. His energy siphoned out of him, the agony keeping him perfectly still. He willed the intensity of the throbbing to ebb, so he could clear his head and figure out his next move.

"Look at you. You're a mess." Brewster pointed the gun at Dallas, clutching it in both hands. "And you've outworn your usefulness."

"I'd think twice about that," came from the open doorway.

Gwen took a step into the room, holding her Glock. She stood with her legs apart and her aim directed at Brewster's head. Her face was unlike anything Dallas had ever seen from her before—she was in total control.

Brewster stuck up his free hand while keeping his gun pointed at Dallas. The red in his cheeks faded.

"Not me. You're aiming at the wrong guy." His voice trembled. "He's the one working for Robertson. I'm here to save you. He's supposed to kill you after the trial is over—you and your father."

She never blinked and never lowered her gun. Dallas rested his head against the wall, fighting his pain and finding his voice.

"Gwen," he called out in a raspy tone, "if I'd wanted to kill you …"

Her attention locked on Brewster. "I'd be dead already."

Dallas never had time to react or call out before Brewster pivoted from his right leg to his left and spun his gun toward the door. The *crack* reverberating around the bedroom deafened him.

Brewster's head snapped back and his legs buckled. He landed on his back, facing the ceiling. Blood, trickling from the wound in his forehead, rolled down his cheeks and pooled on the rug until his face became a dusky gray.

Dallas sagged against the wall, thanking God the ordeal was over. He turned to Gwen, who still had her gun on Brewster, and an overpowering foreboding came over him.

Who the hell is Gwen Marsh?

And then, like turning off a faucet, her demeanor changed. "Are you all right?"

Dallas wanted to stand, pull her into his arms and thank her a thousand times over for saving him, but the handcuffs kept him pinned to the floor.

"Get these cuffs off me. Find the key. Brewster must have it on him."

He waited as she crept closer to the downed man. "Kick the gun away first." Dallas grimaced when the throbbing flared again in his shoulder. "Before you get the key. Make sure he's dead."

She pressed the toe of her shoe against the gun that had fallen out of Brewster's hand. She nudged it a few feet away, and then leaned over, checking his carotid artery. Without showing any signs of revulsion, she went through his pockets while holding on to her gun.

His initial instincts about her had been wrong. This wasn't some vulnerable, scarred, recluse wrapped up in her animals. She was a cold and calculating woman with nerves of steel. Not many people could do what Gwen had without breaking down. Maybe her medical training had hardened her for such a task because no matter how much she claimed her father had trained her, he'd never counted on her ending up here.

"Got 'em," she announced before hurrying to him.

She set her gun on the floor while he showed her the handcuffs. His shoulder smarted like hell, but when the metal bracelets fell from his wrists, the unbearable burning in his side lessened.

He held his tender ribs, worried about her composure. "Are you all right?"

She dropped the keys and handcuffs in front of him. "I'm fine."

He reached for her pistol and flipped the safety. "You should have told me you brought your gun."

She sat next to him and wiped the blood from his lips. "What about Crawford?"

"Brewster killed him." He saw his blood on her hand and noted how it wasn't shaking. "He wanted you. You were to be the insurance policy to get your father to recant his testimony against Robertson."

Gwen hooked her arm around his back and helped him from the floor. "There's going to be hell to pay for this."

He took in her profile as she guided him out of the room. She didn't have the wild-eyed look or shakes of a woman who had just been through hell. In his experience, no one was ever "fine" after killing a man. There were tears, hyperventilating, and a whole lot of trembling. It had messed him up after his first kill, but Gwen didn't exhibit an inkling of distress.

"Most people aren't so together after killing someone."

She kept her gaze on her open bedroom door as they moved along. "It's not like it's the first time I've watched someone die."

"Watching someone die isn't the same as pulling the trigger."

203

She maneuvered him through her bedroom door. "Death is death. When you work with it day in and out, it doesn't matter who pulls the trigger because you've become numb to it."

He took in the shock of her green curtains and carpet, wondering why her comment struck him as odd. Nurses fought to keep people alive. She made it sound like she'd given up on saving anyone.

Gwen eased him onto her comforter. "What do we do now?"

He winced as he struggled to get his phone out of his back pocket. "I'll make a call."

"I'll get some ice and medical supplies while you get us some help."

She was at the door when a firestorm shot up his left side and ended at his shoulder.

"And when you come back …" His breath caught in his chest. "We need to talk."

She halted at the doorway. "About what happened with Brewster?"

Dallas swiped his thumb over his cracked phone screen. "No, about who you really are."

CHAPTER TWENTY-TWO

Dallas fought to stay upright, but the burning in his chest added to the hammering behind his eyes. The bones in his face throbbed and his shaking hands made it hard to hold the phone. He hoped she returned with something to keep him from passing out. He couldn't leave her alone. Another assassin could be waiting to strike.

The other end of the line rang and rang, then a man's irritated voice came through the speaker.

"Dallas?" Lance's rumbling filled his ears. "This better be good. I'm in the middle of dinner with a very beautiful—"

"I've got two dead FBI agents." Dallas wiped more blood from his mouth. "I need a crew to take care of the bodies."

"You and Gwen okay?"

Dallas winced as he struggled to get comfortable. "A bit bruised, but we'll survive."

"What happened?"

"One of the FBI guys, Brewster, was a mole working for Robertson. He wanted to kidnap Gwen and get Ed Pioth to recant his testimony."

"Our friend suspected Robertson had somebody on the inside with the feds but wasn't sure who. When you came on board, I figured he would find out sooner or later. You have a talent for bringing out the worst in people."

"So he used me? That son of a bitch." He sank into the bed.

"You could have said something."

Lance chuckled. "Please. He uses everybody. You should know that by now."

Dallas let it go. He still needed to get what Carl wanted. Otherwise, he would have bigger problems.

"How will you get rid of the bodies? I don't need this to come back to me."

"I know someone who can take care of the details," Lance assured him. "I'll have a crew come by and clean up."

"We'll be here." Dallas swayed, every part of him aching and throbbing. "Brewster told me the feds pulled out. Is that true?"

"Afraid so. You'll be on your own until the verdict's read. Once there's a conviction on Robertson, our friend will see to Gwen and her father."

Lance sounded too cocky. "What if the jury finds him not guilty?"

"They won't." Lance hung up.

I should have known.

Dallas put his phone on the bed and hugged his left side. Every part of him hurt.

He gently eased back on the bed. Once the cleaners had gone, he could regroup and plan how to keep Gwen safe until the verdict came.

The creak of the floorboards forced him to sit up and reach for the Glock. He saw her, with the peroxide and gauze tucked under her right arm, standing by his bed.

"I didn't hear you come in."

Gwen lifted the vodka bottle. "I thought you could use this." She put the gauze and peroxide on the bed.

"Later." Dallas put the gun down on the bed. "There's still a lot to do."

She handed him the bottle. "I suggest you take a shot of this. You look like you're about to pass out."

He unscrewed the cap and took two long sips, then winced and touched his mouth.

Gwen poured the peroxide into a swath of gauze. She traced the right side of his face, inspecting the dark bruise forming.

"What did he hit you with? The gun?"

"Among other things." He handed her the bottle. "You sure you don't need any?"

"No, maybe later I will," she admitted.

The alcohol had helped clear his head, but not erase the picture of Brewster's face as the bullet hit him.

"You were pretty good in there. Who taught you how to shoot like that?"

She unbuttoned his shirt. "Learning how to shoot was a requirement in my household."

Gwen pushed the shirt over his injured left shoulder, but Dallas didn't squirm or gasp. He couldn't let her see how weak and vulnerable he felt.

"Brewster wasn't some buck out in an open field. Your shooting was accurate, deadly, and showed exceptional skill."

She ran her fingers ran over the contours of his injured shoulder. "My father sent my brothers and me to the best combat training schools."

He gripped her hands and held them, pressing his lips into a thin line. "That would explain a few things but not how you kill a man without batting an eyelash." He took in the way the light changed in her eyes. "Who are you?"

She wiggled out of his grasp. "I'm not a shrinking violet afraid of confrontation or in need of a man to take care of me. All my life, I've been trained to protect myself in any situation. What you saw in there was years of what my father called *prep work*." She sat on the bed next to him. "But there were things he neglected to teach me. Like how to get along with people or have a relationship."

The comment touched him. There were so many things he could say to reassure her, but none of it would sound genuine. Relationships confused him as much as Gwen, but instead of sharing that, he patted her thigh, eager to change the subject.

"In case I forget to tell you this later, thank you for saving my ass."

She nudged him with her shoulder. "Well, I'm a sucker for a fine ass."

The loud chimes of the doorbell rose from downstairs.

He flinched at the intrusion, wanting a few more moments alone with her.

"That was fast. Lance must have had men close by." Dallas carefully pulled his shirt over his left shoulder. "Let me do the talking."

"What will they do with the bodies?"

Dallas slowly got to his feet and swayed. He blinked, concentrating on her, and pushed aside his wooziness.

"I have no idea, but I'm sure they will get a place ready for them."

She held his hand, but he pushed it away, refusing her help.

"What does that mean?"

"In Carl's world, it means to look for a special burial spot for bodies. Where Brewster is found will send a clear message to the people he works for. It's a way men like Carl use intimidation to stay in charge."

"What happens when the FBI finds out about Brewster? What will they do?"

"Nothing. Brewster will be ruled a self-inflicted gunshot wound, and Crawford will be reported as killed in the line of duty."

She raised her chin. "How do you know that?"

"It's what they always do when they find a mole."

She shivered and covered her arms. Dallas wished he hadn't been so brutally honest with her, but after her performance with Brewster, he saw her less like a woman and more like him—shatterproof.

"It's a warning to the people who were paying him. Every leak, every mole, every double agent when killed is labeled a suicide. It's a badge of disgrace and the ultimate act of revenge."

Gwen frowned, deepening the lines in her forehead. "Why is it revenge?"

Dallas rested his good shoulder against the doorframe, willing the pain away. "When I started at the FBI, I was taught that the ancient Romans compared the suicide of a soldier to desertion. There can be no greater humiliation than for a soldier to desert his post. In so doing, he disgraces his family and his name. His existence is wiped clean from the records and his life is voided from every archive, like he never existed."

She gazed into his eyes. "Is that what you do? Wipe everyone from your life, like they never existed."

The doorbell rang again.

Dallas turned away. He had to keep his walls high to maintain that wedge between them.

"We can't keep Lance's crew waiting."

❦

The icy night breeze coming in through the open glass doors helped to keep Dallas focused as the men dressed in black suits carried their buckets, brushes, and boxes of collected evidence, and scurried down the brick walkway to a group of black vans. The stillness of the street, the quiet from the neighboring French Quarter added to the eerie atmosphere.

The crew had worked under cover of darkness and carefully removed Brewster and Crawford's bodies, keeping the black bags hidden in a steel cart they loaded into one of their vans. Once the black sedan was discreetly towed away and all the debris from the altercation extracted, Dallas shut the doors and allowed the fatigue he'd been suppressing to take over his limbs.

He shuffled to the alarm pad and punched in the new code he'd programmed after spending an hour figuring out the system.

Gwen slid next to him. Her hand went to the small of his back, sending a warm rush through him.

"We'd better see to your injuries."

His exhaustion receded as he turned to her. Dallas wished he had more time to discover who she was, and why she'd felt compelled to lie to him, but while the team had worked to clean the mansion, he'd realized his job wasn't her. He was there to get what Carl wanted. Her games were her affair.

"What did you have in mind?"

Gwen took his right hand. "The perfect thing to relieve your aches and pains."

He limped along, her touch chasing away the tension of their chaotic evening. Why she soothed him was another mystery—one he would never solve.

Their footfalls echoed around the foyer as they made their way to the curved staircase with its winding banister. She went slowly to allow his battered body the chance to tackle each step. Coming down the steps to greet the clean-up team had hurt a whole lot less than going up. Every movement sent a jolt of pain through his back as he eyed the top, praying for the torture to end.

Once he had conquered the stairs, the last few feet to her bedroom door seemed to go on forever. When the streetlights filtering through her balcony windows appeared, he was ready to collapse.

She left him standing in front of the four-poster bed and ducked into her bathroom.

He swayed a little, eager to climb onto the comforter and sleep for days, but the specialist in him refused to give in to his urge.

He perked up when she walked into the bedroom, carrying a long towel.

"Take off your clothes and put this on." She shoved the towel into his chest.

"Why do I need this?"

"For once, do as I say."

He liked the way her voice dipped when she gave commands. It was like she had done it many times before.

Dallas chucked the towel to the bed and went to remove his shirt, but could barely raise his arms above his head.

"Let me do it." Gwen moved his hands away. "You're in no condition to argue with me."

She lifted the bottom of his shirt, exposing his chest. She worked the material over his shoulders, gently freeing up his good shoulder and then his bruised one.

He liked the way she tended to him, clucking as she examined the dark bruises forming on his side.

She rested her hands on the fly of his jeans, and he reconsidered being alone and naked in her room.

"Perhaps this isn't a good idea."

She lowered the zipper. "Relax. If we don't see to your bruises now, you'll be unable to move in the morning."

She had to help him out of his jeans. The infirmity made him feel useless, but her encouraging touch eased his embarrassment. He kept reminding himself she was a nurse and knew what she was doing, even if he didn't.

Left in his briefs, he shivered as the cold closed in around him. Gwen wrapped the towel around his waist and seated him on the edge of her bed.

He furrowed his brow as she retrieved a jar from her nightstand. "What's that?"

She applied a dab from the jar to Dallas's left shoulder. A trace of sweet potato lingered in the air.

"It's yam cream. Best stuff in the world for bruises. It also has feverfew and white willow bark for inflammation."

The cream warmed his skin as she smoothed it over his tender shoulder and left ribs. The rush gave him a smidgen of relief.

Her fingertips became more insistent and dug into his flesh. White-hot shooting pains sent starbursts across his vision.

He hissed and reflexively pulled away. "Damn it. That hurts."

She kept working his sore muscles. "I know, but it will help you."

Dallas squeezed his eyes shut to block out the pain. It didn't help. He grunted, grimaced, and cursed through ever poke.

Her prodding fingers worked their way down to his sore ribs. Spikes of electricity took away his breath, but he didn't want her to stop.

"Where did you learn about this stuff?"

"When you ride horses, you tend to get knocked about a bit. I've used this for years. It's better than a shot of vodka and two aspirin."

The warmth turned into a pulsating heat that traveled from his shoulder and down his back. His pain lessened, and Dallas gained a new appreciation for her healing skills.

"Who do you get to rub the cream on you?"

She picked up the jar and lifted out a dab. "Never had the desire for anyone to do that for me."

"Maybe you should spend more time with other people and away from your horses. Might help you find someone."

Gwen gently swirled the cream on his left cheek. "I could say the same thing to you."

"I've made it just fine the way I am for the past thirty-eight years."

"You sound like me."

She was right. They were two people burned by relationships and afraid of starting again. But she didn't have a business that made any relationship impossible. The only person who would understand his commitment was another specialist. And his experiences with women in his game had never ended well.

Dallas might not have had a choice about his future, but she still did. He wanted her to find what he could never have.

He hooked her waist and pulled her close. "You deserve someone who can make you happy."

"Do I?" She lowered her chin. "I've been wondering what exactly it is I deserve. Maybe this whole Robertson fiasco has made me realize there are things I need to change in my life."

His pulse quickened. "What things?"

"You were right about me. I am hiding something." She flopped down on the bed. "I made a promise to a patient once. A man I cared for up until he died. His name was Earl Yeager."

The trauma of shooting Brewster had probably brought on her confession. He'd seen it before, and so had Simon La Roy.

"The best times to get information from a target is when they're vulnerable."

Dallas hated what he was about to do, but he had to close the job.

"Perhaps it's time to let go of this promise," he suggested, setting her up for the squeeze, as his specialists called it—the moment when a target spilled all. "If it's eating at you, maybe it's best to relieve yourself of the burden."

He waited, observing the rise and fall of her chest, and cursing himself.

The muscles in her neck jumped out like rope behind a sail. She twirled a lock of hair around her finger while her lips became thin and firm.

Whatever it was, Dallas could see she was having a hard time letting go.

"He asked me to do something for him, and up until now, I've been reluctant even to try. But I was thinking … I was hoping you could help me."

Dallas felt almost sick as he slipped his right arm around her shoulders, encouraging her. "I will do whatever you need me to do."

Gwen wriggled out from under him. She hurried across the room to the brown leather purse on the dresser.

He went after her, ignoring his agony. He was too centered on her secret to care about his discomfort.

She rummaged through the purse, and when she faced Dallas, she held up her closed right fist.

"He gave me this." She opened her hand and showed him a small gold key. "I know it's a safe deposit box key, but I have no idea where it goes."

On assignments in the past, he would have reveled in her confession. He felt no surge of victory, no elation, no pride in what he had done. All that flowed through him was the acrid sting of regret.

"Do you know what's in this box?"

She shook her head. "He never told me. He made me promise to give it to his family. It's just that … I don't know how to find them."

Gwen closed her hand around the key before he could examine it. She returned it to a back pocket in her purse.

His stomach sank. The answer had been within his reach, and she hadn't handed it over.

Damn it!

He clasped her shoulders, wanting to shake her reluctance from her. "I can try to find his family. I'll do what I can to track them down."

"Thank you." She eased away from him, a slight blush on her cheeks. "Now, you need to rest. Take my bed for the night. I doubt you'll want to sleep in your room after … I can sleep on the floor."

The image of her being put out because of him added to his guilt. "No, I can find another room. There are plenty."

She reached for one of the posts on the bed. Her fingers shone white against the dark wood.

"I don't want to be alone," she whispered.

Dallas sighed as he watched her trembling chin.

She's finally letting it all soak in.

He went up to her and pried her fingers from the post, eager to get her mind off Brewster. He took her hand and sat on the bed.

"It's a big bed. We can share it. I promise I will be a complete gentleman."

Her posture crumpled. "Have you ever been a complete gentleman?"

"I've had my moments."

She gave him a curt nod. "We can give it a try."

Gwen kept her head down as she gathered up her nightshirt and scurried to the bathroom, shutting the door behind her. She was no longer the woman who had boldly shot Brewster.

He sat on the bed, his fingers digging into the comforter, while he eyed her brown leather purse. The sweetness of the yam cream encircled him as he toyed with taking the safety deposit box key.

He couldn't cut and run. Not yet. He needed to make sure she was safe. When the trial was over, and her future decided, he could walk away with a clear conscience—well, almost clear.

Another day or two won't matter.

He could postpone the inevitable weight of his regrets, but his readiness to delay surprised him. A specialist was only to think about the job—the job was all that mattered. He would have to learn to embrace that mindset again if he wanted to survive in the business. To think only of his assignment, and forget about the person he was about to destroy.

CHAPTER TWENTY-THREE

The afternoon sun streamed through the gaps in the pergola, producing a checkerboard on Dallas's bare chest. A cool breeze skirted over the brick patio wall and teased his skin as he reclined in a chaise lounge, his belly full of ham and eggs. He raised his head and caught his reflection in the glass doors—he looked quite a sight. He had a bruise under his right eye and along his right cheekbone. His entire left shoulder, part of his side, and along his back were varying shades of black, blue, and yellow.

He longed to give in to the wash of fatigue sweeping over him, but the phone gripped tightly in his left hand reminded him why he couldn't let his guard down just yet.

The text from Lance an hour earlier still appeared on the screen.

> Stand by. The jury has reached a
> verdict.

The phone rang, and he scrambled to sit up, wincing.

"Any word?"

"They just announced the verdict five minutes ago," Lance said. "Guilty. The judge remanded Robertson into custody right away. It seems the feds think he's a flight risk."

Dallas's thrill of victory was short-lived as he thought of Gwen. "Now what?"

"You can take Gwen back to her farm. The feds are pulling

out as we speak."

"Their job is done," he agreed, scrubbing his face. "Who is going to keep an eye on Ed and Gwen now?"

"Our friend is putting men around Ed's house and will send two men to cover her place. He also wants to know if you got what he wanted."

Dallas peered at the bricks set into the patio wall, his misgivings eating at him. "Yeah, I got it."

"Any idea when you'll be heading back?"

"I'll make reservations today." He dreaded returning to the snow and emptiness of New York. "I'll let you know when I'll be flying out."

His husky voice had lost its intensity. Either his injuries had gotten to him or the job had. Whatever the reason, it was time to go.

"You okay, Dallas? Doesn't sound like you're too excited about getting back. You sure you want to leave?"

He willed away his weariness and firmly said, "My responsibilities are there."

"I'll be waiting for your call then." Lance's gravelly voice softened. "Have a good night. Try and enjoy yourself."

Dallas could almost hear him grinning as he hung up.

He stared at his phone, debating his next course of action. His restlessness reignited as he tapped his office number. Something wasn't right—the job wasn't finished. But he had the information Carl wanted. All that was left was to take the safety deposit key from her purse and hand it off.

"I can only assume this call means you're heading back," Stokes said when he answered.

Dallas scanned the patio, debating how to break the news to

Gwen. "If the airlines can get me in, I should be back in the office in a day or two."

"I'll let Cheyenne know."

"I take it you and Cleveland haven't come to terms yet."

"Hey, I'm a likable guy, but the raging beast is so moody. Kind of like you." Stokes became serious again. "Glad you're heading back. It's getting hairy without you."

The corners of his mouth turned downward at the prospect of burying himself in work once again. The organization was his top priority, but his zeal for it had dimmed. Even images of his Central Park penthouse didn't conjure warm thoughts of home. It had been Simon's home, never his.

"I'll text you when the job's done."

Gwen walked through the patio doors right at that moment. He squeezed his phone, hoping she'd not overheard too much.

"What's done?" she asked, coming up to him.

He tossed his cell to the chaise lounge and pinched the bridge of his nose, not wanting to look at her.

"Lance called. The verdict came in a few minutes ago. They found Robertson guilty. The judge remanded him into custody right after the trial."

"I can go home?"

Her enthusiasm reminded Dallas of where she belonged—on her farm with her animals, and far away from him.

He struggled to ease his legs over the side of chaise. "We can go first thing in the morning."

"Why not now?" Her bubbly tone was that of an exuberant child. "We need to get back to my horses."

His feet touched the slate, and he hunched over, the heaviness in his limbs reflecting the conflict swirling in him—guilt for leaving her, but also glad to get away.

He picked up his phone, cursing his emotions. "Go and pack."

Gwen pumped her fist into the air. "When we get back, you can cook a celebratory meal. In the morning—"

"I'm not going to stay." He kept the chill in his voice on purpose. "The trial is over and I need to get back to New York. I'll try and get a flight out tomorrow."

Her arm fell to her side, and her happy glow fizzled. "I see. Your job is done."

She turned to go, but Dallas held her arm. He didn't want it to end like this—not with malice or regret. He needed her to understand why it had to be this way.

"This isn't the job. It's me. I can't stay.

She stiffened against his touch. "I forgot about who you are for a moment. I'm sorry I got carried away."

He ran his hand through his hair, wishing he could explain about his life. "I don't want you to—"

"Let's just leave it where it is, shall we?" The detached formality he'd received from her on that first day returned. "Anything else would be a lie."

She hurried through the glass doors, disappearing into the house.

Dallas caught sight of the tall, lean man in the glass doors, but he didn't recognize the dead blue eyes staring back at him. Perhaps the first assignment after so long an absence was the most difficult. When he got back to New York, things would get easier. He would master his emotions as he had before.

Give it time and you'll forget how to feel.

That was the mantra Dallas seared into his brain as he headed into the house.

CHAPTER TWENTY-FOUR

The green pastures of Gwen's farm should have sent a surge of relief through Dallas, but the closer the car got to her gate, the sharper the sting of his regret. He'd spent the entire drive planning what to say before he left, and once he'd parked in front of her cottage, all his practiced speeches vanished. He let go of the steering wheel and flexed the blood back into his numb fingers, having been unaware that he'd clenched his hands.

Gwen was out the passenger door and across the clearing to the barn before he cut the engine off. He toyed with the idea of going after her, but then, on the seat next to him was Gwen's open purse. The last tie binding him to her was within his reach.

Take it and go.

He turned to make sure Gwen was still heading toward the barn before he rummaged through it. He removed the Glock stuffed into the purse and set it on the seat next to him. He fished out her wallet and keys, and then went through the little compartments that made up a woman's purse. There were a lot of them.

A high-pitched, piercing scream came from the barn.

Dallas's galloping heartbeat thundered in his ears when he turned toward the barn, scouring the open countryside. He grabbed the Glock and scrambled from the car.

He raced toward the barn, the long grass slapping at his jeans while disturbing images of what he would find pushed him to run faster.

At the barn doors, he stopped and listened, ready to shoot. A woman's sobbing came from one of the stalls at the rear of the barn. The aisle had no debris, blood, or anything that would alert him to the situation. Only sawdust and hay bales littered the floor. He hugged the stall doors, taking advantage of their cover, and followed the sound of crying.

Dallas arrived at the last stall, peered around the door, and came to a standstill.

The palomino mare Gwen had ridden was on her side with stiff legs and a bloated belly. Flies covered her mouth, and her tongue hung from her lips a dusky shade of blue.

Gwen lay stretched over the poor creature's neck, her shoulders shaking as she wept.

He lowered his gun and stepped into the stall, but then the stench accosted him.

She wheeled around and glowered at him with her red and watery eyes.

"Those bastards. I checked the other horses before I found her. None of them have had any water or hay in days. It's as if they never lifted a finger to care for them."

Dallas went to the water bucket in the front corner of the stall. It was bone dry. The feed bucket was also empty, and around the stall, mounds of manure and muck were ankle-deep.

He recalled the grooms Gwen had left in charge the day they'd headed for Carl's. The two young men seemed so eager to learn the ropes of her farm.

"I heard your scream in my car on the other side of the clearing." He glanced outside of the stall, and his hand closed around the Glock. "If those two grooms are on the property, why didn't they come running?"

She pushed away from the dead horse, her gaze reflecting the same uneasiness climbing his spine.

Gwen joined him at the stall's entrance. "Maybe they left."

Dallas waited, eager to pick up any sound. There was only the whisper of wind through the barn and the rustle of the other horses.

The hair lifted on the back of his neck. "Or maybe they're still here." He took his phone from his back pocket. "How fast can the local sheriff get here?"

"Fifteen minutes. That's if they come from the closest station."

Cut off with no close back up, Dallas weighed his options. The last thing he needed was to get the local police involved. He didn't want the headache of explaining where he'd gotten his guns.

"Let's check the grooms' apartment before we call anyone. How do we get inside?"

"Through the tack room."

Dallas cautiously stepped from the stall, keeping one eye on Gwen and the other on the aisle.

"Stick close to me."

He moved slowly, listening and checking the stalls for signs of what might have happened to the two grooms. Gwen's heavy breathing assured him that she remained right behind him.

They stopped at the flimsy wooden door of the tack room. Dallas pushed Gwen behind him before slowly nudging it open with the tip of his gun.

The scent of oiled leather mixed with the musty, sweat-soaked saddle blankets came from inside, but there were no sounds, no light coming from the apartment entrance at the back of the tack room.

Dallas signaled for Gwen to wait and then slipped into the darkened room. The walls had an array of saddles, bridles, and halters hung on hooks or secured to posts. Everything appeared to be in place. No debris cluttered the floor, and nothing seemed thrown around—no signs of a struggle.

He collected Gwen, shut the door, and then tiptoed with her to the apartment entrance, which was located next to an old refrigerator.

"The stairs are behind that door," she whispered.

He pointed at the ground. "Stay in this room. Keep the door shut. If you see or hear anything, call for help."

She touched his arm. "Be careful."

Dallas wanted to tell her everything would be fine, but instead, he eased the door open.

Sunlight streamed into the tack room, illuminating the equipment on the walls. He stuck his head through the door and listened.

Nothing.

After a few seconds, he climbed inside the short, enclosed staircase. "Keep this door closed until I get back."

Gwen's eyes appeared as two slits as she nodded.

He crouched on the first step, pointing his gun at a closed white door at the top of the stairs and waited for her to secure the tack room door.

Once the handle clicked into place, he moved, very slowly, up the staircase.

Sweat trickled from his brow, but he didn't wipe it away. He kept his hands wrapped around his gun, ready to fire.

Dallas was close to the top, mindful of keeping as quiet as possible, but when he shifted his weight onto the next step, a loud creak erupted from the stairs.

He froze, and his gaze locked on the door, waiting for it to fly open.

Seconds ticked by, but there were no sounds from the apartment.

They're either waiting to jump me, or not in there.

He headed up the last few steps, formulating a plan. He stayed low when he reached the door, and strained to pick up the slightest movement from inside.

Dallas psyched himself up for his charge into the room. His legs trembled, and his left side throbbed, but he shut out the pain and concentrated on how to get into the apartment without getting killed.

He put his hand on the knob, but then the door swung open. The slow creak echoed throughout the staircase.

He got down low and braced himself for an assault, but no shuffling, men shouting, or gunfire broke through the eerie silence.

Dallas raised his head and peered into the apartment. The overhead fixtures were out but two large windows at the back filtered sunlight into the single-room setup. One wall had white cabinets, a compact refrigerator, and a range. In the center was a red sofa, armchair, and a television on a round table perched atop a green rug. On the other side, against the wall, were bunk beds with white comforters.

Everything appeared neat and orderly.

He kept low while moving into the room, checking both sides of the entrance. The scent of coffee hit him, and then something else—the acetone reek of death.

Dallas moved deeper into the apartment, and the offensive odor got stronger. He attempted to cover his mouth with his sleeve and keep his gun raised. His eyes watered when the smell overpowered him.

He headed to the middle of the room to start his sweep for any clues. The linoleum floor dulled his footfalls, but as he got near the sofa, something hanging from the top of the bunk beds caught his attention—a human arm.

He inched closer, noting the mottled color and black fingers. It peeked out from the comforter haphazardly thrown over the top bunk. A large lump beneath the fabric sent a quiver of despair through Dallas. Someone had already decided on the fate of the grooms.

The smell got worse as he lingered next to the bunk bed. He removed one hand from his gun and took a deep breath through his mouth before tugging back the cover.

Contorted, decomposing bodies twisted into a macabre heap of hands and arms crushed under torsos made him recoil. The young men's heads had been set at frightening angles leaving their mouths opened and revealing their blackened tongues.

Dallas covered his nose and mouth before getting closer to search for a cause of death. The pooling of blood, their coloring, and the lack of rigor mortis gave him an estimation when they had died—probably the same day he and Gwen had left. He examined their faces and heads for evidence of beating or gunshot wounds.

He found fresh bruises on their cheeks, torsos, and shoulders. The distorted shapes of their noses indicated severe breaks. One of the men had lost two teeth, the dried blood had turned black on his lips.

Dallas found a trail of blood on the side of one man's face and followed it. Then, beneath his thick black hair at the back of his head, he found a bullet wound.

The stink became too much. He stumbled backward, putting the pieces together. His tears retreated, and then the cold reality of their compromised position clawed at his insides. Vulnerable and easily out gunned, he couldn't protect her if the men who did this came back.

I've got to get her the fuck out of here.

He jogged out of the room and bounded down the stairs.

When he pushed open the door, she was there, waiting with his phone in her hands.

"What did you find?"

He went up to her and clasped her hand. "We have to leave."

She pulled against him as he dragged her to the tack room door. "Why? What is it?"

Dallas stopped and faced her. "The grooms are dead. They were beaten and then shot. And whoever did it is going to come back for you."

Her gasp carried around the small room. "Me? Why? The trial is over. Robertson is going to prison."

The cold clung to his sweat-soaked shirt. The smell of the dead men was still with him, and the expanding knot in his stomach urged him to leave.

"Robertson may not be the only one after you. There are others Carl knows. Men who want the information you have."

He couldn't see her reaction. The dim light from the stairs kept her face hidden in shadows.

His mind raced, trying to decipher what she was thinking, but a funny inkling of relief broke through the taut wall in his chest. Perhaps it was a good thing she knew others were after her. She might give him the key without a fight.

Gwen eased closer to him. "That's why Carl sent you. He

wanted what Earl gave me. He asked me about it a dozen times, but I never understood why it was so important to him." Her eyes came into the light and appeared like two wary slits. "Then you show up, asking all those questions. You're not a bodyguard. You came to get a dead man's secret."

The warmth drained from his cheeks. For a target to know what a specialist wanted was disastrous.

Fuck.

He tugged her hand, not wanting to debate her when there still might be killers on her property. "We can talk about it in the car." He raised his gun. "Right now, we have to get out of this barn. When we step outside, stay close to me. We'll head straight for my car."

He opened the door and stuck his head into the aisle, investigating the back of the barn.

The same peaceful scene greeted him as when they had stepped inside the tack room. There was only the wind and the rustling of the horses in their stalls.

He eased onto the barn floor. Dallas had never thought he'd be so glad to smell shavings and manure again, anything to get the foul odor of the dead men off him.

Gwen followed, sticking close while they made their way to the horse's stalls.

A few horses stuck out their heads, one pawed the ground. When they saw Gwen, they became agitated. The strawberry roan let out a long, loud whinny that shattered the stillness in the barn.

"They're hungry," she said. "They need to be fed."

He feared the noise might alert anyone hanging around of their position. "We're not stopping."

They reached the first of the stalls, the open barn doors only lay a few feet away, but then, Gwen left his side.

His hands tightened on the gun. "What are you doing?"

At the first stall, she shot back the bolt holding the door in place. "Letting them out."

She yanked the heavy door open. The strawberry roan inside walked out, his nostrils flaring.

The hungry horse went straight to the hay bales stacked next to Dallas.

Gwen was already at the next stall, working the bolt. "They can get water from the trough in the field, hay from the bales stacked in here, and grass in the paddocks." The clang of the metal bar slamming back echoed around them. "It will be enough until I come back."

Dallas went to Gwen's side and stuck close while she set each one of the horses free. He wanted to urge her from the barn but gave her the extra time to see to her horses. She wouldn't leave them to die, and neither could he.

The aisle quickly crowded with the timid creatures who appeared unsure of what to do.

The cover they offered gave Dallas an idea, solving the problem of how to get Gwen across the open field in broad daylight without being an easy target.

"Chase them outside," he told her. "Into the field. We'll stay with them until we reach the car."

Gwen raised her arms and calmly herded a few of the horses to the open barn doors. Some snorted, stomping their feet with protest, and one pinned his ears back as she coaxed him.

But once outside, many of the horses broke into a trot and raised their tails.

Dallas grabbed Gwen's hand and started jogging with the

horses toward the house.

He searched the surrounding fences, and line of trees for any sign of the men who had killed the grooms. The grass brushed angrily against his jeans as he struggled to keep up with the slender bay.

Apprehension raked across his gut when the horse pulled up and stuck his nose in the grass. The car wasn't far away, but they would be the most vulnerable in those last few feet.

His shoulder throbbed, and sharp pains kept shooting from his left side as he ran, but he refused to slow down. He kept his attention on Gwen with only one goal in mind—getting her away from the farm.

They closed in on his red car. He dug out the remote from his pocket and opened the doors. Ten feet ... five feet ... and then they when he touched the handle on the door, he yanked it open.

Gwen ran into the car right next to him. He covered her head with his hand and shoved her in the driver's side door.

He waited as she climbed over the center console and got in her seat. He hurried in after her and slammed the door closed.

Gwen peered out at her Acadian cottage, her lower lip trembling.

He followed her gaze to the front porch. Not a hint of light shone through the windows. The only sound the gentle tinkling of wind chimes at the end of the porch.

"What about Lawrence?" she asked in a shaky voice. "If the grooms didn't feed the horses, then—"

He pushed the ignition button, and the engine roared. "We can't risk it."

Dallas slammed the car into drive and hit the gas, taking a sharp turn to head back through the open gate.

230

Gwen secured her seat belt. "We need to go to my father's. He can protect us."

He noticed the way her voice cracked, how she clutched his phone, and the grim line across her lips. He wished he could reassure her, and tell her the farm and her animals would be fine, but he couldn't. Later, when they were safe, he would soothe her fears. For now, he needed to concentrate on her.

"I have to make a call."

He took the phone from her as the car passed through the gate.

After he dialed Lance's number, a surly voice came over the speaker.

"Don't you ever text like a normal person?"

Jazz music and other voices drifted through the car.

Gwen's wringing hands concerned him. "I've got two dead grooms in the apartment above Gwen's barn and God knows what else waiting in her house."

"I'm at a brunch." Lance raised his voice over the music. "Let me go outside."

Dallas waited as the background noise dissipated.

"All right, go ahead," Lance instructed.

"This was professional. They beat the grooms before they shot them. They were probably questioning them."

Lance's easygoing tone took on a hard edge. "Get her in your car and get your asses out of there."

"Way ahead of you." Gwen's tears tore at him. "Gwen wants to head to her father's. Is it safe?"

"Yes, go to Ed Pioth's. Our friend has his men there. I'll let him know you're heading that way. He can send men to her farm. They'll clean up whatever mess they find."

Dallas hung up and pressed the accelerator, eager to get far away from her farm. He wanted to console her, but her safety was paramount.

"Carl will send people out to take care of everything. They'll check on Lawrence for you, too."

She turned toward the window, hiding her face. "Like he sent you to take care of me?"

The cold fury brimming in her voice confounded him. What could he tell her to salvage his assignment? He still needed the goddamned key.

His grip tightened on the steering wheel. "He sent me to look after you. He said others were interested in the information you had. These men were going to kill you until Carl intervened."

She wiped her eyes. "All the bullshit you fed me about keeping me safe … You're no different than the men who want me dead." She tossed her head back. "And to think, I was beginning to like you."

"Do you think I would have taken you to Carl's, fought Brewster, dragged you out of that barn if I didn't want to keep you safe? I'm not the enemy here. The men who want you dead are the ones you should be pissed with."

She wrapped her arms around her chest. "Deceiving someone is just another way of killing them. Lies can destroy a person just as easily as a knife or gun."

He stepped on the gas, fed up with her righteous attitude. The car's rear end shimmed on the gravel road.

"You haven't been exactly honest with me, either." He dug his nails into the steering wheel. "When are you going to tell me who you are?"

"You know who I am." Her strained voice rose in the car. "I'm not a liar or a cheat or a manipulator like you. Don't you dare jump all over me because you can't handle facing what you are. I don't have to pretend to be someone else to get people to trust me."

To argue with her was pointless—arguing with a woman, target or not, never got him anywhere. Dallas checked the rearview mirror, getting his head back on the task at hand.

"And if I had told you why I was sent from the first day we met, what would you have done?"

"Given you what Carl sent you to get and kicked your ass off my property." She turned back to her window. "But you chose a different outcome for both of us."

"No, you chose this outcome, Gwen. I was doing my job."

His phone vibrated in his lap. Dallas tore himself away from her profile and read the incoming text.

> I'm to collect the information our friend wants when I take you to the airport in the morning. You have ten o' clock flight to New York on American. Check your email.

Lance's message added to the anvil pressing on his chest.

He tucked the phone under his thigh. After tomorrow, his assignment would be over, and he could get back to his people and his business. It was where he belonged.

CHAPTER TWENTY-FIVE

Dusk had stimulated the lights along the historic Garden District street, and their odd yellow glare sent streaks across the road in front of Dallas's car. Patches of menacing shadows created by the thick oak trees along the sidewalk awakened an uneasy twinge. He knew nothing about Ed Pioth's home, the layout, the men covering it, and after everything he'd learned about Gwen's father, he dreaded their encounter.

He followed Gwen's directions until he eased in front of a classic double-gallery home, reminiscent of the postcards showcasing this section of the city. Two heavy-limbed oaks on either side of a brick walkway lovingly embraced the home's romantic wrought-iron balconies and white Corinthian columns. A white front door had a fanned transom and along the porch were a few white rocking chairs. With gray stucco exterior and high and arched windows, the structure gave an impression of strength and authority—qualities Dallas suspected the occupant admired.

He remained behind the wheel, scanning the walkway, house, and surrounding street for any sign of Carl's men. The shadows beneath the trees hid any signs of movement, but then a bald, bulky man in an ill-fitting suit stepped into the beam from a front porch light.

"Stay in the car," he directed in a dark tone.

The thick scent of gardenia brushed past when he climbed out. He put his hand on Gwen's Glock still nestled into his jeans as the stranger came down the walkway.

Dallas sized up the bulky man's hands, where they were and if they had anything in them.

"We've been expecting you, Mr. August."

His croaky voice broke the creepy silence enveloping the street.

"Mr. Bordonaro wanted you to know that if there's anything else you require to let me know. My name is Evan."

Dallas gave Evan's round face a quick going over. "What about the rest of your party?"

Evan nodded to the street. "One in the Camry over there."

A nondescript black Camry parked a short distance away remained close enough to observe everyone coming and going from the entrance.

"There's a man on the back porch, and I get the front porch," Evan announced with a nod.

"More thorough than the feds were willing to be." Dallas went to the car and opened Gwen's door. "It would seem we're well-protected."

She smirked as she climbed out. "I guess that makes you obsolete."

"Not quite." Dallas took her elbow and urged Gwen to the back of the car.

Evan inched closer to the trunk. "Mr. Bordonaro made it quite clear that every effort was to be made to keep Mr. Pioth and Ms. Marsh safe."

Dallas retrieved his overnight bag, still nervous about their situation, but resigned to make it work.

Gwen left his side, jutted out her chin, and walked up to Evan.

"What about my farm?" She stubbornly folded her arms over

her chest. "Will they be just as thorough there?"

"Yes, ma'am." Evan smiled, looking more menacing than friendly. "My guys went over there right after Mr. Bordonaro called. I promise when you return home, everything will be as it should be."

Gwen uncrossed her arms. She went to the trunk to retrieve her overnight bags, but Evan grabbed them first.

"Allow me, ma'am." He lifted her bags and picked up Dallas's suitcase as well.

Gwen cocked one eyebrow at Dallas, appearing pleased.

Dallas made the trek to the door with mixed emotions. One part of him was glad the ordeal was near an end, another dreaded the evening to come, and the conversation he and Gwen had to have.

The moment they climbed the steps, the front doors flew open. Dallas reached for his gun but stopped when he saw an older, very tall, muscular man with a full head of gray hair and bright blue eyes.

This must be Ed Pioth.

His intimidating size, bulging biceps, pinched mouth, and dark expression led Dallas to believe he was about to get punched in the nose.

"You're the bodyguard Carl hired. I'm Ed Pioth. Everyone calls me Ed." His booming voice carried across the porch.

Dallas stepped inside the home. "Ed, it's a pleasure to meet you. I'm Dallas August."

He shook his hand and noted how Ed's keen gaze evaluated every inch of his face. Dallas had seen his type before—the suspicious ones who judged a person in the very first seconds of a meeting.

Evan came in and deposited their bags on the floor. Then he gave one last nod to Ed and quietly shut the front door.

Near the entrance were a few framed family photos. All were of two tall, muscular blond men in an assortment of football uniforms, track clothes, and military gear.

"I heard about the farm." Ed came closer. "You all right?"

He made no move to comfort his daughter but stared as if he were waiting for her to break down.

Gwen's stiff body language told Dallas she wasn't comfortable in the home. Perhaps the events of the day had been too much, but the warm welcome he'd expected she would receive never materialized.

She held her head high. "My farm is a mess, but Evan assures me they will have it fixed by the time I get home."

"You look like hell." Ed motioned to Dallas's face. "You got quite a shiner there."

"Looks worse than it feels."

Ed inspected the bandage on Dallas's finger. "Was that from Brewster, too?"

"Just had an accident. I was chopping vegetables in the kitchen."

Ed's raucous laugh reminded Dallas of a foghorn—blaring and obnoxious.

"Why were you chopping up vegetables? That's a woman's job."

"Don't start." Gwen got between them. "Dallas doesn't need to hear your antiquated thoughts on the role of women."

"Antiquated?" Ed sobered and stuck out his chest. "I told you it would take a man to protect you and I was right. You should be grateful you had a former FBI agent to keep you alive."

Dallas stepped in, wanting to cool the hostility between father and daughter. "I didn't realize you had checked up on me."

"Of course." Ed put a demonstrative arm around Gwen's waist. "You think I would let just anybody move in with my little girl?"

Gwen quickly shimmied out from under Ed's grasp.

Her father might have been affectionate, but Gwen didn't seem to share the same regard.

Ed guided them along the short entrance hall and to a spacious foyer. A nine-tiered, tear-drop crystal chandelier hung from a white plaster medallion inlaid with roses.

More photographs of Ed's male progeny crowded the walls of this room as well. They were standing behind a ten-point buck, holding fish caught in a boat, or wearing tuxedos with corsages in their hands. The brothers seemed to be everywhere.

Ed stopped at the base of a curved staircase with a thick walnut banister carved to resemble a grapevine. "I'm glad you were there to keep Gwennie safe from Robertson's thugs."

Dallas set his overnight bag on the floor, "Are you sure it was Robertson's people?"

"Who in the hell else would it be?" Ed's loud voice shook the room. "After what happened at Carl's, he was out to get my daughter."

"But it could have been associates of Carl Bordonaro's," Dallas asserted, hoping the man would understand.

Ed's face reddened.

Dallas hadn't been sure about Ed's role in his daughter's dilemma until that moment, but he still wasn't convinced her father knew about the information she possessed.

Gwen frowned at her father. "Do you know the real reason

Carl hired him?"

Dallas ran his hand over his mouth, cringing. This wasn't how he'd wanted to handle the situation. He needed Ed on his side. If Gwen turned Ed against him, he might get kicked out of the house and never get a hold of the key.

"Gwennie, please!" Ed held up his hands. "You know Carl wants only the best for you."

Her tone turned icy. "Does he? Then why send him to lie to me?"

Ed's brows came together. "Lie? Who's lying?"

She dismissively waved at Dallas. "Carl sent him to get information from me."

Dallas arched his back, waiting for the impact of Ed's fist on his jaw.

"Is this true?"

Ed's hushed voice raised Dallas's curiosity. He expected to see his red cheeks and a cold sneer charging at him, but instead, Ed appeared as collected as the moment Dallas had walked in the door.

Though he was unsure of how to phrase his answer without pissing Ed off, Dallas knew he had to come clean.

"Carl feared for Gwen's safety and sent me to protect her from associates of his who wanted to know what Earl Yeager told her before he died."

Instead of glowering at Dallas, Ed turned to his daughter, frustration brimming in his voice. "Did you give him what Carl wanted?"

"No!" Her voice crept higher. "Mr. Yeager gave it to me. I promised I would carry out his wishes, not hand it over to this ..." She glared at Dallas. "Liar."

Ed's gaze darted between Dallas and Gwen as the tension

between them choked the air.

Dallas took in Gwen's scowl, wondering how he would get anything from her. The entire assignment had blown up in his face and it was his fault. Stokes was right—he'd been too rusty to return to the field.

Ed cleared his throat. "Gwennie, why don't you go upstairs and get settled in your old room? I want to have a word with Dallas."

Her shoulders deflated. "Whatever you two have to say, it involves me."

"This has nothing to do with you." Ed went to the newel post carved like a cluster of grapes and tapped the wood. "There's business Dallas and I have to discuss."

"Which is what?" she demanded, tilting her head. "I want to hear it."

Ed closed his fist on top of the newel post. "Go upstairs and let me handle this mess before someone gets killed."

His eyes glowed with a savage fire, and suddenly Dallas realized why Ed Pioth had been so important to Carl. He could be formidable when pushed, and probably as ruthless as the men he'd done business with for years.

"Gwen, why don't you go on upstairs?" Dallas nodded up the staircase, wanting to soothe her dented pride.

"Fine. I'll go." She picked up her overnight bags and swung them over her shoulder. "If you need me, I'll be punching a pillow."

Dallas tried not to grin as she bounded up the steps.

Ed waited until Gwen turned the corner on the second-floor landing. His gaze remained on the staircase for a few moments, and when he faced Dallas, his hand slid from the newel post.

"So this was all about her taking care of Earl Yeager. I told her not to do it. I never liked Earl. He ran a lot of dirty businesses in town."

Dallas inched closer. The man knew more about why Carl wanted the information than Gwen. Ed had spent years as a confidant of the wise guys who ran the city. He had a better understanding than his daughter of what to do and not do to stay alive.

"Carl and several of his associates think Earl disclosed something to Gwen before he died. It seems there are quite a few men who want this information. Whoever went through her house and killed those two grooms was looking for it."

Ed ran his hand across his chin. "Any idea what it is?"

"Gwen showed me a safety deposit box key Earl Yeager gave her. He wanted it to get to his family. I need that key. I'll give it to Carl, and then, perhaps, Gwen will be left alone."

Ed studied Dallas with his lips drawn in a firm line. "Carl wanted you to get this information out of her by any means necessary, I'll bet."

Dallas figured there was no point in sharing what he'd intended with Gwen. Ed had already figured it out.

"I'm leaving first thing in the morning. I haven't told Gwen. I won't be seeing her again."

The muscles quivering in Ed's jaw belayed his irritation.

"You're leaving when there's still a big mess to clean up."

"The decision wasn't mine," Dallas assured him.

Ed folded his arms over his broad chest, staring down at him. "You know, I might be an asshole, but when it comes to my kids, I want the best for them, especially Gwennie. When she came to us from that orphanage, she was so small and so malnourished I didn't think she'd make it. I've bent over backward to make sure she grew up tough, to overcome the bullies who made fun of her or teased her because she didn't look like her family. But when she showed up here with you, I saw a change in her. A softness I'd never noticed before. When you leave, you'll take all that away."

His words sucked the air out of Dallas, but what could he do? No matter how much Ed wanted something else for his daughter, it would never happen—not with Dallas.

He picked up his suitcase and overnight bag. "Where do you want me to sleep?"

Ed relaxed his firm stance and pointed up the stairs. "There's a guest bedroom across the hall from Gwennie's."

Dallas moved toward the elegantly carved staircase, wishing he could assure Ed that there was nothing between him and Gwen, but he wasn't so sure. His relationship with her had grown more complicated by the day. Perhaps walking away without a word was for the best.

"Long goodbyes do no one any good," Simon La Roy had once professed. *"End the job in one clean break. No one likes a specialist hanging around where they're not wanted."*

Dallas climbed the steps with images of Gwen's unusual smile building a thickness in his throat.

Simon always was a heartless prick.

CHAPTER TWENTY-SIX

The glimmer of the streetlamps came right through the sheer guest-bedroom curtains and shone on Dallas's bed. He couldn't shut out the confounding light no matter how many times he adjusted the curtains. Fed up, he tossed aside the gray covers, sat on the edge of the bed, and stared at his bare feet, wondering how he would ever get to sleep.

The cherubic-faced angels carved into his headboard, their puckered lips caught in an eternal kiss, brought back the memory of kissing Gwen. The perfection of her skin, and her intoxicating essence remained with him. He'd avoided her since entering his room, choosing to spend his time on emails. The distraction had worked, but once done with the problems of his organization, his thoughts had drifted back to her.

There's only one way to get her out of my head.

Spurred on by restlessness, he put on a T-shirt to stave off the chill, and still in his pajama bottoms, crept out of his room.

The dark landing had shards of light here and there peeking in from the street. Dallas groped along the hall until he reached the stairs.

He descended the steps, the light coming through the transom above the doors guiding his way. The quiet of the house washed over him. He glanced at his watch—it was well past midnight. It seemed he was the only one who couldn't get to sleep.

He touched the cold wood floor, and then the streetlights

landed on a table by the entrance. Atop the table was Gwen's leather purse.

A hitch caught in his chest—the one thing he needed most was within reach. He zipped open the purse and had stuck his hand inside when a flickering light shone on the wall next to him. It glinted off the glass of a few framed pictures of Ed's sons. He turned and saw an orange, fiery glow peeking through a pair of cracked pocket doors to the side of the staircase.

He wasn't the only one up, after all. Flooded with curiosity, he stepped away from the purse. He'd come back to it.

Dallas stopped at the pocket doors and peered through the crack. Firelight from the hearth filled the room. The *snap* and *crack* of the logs carried out into the foyer. He browsed the dark paneled walls and plush gold chairs, but it was the painting of a captivating woman above the thick walnut mantle that captured his attention.

She sat in a wing-backed yellow chair with her shoulder-length golden hair caught up in a breeze. Her skin was creamy porcelain, her brilliant green eyes gave off a hint of mischief, and her sharp nose and prominent cheekbones reminded Dallas of the men he'd seen in the pictures displayed throughout the home.

Then a head with long black hair popped up from the plush gold sofa. A woman's thin arms stretched upward, and a languid yawn carried to the door.

Dallas hesitated, unsure of where to go. He needed the key from her purse, but this might be his last chance to be with Gwen, to spar with her and revel in her fiery obstinacy. Perhaps just this once, he could break the rules and say goodbye.

"Your father has a beautiful home," he said, walking into the room.

Gwen spun around to him.

"Dad treats this house as his fourth child." She watched as he came across the hardwood floor. "Between the termites, the continual problems with sinking foundations, and the constant maintenance, he pays more attention to it than my brothers and me."

"Your brothers do seem to be everywhere."

"The house is a virtual shrine to them. Colin and Jackson were sports stars." She returned her gaze to the fire. "Dad had to figure out something to do with me, so he took me to the local stables and stuck me on a horse at four. My brothers complained my father spent more time at horse shows than at football games, but that's not entirely true."

He came alongside the sofa, taking in her long-sleeved white shirt and jeans. "Meeting your father has given me a little more insight into you. He's tough and made you tough, too."

"Tough enough for a woman, my father would argue. In his eyes, I'll never be quite good enough."

He studied her profile, questioning why she wasn't shouting, causing an uproar, or engaging in another war of words. He'd kept away to avoid an altercation about his reasons for being there, but as she sat on the sofa, almost appearing comfortable with him, her behavior confounded Dallas more than her brutal stubbornness.

The firelight shimmered off a bottle stuck between her crossed legs.

"Where did you get that?"

She lifted a half-full bottle of vodka. "Dad doesn't keep liquor in the house, so I smuggled it in. I put it in my bag back at Carl's. I remembered it when I couldn't get to sleep."

The reason for her mellow mood revealed, his trepidation melted away. "Can I join you?"

She waved him to the sofa, wobbling as she moved. "Go right ahead."

He sat and became hypnotized by the firelight on the portrait. The lines and color of the subject's hands and the way her long dress draped around her ankles impressed him. It was a piece worthy of Carl's collection.

"Is that your mother?"

She took a long swallow of the vodka and then nodded.

"It was a present from my father right after they adopted me." She held out the bottle to him. "Do you want some?"

Dallas took the vodka, inspecting her flushed cheeks and the dots of sweat on her brow. "How long have you been down here drinking?"

She rested her head on the sofa. "A while."

He brought the bottle to his lips and took a long deep swig. The burn hit the back of his throat, and he shuddered with relief.

She turned to him. "What brought you down here, other than your usual bullshit?"

He swallowed hard, caught off guard. "My usual bullshit?"

"All that stuff you carry around like a fifty-pound weight." Gwen waved an unsteady hand at his face. "I can see it in your eyes like a loathsome secret you can't share with anyone. Sometimes you look just as lost as I feel."

"You're not lost." He set the bottle on the floor, wanting to stay sharp. "You know where you're going and what you want."

Her heavy sigh rose over the snapping of the fire. "You have no idea what I'm talking about."

He inched closer, admiring the curve of her jaw. "Explain it to me."

She rocked her head forward, glaring at him. "Why do you

care? You came to get my secret. That's what you do—steal secrets and pass them on to the highest bidder." She wrinkled her brow. "How do you sleep at night?"

A lock of her hair tumbled over her shoulder. He wrapped the silky curl around his finger.

"I don't steal secrets. Whatever you think of me, I came here to protect you."

She nodded, and her head lolled to the side. "And you've done that. Job over. You can go home and forget about me."

He let go of her hair and sat back, perturbed by his constant hunger for her. It kept him from stealing the key and walking away. He hoped it died once he returned to New York.

"Forgetting you is going to be difficult."

She rested her cheek on the sofa, tilting her head, and dissecting his face with her gaze. "I thought you hated me. I got on your nerves, frustrated the hell out of you, never listened to a word you said and—"

"Got under my skin in the process."

He put his face closer to hers, and something broke inside him. It was like a tall wall tumbling after a great siege, and all the emotions he'd kept locked away were free.

"You're aggravating, smart-mouthed, deceptive, probably lying about any number of things at this very moment, but there's something I can't quite put my finger on that makes me want to kiss you and never stop."

She sat up and peered into the fire. "It would never go anywhere. You have your world, and I have—"

"Your horses." He slid closer, touching his shoulder to hers.

"Do you ever think about how we might have ended up if we hadn't met like we did? Without the lies, suspicions, and

247

animosity. Like two ordinary people who want to get to know each other?"

He nodded, intent on letting the truth pour from his lips. "I've thought about that a great deal, especially when I remember how you rubbed that cream on me."

Her airy, happy giggle gave him a glimpse of the woman she kept hidden behind her tough exterior. He knew the vodka had let her guard down, but he liked her this way. It was the most honest he'd ever seen her.

"I keep thinking of you in my kitchen." She rocked her head back. "I would sneak out of my office and watch you when you weren't looking."

The heat warming his insides stalled, and he drew his brows together. "Your kitchen? What did we do in your kitchen?"

She turned to him, and the rosy hue on her cheeks became a blazing shade of scarlet. "I hate to admit it, but watching you cook was a real turn on. It is for most women."

Dallas's chuckle circled the living room and a weight lifted.

"Now you tell me." He crumpled into the sofa. "I kept trying to get closer to you, to get you to see me as more than a bodyguard, to not hate me, and the answer was there all along. How did I miss that?"

Gwen nestled against his shoulder. "Yeah, well, it took me half a bottle of vodka to figure out how I feel about you."

He put his arm around her, pulling her to his chest. "And what have you decided?"

She ran her finger over his lips. "That whatever reason brought you to me, you're not the man I thought you were. You're so much more."

He touched his forehead to hers, relieved. It wasn't forgiveness she offered him, but a respite from his inner turmoil. He could take the key and walk away right now without any regrets. Hell, he would have one, and that was what kept him on that sofa—the hope of a few minutes of peace in her arms.

"What are we going to do about this?"

She dragged her finger from his lips to his chin and down his neck. "I've got my yam cream upstairs in my room."

He studied the contours of her face, hesitating.

Gwen pulled out of his embrace and took his hand, locking her fingers with his. "I suggest you come with me."

Dallas's guilt kept him on the sofa. She was tipsy, and he had an early flight.

"Are you sure? I can't—"

"I'm sure about you." Gwen yanked him to his feet. "I'm not under any false illusions about us. I want you for as long as I can have you. One night or one hour, I don't care anymore."

She threw her arms around his neck and kissed him with wild abandon.

Dallas forget all about Carl, the safety deposit box key, and his job. In that instant, he only wanted her. He eagerly embraced her, crushing her slender body to his. He returned her kiss with all the passion he'd been denying since first gazing into her hypnotic eyes.

She pulled away and urged him out of the living room.

They arrived at the base of the stairs, and she let go of his hand. Gwen ascended the steps, swaying her hips seductively as she climbed.

Halfway up, she stopped. She kept her back to him as the long-sleeved shirt around her fluttered. Then she dropped the shirt over one shoulder, exposing her beguiling skin. Gwen tauntingly lowered the fabric over her other shoulder. Then, she slowly eased the shirt down her back, and with a flourish, draped it over the banister.

His insides tingled when he saw her naked back and soft curves. Hungry to get his hands on her, he hurried to catch her, but Gwen darted up another few steps, staying out of reach.

She reached the top of the stairs and kept her back to him as she slid off her jeans. Gwen took her time climbing out of them, and when she faced Dallas again, she held the jeans in one hand while discreetly covering her breasts with her bandaged arm.

She grinned and dropped the jeans to the floor.

Dallas rubbed his chin, hell-bent on taking her to bed.

"Since you're still technically injured, I thought I would make it easier for you." She ran her fingers along the waistband of her white panties. "Think you can handle the rest?"

A burst of energy charged through him, and he took the stairs two at a time.

He reached the top, and Gwen ran toward her bedroom door.

It wasn't until she'd almost made it into her room that he enveloped her in his arms. He kissed her, letting go of all the longing he'd suppressed, and pushed her into her darkened bedroom.

With a swift kick, he shut the door. The glare from the streetlights streamed in through the window, guiding them to a wrought iron princess bed draped with yards of sheer fabric woven into the canopy.

She laughed into the recesses of his neck as he batted aside the bothersome material. They fell into the full-sized bed, clinging to each other. Creaking filled the bedroom while Dallas appraised their tight accommodations.

"Do you think we will both fit on this thing?"

"We'll fit." She cupped his face and kissed him.

Her soft skin smelled of jasmine and her lips tasted of vodka. Her gentle moans as he kissed her throat cast away any reservations he had about being with her. He needed this, and so did she.

He worked her panties down her legs while nipping her breasts, consumed with tasting every inch of her.

"The more I'm with you, the more I want you," Dallas murmured against her chest.

Gwen tugged at his shirt, and a crushing pain from his shoulder made him fall across the bed.

"Damn it."

Gwen sat up on her elbows. "Sorry. I forgot about your war wounds. Do you want to postpone?"

"No." Dallas rolled on his back and almost fell off the edge of the bed. "We're going to make this work."

Gwen positioned him in the center of the bed. "Leave everything to me."

She climbed on top of him and straddled his hips. Her hair tickled his bruised right cheek as her soft lips kissed his chin and nose.

"Now I get to show you the second-best thing I'm good at."

"I wouldn't exactly say the second-best thing." He gripped her hair, luxuriating in its silkiness. "I've been quite impressed with your performance so far."

Her kisses worked down his chest while she nudged his pajama bottoms over his firm butt. After flinging his pants aside, she gently coaxed his T-shirt over his shoulders.

He liked the way Gwen took control, undressing him while he kissed her breasts. A woman who knew what she wanted had always been a turn on for him. He'd forgotten that; he'd forgotten so many things about who he was before Nicci. But Gwen had revived the Dallas he'd once been—a man who had lived for the job.

Her insistence, the way she bit his neck, and the hunger in her hands drove him mad. She seemed as desperate for him as he'd been for her.

He tasted her pink nipple, sucking hard. She gasped and ran her hands through his hair, adding to his frenzy for her.

His fingertips stroked the soft skin on the inside of her thigh. "You wouldn't happen to have any condoms hidden in this room."

She bit his earlobe. "In my father's house?"

"Do you want to run to the store, or should I?"

"I can't wait that long." Her arms went around his neck. "I want you inside of me now."

The calculating specialist in him crumbled. He silenced his nagging doubts about her, quieted his cautious voice telling him to stop. It was the only night they would have together. Dallas wanted to forget about what tomorrow would bring.

He grabbed her hips, lifted her over his erection, and took her with one forceful thrust. He guided her hips, encouraging her to ride him, forcefully, relentlessly.

Gwen dug her nails into his chest as he entered her again and again.

Overcome, Dallas forced her hips to move faster, taking him as deep as she could.

Gwen groaned, arched her back, then she bucked. He held on to her, enjoying the guttural sounds she made when she came.

Dallas tensed, sending tendrils of pain through his shoulder and back, but he didn't care. He grunted and slammed into her with one last thrust before his climax exploded.

Their panting reverberated throughout the darkened bedroom. He lay beneath her with his arm draped over her back, attuned for Ed's pounding footsteps, or a bang on her door, but the quiet house remained like a tomb. The only sound was her faint breath against his cheek.

Perspiration covered his brow, and as Dallas reached to wipe it away, Gwen stirred.

He gazed at her, mesmerized by her beauty. A fleeting hope for more than one night with her drifted through his head, but the specialist in him snuffed out his longing. He'd been down this road before with a target, and he couldn't go through that hurt again.

She kissed his lips, arousing a white rush of heat.

"I didn't expect that."

He nuzzled her cheek. "What?"

"To become so lost in you." Gwen rolled over. "Neither one of us are the kind to give in to our desires."

He gathered her up in his arms to make sure she didn't fall off the narrow bed. "And yet here we are."

"Any regrets?"

"Never. We both wanted this, even if it took some vodka to give us the courage."

"We've both built a lot of walls around us. You more than me, I think." She raised her head. "And when you go, those walls will go right back into place."

He longed to tell her he wouldn't leave, but the forces driving them apart were stronger than the ones keeping them together.

"Have I ever showed you what I'm good at?" he murmured into her cheek.

"Other than cooking."

He took her lower lip in his mouth and raked it over his teeth.

"That's the second-best thing I'm good at."

She ran her fingers through his short hair. "Getting beaten up?"

He chuckled into her neck. "That's the third."

Gwen sighed and reclined on the bed. "Does it involve a gun?"

His hand slipped between her thighs and gently spread them apart. "Now you're getting warm."

CHAPTER TWENTY-SEVEN

Faint rays of golden sunlight stretched across the princess bed, rousing Dallas from a deep sleep. He glanced at his watch and grimaced—he'd overslept. Gwen's head lay across his chest, her hair draped over his shoulder. He gently nudged her aside, trying his best not to wake her as he wiggled out of bed. The way she slept, curled up like a child, damn near made him climb back in.

In the pale light, he got his first good look at her bedroom. Horse show ribbons decorated the walls, and trophies cluttered the oak dresser. On the bookshelves, copies of classic Jane Austen novels sat next to those of Stephen King. There were assorted ticket stubs from various rock concerts preserved beneath a glass countertop on a white desk. Inserted into the edges of a vanity mirror above a white dresser were a few pictures of two men in desert fatigues. They both had their father's coloring and muscular physique.

He padded across her room, picking up his clothes as he went. He opened the door as quietly as possible and then ducked into the hall.

Once safely in his bedroom, he quickly flung what clothes he had unpacked into his suitcase and headed for the shower.

While waiting for the water to warm, he remembered the way Gwen had kissed him and ridden him. Frustrated, he turned the tap to cold and jumped into the shower.

He shivered beneath the water, but he needed this—to feel

something, no matter how painful, before he returned to New York. Once he stepped back into his world, he would become numb again. Dallas would disappear behind the uncompromising professional he'd been before New Orleans, and before Gwen.

☙🕉❧

His senses dull, his eyelids heavy, and the ache from his shoulder nagging at him, Dallas set his suitcase and overnight bag by the front door. He didn't want to think of Gwen still asleep in her bed, or the night they had shared. Instead, he concentrated on the long day ahead and business matters needing his attention the moment he got back to New York.

The bitterness of coffee and chicory drifted by and he perked up his head. Perhaps a quick cup would help him. He turned, about to head toward the kitchen, when Gwen's handbag on the table brought him to a halt. He'd forgotten all about the key. He checked his watch and the bite of urgency to finish his job took hold.

Do it. Lance will be here any minute.

Dallas did a quick scan of the hall and stairs—he was alone. He quickly lost himself in the purse's small compartments, which hid anything from lipstick to loose change. The key wasn't in any of the compartments or hidden in a side pocket. He was tempted to dump the contents of the damn thing on the floor.

He stood back, scowling at the purse and running his hand through his hair.

Where the fuck could it be?

He rechecked his watch. He still had time to question Gwen about the key.

Dallas set his foot on the stairs, and planted his hand on the newel post, ready to get tough with Gwen, but then stopped in mid-stride.

What am I doing?

He already had the information Carl wanted. Gwen had told him about the safety deposit box but knew nothing about the contents or the location. He didn't need the key to fulfill his assignment. If Carl wanted the key, he could get it himself.

The bitter taste in his mouth receded, and he turned away from the staircase. The lure of coffee guided him down a long hallway, and he pushed all worries about Gwen and her future aside. Once her secret passed into Carl's hands, she would be safe from further danger, free to live a quiet life on her farm.

He stepped into the kitchen and the bright yellow walls, shiny white-tile countertops, and ribbons of sunlight streaming through the windows sent his hand to his eyes. Momentarily stunned, he squinted while waiting to regain his vision.

"You heading out?"

The glare cleared. Ed appeared at a round, wooden table in the center of the kitchen, a coffee mug in hand.

Cabinets done all in white rose behind him, a dated white built-in refrigerator and white dishwasher set in the center. There was an old cast-iron sink, and several appliances cluttering the countertop. Dallas spied the coffeemaker's full pot and the pang of guilt from his night with Gwen morphed into an unshakable need for caffeine.

"I'll be leaving in a few minutes." Dallas slinked up to the coffeemaker. "Thought I would grab a cup before Lance Beauvoir shows up."

He liked the assortment of framed recipes arranged on the

yellow walls. It filled the room with mouth-watering pictures of cakes, pies, and cookies.

"Lance Beauvoir, now there's a character," Ed admitted.

Dallas selected a mug and examined an antique six-burner stove set up at the end of the counter.

"Yeah, Lance is something."

"When Gwennie first told me about you. I got in touch with Lance." Ed wrapped his hands around his mug. "He told me a good bit about you. He likes you, and Lance Beauvoir doesn't like very many people."

Dallas filled his mug. "Lance has been a good friend."

"And my daughter? What has she been to you?" Ed stiffly stood from the table, no longer intimidating. "For what it's worth, I understand you haven't been given a lot of choices here. I know you're leaving, and it's over, but at least my Gwennie had some happiness with you." He pulled something out of his pants' pocket. "I believe this is what you were looking for."

In his hand was a small gold key.

Dallas put down his mug. He stepped closer and took the key from him, clenching it in his closed fist while a sinking feeling came over him.

"Why give this to me?"

"I explained everything to Gwennie last night. I made a fire in the living room, sat her down, and told her why you were here. After that, she gave me the key. I was instructed to give it to you before you left this morning."

His chest constricted as he silently berated himself for being such a lousy human being.

"Tell Gwen …" Dallas struggled to find the words.

"I'll tell her something." Ed patted his shoulder. "Not to

worry."

The phone in Dallas's pocket pinged.

Outside. Move your ass.

Regret rolled through him.

"I take it Lance has arrived." Ed held out his hand to Dallas. "Thanks for taking care of Gwennie. Now you try and take care of yourself."

Dallas slid the key into his pocket, dazed by what had happened. People weren't so forgiving in his business. They usually screamed or swung punches after finding out about his deception. He'd never been wished well before.

He hurried from the kitchen, shame burning his cheeks.

When he stopped at the entrance and collected his bags, his gaze traveled up the grand staircase. The longing for one last look clouded his judgment but then the ping from his phone brought him back to his harsh reality.

He squared his shoulders and readied to put her behind him. Dallas opened the front door and sucked in the cold morning air.

It's time to go.

A blue Jaguar waited at the end of the walkway, the tailpipe putting out puffs of smoke while it idled at the curb. Lance Beauvoir, decked out in a form-fitting suit, climbed from the driver's side, waving his hand.

"Didn't you get my texts?"

Lance went around to the back of the car and opened the trunk, an impatient bounce in his step.

"I was saying goodbye," Dallas explained.

Lance cringed. "I never figured you one for goodbyes."

The pain in Dallas's shoulder flared as he lifted his luggage into the trunk. Still wincing, he unzipped his suitcase and removed the Sig Sauer.

He handed the gun to Lance. "Well, there's a first time for everything."

Lance snickered and pitched the gun back into the trunk. "Somehow I don't see you and Ed Pioth hugging it out." He pointed to the bandage on Dallas's finger. "The guy who did that to your finger, did he do that to your face, as well?"

Dallas ignored him and eyed his car parked behind Lance's Jaguar. "I thought we were going to return that."

"It's leased for another week. I can return it later." Lance arched an eyebrow. "The case I gave you with the backup Sig, is it still in the trunk?"

Dallas nodded and reached into the pocket of his slacks.

He pulled out the gold key Ed had given him and tossed it to Lance.

"I believe that is what Carl is waiting for."

Lance closed his hand around the key. "Carl will be very pleased."

Dallas shut the trunk. "I'm glad someone will be."

"Do I detect a hint of regret?"

Dallas glared at Lance over the roof of the Jaguar, wishing he'd called an Uber.

Lance opened his car door. "Hey, I'm not saying anything happened between you two, but if it did, I could certainly understand. I'm just glad you took my advice."

"What advice?"

Lance gave him a mischievous grin. "You got to know the woman. Did I happen to mention I'm envious as hell?"

A violent storm of cutting remarks shot through his head, but Dallas held it all in. He raised his gaze to the elegant second-story balcony of Ed's mansion, taking a last mental picture. A fluttering curtain in one of the windows aroused hope for a final glimpse of her. Then the curtain stilled.

He got in the car and yanked his seatbelt over his shoulder, angry for forgetting what he was.

"You've got it bad." Lance hit the ignition switch. "I haven't seen you that enamored with anyone since Nicci."

Dallas didn't look at him but motioned to the road ahead, ready to put Gwen behind him. "Are you going to talk or drive?"

"I've been known to do both."

"Just get me out of here." Dallas turned to his window and willed the walls around his heart back into place. "My job is done."

CHAPTER TWENTY-EIGHT

The golden streaks from the morning sun had barely crested the New York skyline when Dallas got behind his desk in his Cuomo Towers penthouse. His shoulder still ached despite the aspirin he'd consumed after stumbling out of bed. He would probably need a whole pot of coffee to help him tackle the work that had piled up since he'd been in New Orleans.

He sighed at the work waiting for him on his desk. Stacks of manila envelopes with new clients yet to vet needed his attention, emails on his computer awaited a reply, and a pile of unopened bills required payment. He was too damned preoccupied to deal with any of it.

Dallas read through the notes he'd made on the yellow legal pad. It was his accounting of every room in the penthouse. He had a long list of changes he wanted to implement—ways to make what had once been Simon's his.

He raised his head to his open office door, craving his coffee. "Cleveland?"

"I'm comin'," his security guard shouted from the hall.

The tall man with the bulging arms casually strutted into the office, carrying a steaming mug.

"You've been back for two days, and you still look like shit." He set the coffee on Dallas's desk. "You ever gonna tell me who beat the crap out of you?"

"Nope."

"You gonna tell me what happened? You've been real quiet since you got back." Cleveland didn't wait for a reply. "Can't believe you didn't stay longer in N'awlins. What I wouldn't give to get away from this freezin' ass weather."

Dallas scribbled on his pad. "Would you like a vacation?"

"Sure." Cleveland shrugged. "You gonna give me one?"

Dallas tapped his pen on his pad, half paying attention. "No."

Cleveland peered over his shoulder. "Whatcha doin'?"

Dallas dropped the pen and was about to reprimand his security guard for snooping when he changed his mind. He sat back and eyed the man, curious.

"How would you feel about redecorating this office?"

Cleveland cocked his head. "What brought this on?"

Dallas set his pad on the desk, more determined than ever to implement his changes. "Maybe I've come to terms with owning this business. It's time to make it mine."

"I hope that means you gettin' rid of Simon's pictures and shit."

"Some of his things will go into storage, or maybe I'll sell them. I'll hire someone to come up with ideas." He motioned to Cleveland. "You're the one who kept reminding me about Simon's stuff all over the penthouse. And you're right, we need somewhere we can be comfortable."

The large man came around to Dallas's side and stared at him for several very uncomfortable seconds.

"Did you sleep with that Gwen Marsh woman? Is that why you got a hankerin' to redecorate?"

He sharpened his focus on his security guard. "How the hell did you come up with that? And no, I didn't sleep with her." Dallas clenched his fists at the lie. "You were hired to run my security, not my love life."

Cleveland's glower cooled. "So, you're serious 'bout redecoratin'. For true?"

Dallas scratched his head, daunted by how Cleveland's mind worked. "I've made notes, so if you have any suggestions, let me know."

Cleveland's bellowing laugh bounced off the walls. "Yeah, I got a suggestion. Put Stokes's skinny ass in a new office in a whole 'nother buildin' on the other side of town."

Dallas picked up his pen, ready to get back to work. "I guess that means you two never made friends while I was away."

"Friends?" Cleveland bowed over the desk with a threatening line on his lips. "You're lucky I didn't kill that boy. Otherwise, you'd be bailin' my ass outta jail instead of sittin' there makin' notes about wallpaper and shit."

Dallas arched away. "Is there anything else you want to tell me?"

"Yeah." His security guard stretched his thick neck. "If I have to keep workin' with Stokes, I want a raise."

Dallas chuckled and picked up his coffee. "I'll think about it." He lifted the mug to Cleveland. "And keep these coming."

Cleveland groaned as he marched to the doorway. "You'd better get your ass a secretary before I chuck that coffee in your lap." The door closed with a muffled *thud*.

Dallas needed to have a word with Stokes. He couldn't afford to lose Cleveland. He liked the man too damned much.

His phone rang and forced him to set aside his coffee. The number flashing on the screen made him hesitate. This was another problem he didn't need.

"Hello, Dan. Never thought I would hear from you so soon."

"What kind of horseshit are you trying to pull, August?"

Dan's bellow made Dallas pull his phone back. He knew most of his moods pretty well, but this was new. Intrigued, he closed the email on his computer and gave Dan his full attention.

"You lost me."

"Brewster and Crawford. They were found dead inside a property belonging to Robertson in New Orleans. What do you know?"

Dallas hesitated, still unsure of what he'd heard. "Robertson? Are you sure?"

"I'm looking at the fucking report on my desk."

The strain in Dan's voice forced Dallas to believe the information was credible. It also went along with the message Carl had wanted to send to his former rival—guaranteeing he'd be locked away for a very long time.

"Well, you have Robertson," Dallas told him, a cocky lilt in his voice. "Question him."

"I can't. He's dead. They found him strangled in his cell."

Cold washed over Dallas. "When did this happen?"

"What are you living under a rock?" Dan shouted. "It's all over the goddamned news."

Dallas wiped his face. Carl's influence stretched far. To take out Robertson while in federal custody meant his moles had embedded themselves right under the government's nose.

"I want answers," Dan said, sounding calmer. "The last time we had contact from either of my men was the day they were at Carl's house watching you and the woman. But then the trial went to the jury, and I pulled them. After that, they went silent. The trackers on their phones went dead, and they never showed up at their hotel. But you know what happened, don't you?"

Dallas put his feet on his desk, feeling smug. "Can't help you."

"I could haul your ass in for questioning."

He'd lived under the FBI's shadow, fearing any involvement with them in case his business suffered, but Dallas was done cowering. He'd arrived from New Orleans wanting to make the organization his, but he would have to do more than redecorate—he would have to defend it against all obstacles.

"You won't do that, Dan, because I know about Brewster." He relaxed his grip on the phone as his confidence grew. "He belonged to Robertson. He told me right before he tried to kill me and frame me for Crawford's murder. Robertson wanted Gwen, and was going to use her to sway the trial's outcome his way."

There was no whisper, no noise, no rustling as the silence stretched between them. The void of sound pulsated with the friction that had seeped into their once-friendly relationship.

"Did you kill him?"

The undertones of animosity in Dan's gruff voice prompted Dallas to carefully weigh his answer.

"No, he committed suicide. Isn't that what you're going to put in your report? That he was found dead of a self-inflicted bullet wound to the head on Robertson's property. That way you can scare off any others considering moonlighting for the mob."

"Like I need that headache on my department's record." Dan's throaty chuckle resonated throughout the office. "Brewster and Crawford died in the line of duty, revenge from Robertson for the trial. That is what my superiors will read in my report."

Dallas had spent years under Dan's tutelage and knew the man had survived by treading water in a cesspool of bullshit. He needed a story to appease his superiors and keep his department free of investigation, but for Dallas, Dan's deception was an opportunity.

"What would your superiors say if they knew about Brewster? Or that he wasn't the only mole in your department?" He pictured Dan's red face. "Wouldn't look good for you if that information got out. It might jeopardize your position as head of the Organized Crime Division. Could even lead to an interdepartmental hearing, and I know how much you hate those."

"Are you blackmailing me?" Dan asked in a furious whisper.

"Yes, Dan." Dallas drummed his fingers against his leg, brimming with confidence. "I believe I am."

Dan uttered a tirade of curse words. "I could nail you for Brewster's death and Crawford's. I could have agents at your office with arrest warrants in ten minutes." He paused, and rapid-fire grunting sounds came over the speaker. "What do you want?"

Indignation had Dallas's voice dropping to just above a growl. "We're even. I owe you nothing on Bordonaro, and you stay out of my business. If you don't hold up your end, I'll tell everyone I know about Brewster and the others in your department. Men owned by Robertson, Bordonaro, and probably a whole lot more."

He waited, knowing he'd pushed too far but no longer giving a damn. In some poker games, you had to go all in to see what another player was hiding—he'd just done that with Dan. Everything was on the line, and it was liberating.

"Fine." Then Dan's voice turned deadly. "We're even, but cross me, and you won't live to be arrested. And I'll do it myself."

The line went dead.

Dallas set his phone on the desk, feeling a boulder lift from his being. He'd gotten Dan off his back, protected his business, and kept Carl from the clutches of the FBI. For the first time in over a year, he felt like celebrating—he'd pulled off a fucking miracle.

"You're up early," Stokes said as he walked in the office.

Dallas refrained from mentioning his conversation with Dan Wilbur. Stokes didn't need to know about the efforts he went to for the organization. That was his secret to keep.

Stokes came alongside the desk, and Dallas marveled at his impeccably tailored suit and silk tie. He knew a lot of specialists had their quirks, but Ray's affinity for fine clothes seemed to stand out.

Stokes leaned in front of him, his gaze lingering on Dallas's bruised cheek. "Are you going to tell me how you came to look like that?"

He let the comment slide. The less Stokes knew, the better.

"What are your thoughts about redoing this office?"

Stokes's eyebrows rose. "What has this got to do with the bruises on your face?"

Dallas picked up the pad and showed it to him. "Nothing. But since I've returned, I've been considering changing some things around here."

He looked over the notes. "Does Carlsbad go with all of Simon's pictures?"

Dallas chuckled. "You need to lay off Cleveland. He's bigger than you and better with a gun."

He returned the notes to Dallas's desk. "And I'm better with a blowtorch, but let's hope it doesn't come to that."

His assistant strolled across the office to the open door.

Cleveland appeared out of nowhere and came charging into the office, practically knocking Stokes to the side.

"Hey, watch the suit, Columbus."

Cleveland ignored him and marched up to Dallas's desk, carrying a basket stuffed with apples, pears, oranges, bananas, and grapefruit. Wrapped in yellow cellophane and topped with a red bow, the oddity looked ridiculous in the large man's paws.

He plopped the basket in the middle of a pile of bills. Papers scattered everywhere.

"What the hell?" Dallas barked, arching away.

Cleveland waved to the fruit basket. "This just came for you. Figured you'd want to see it."

Dallas shoved the basket away and mumbled, "I'll see it later."

"There's a card. From that Mafia guy." He dropped the opened card on the desk. "And he sent this." He held a brown envelope in his other hand.

Dallas sat back and cocked an eyebrow. "You read the card?"

Cleveland raised his chin, standing up to Dallas. "He says 'thanks for the help and Gwen's back with her horses. Safe at last.' What's that 'safe at last' crap mean? Is she safe 'cause she's rid of your sorry ass, or safe 'cause of some other reason?"

Dallas ran his finger over the top of the card, reading a million different meanings into Carl's note. Part of him wanted to throw the card away, not caring about Gwen's circumstances, but their night came back to him, and suddenly he did care, more than he wanted to admit. But then why would Carl send the basket if he didn't have something further to share?

Dallas picked up the note and deciphered the messy handwriting.

"I have no idea what it means."

Cleveland leaned over his shoulder, his hulking mass warming the air. "Well, ain't ya curious? Don't ya think you should call and check on her? You want to know."

He dropped the note on his desk. "No, I don't. The job is done."

Cleveland set the brown envelope in front of Dallas. "Done, my ass." He removed the fruit basket. "That one I didn't open. Felt like money."

He marched toward the office door and then kicked it closed with his thick boot.

Dallas stared at the unopened envelope, waffling. He didn't want any more reminders of Gwen, but the thickness of the contents sparked his curiosity.

Dallas shook his head and snapped up the envelope. "It better be money."

The moment he tore off the top, he realized it wasn't money. Photographs, a dozen of them, perplexed him. The pictures spilled onto his desk, and Dallas got a better look at the subject. Taken from far away, they were of a woman, either riding a horse, walking across an open field or standing outside a white Acadian cottage.

He leaned forward, getting a better look, and then his bewilderment turned to remorse. They were pictures of Gwen on her farm, tending to her animals and appearing at peace.

Safe at last.

The sting in his chest faded and the resolve he had to let her go took hold, reaffirming he'd made the right choice.

He picked up one of the pictures to get a better look, and then something odd jumped out at him. The woman in the photos looked like Gwen, but her large hands and the way she held her head was off. Dallas flipped through the other shots, hunting for one that offered a better view of her face.

It was the last in the dozen he'd been sent—a close-up shot of her peering into the distance, perhaps curious about the photographer. Her brow had deeper creases than he remembered, her mouth was wider, and her eyes appeared smaller and closer together. The color was also off. They were deep brown and not hazel.

A prick of pressure surfaced in the center of his chest as he carefully examined each picture, dissecting every detail and comparing it to the woman he knew.

After twenty minutes of poring over the photographs, he sat back and covered his mouth.

It isn't her.

The distinction between Gwen and the woman in the pictures was subtle. She had the same size and build, but her face wasn't as pretty, and she appeared a little older and more careworn. Someone keeping an eye on her at a distance—like an FBI agent—would never see the difference. But someone close to her, living in her home and interacting with her, would spot the inconsistencies.

A tornado of images, all of Gwen, inundated him. The pressure in his chest turned to burning. He got to his feet, opening and closing his hands to fend off his rage.

Unfuckingbelievable!

He charged the windows overlooking Central Park, a hundred ideas running through his head. He wanted to call Lance, talk to Carl, confront Ed Pioth, but first, he had to see for himself that it wasn't his Gwen on the farm. And once he knew for sure, he would hunt down the person who had set him up.

He put his hands on the window, rallying his control. He had to be smart about this. Dallas couldn't talk to anyone until he had answers. Once he got the proof he needed, he would use every means at his disposal to find the traitorous bitch. And then, he would tear her apart.

CHAPTER TWENTY-NINE

The sweetness of fresh-cut grass teased Dallas as he climbed from the rental car outside of Gwen's gate. He set his hand over his stomach, hoping to relieve the funny quivering that had been with him since leaving the New Orleans airport. Anger had driven him to get on a plane and come to her farm, but now that he was there, the distasteful acidity of doubt filled his throat.

The expanse of clear sky seemed to reassure him that everything was as he had left it. The white Acadian was there, as was the wrap-around porch and array of potted plants. Even her old blue truck still sat tucked beneath the shade of the tall oak. Horses roamed the paddocks or grazed in the pasture behind the red barn, and the quiet was still hanging around, unnerving him just as it had on that first day.

Then, through the barn doors, a woman riding a sleek bay came out to the field. She sat atop the majestic animal, and his thick neck arched as he trotted. Her long black hair floated behind her, not set in Gwen's usual ponytail.

The relationship between horse and rider fascinated him as he took in the synchronized movements, but something felt off. The grace he had seen when Gwen rode the same gelding in the field wasn't there. This rider was stiff and lacked his Gwen's gentle hands. The animal even moved differently. The change in his trot was subtle, but he seemed less formal and more at ease. The way Gwen had mesmerized him on horseback had vanished completely.

The woman spotted him and turned the horse toward the fence. She came closer, and more differences caught his eye—her large hands, thicker waist, and broader shoulders. When she was almost on him, Dallas saw her eyes—brown and threatening.

"Can I help you?"

The deep throaty voice wasn't Gwen's. It had none of her airiness or sassy charm and was almost flat to his ears.

He anxiously watched as she got down from the horse and came closer. Her hips did not have Gwen's alluring sway. Her face was a bit longer, her skin lacked that velvety quality he'd grown addicted to, and her nose was stubbier, chin pointier, and her features were without Gwen's air of stubbornness. The resemblance was very close, but her world-weary expression and critical gaze weren't that of the spitfire he'd known.

"Look, if you're a salesman, I'm not interested so you can—"

Dallas took a step toward the metal gate. "I'm looking for Gwen Marsh."

The horse nudged her arm, and she stroked his long nose. "I'm Gwen Marsh."

He'd been rehearsing his reaction, letting it consume him during the long flight from New York, and had practiced everything he would say. However, standing in front of the woman he'd wanted to vent his frustrations on, his words suddenly seemed anticlimactic.

He rubbed his face, attempting to clear his head. He wouldn't get anywhere shouting.

"I don't know what's going on, but I was out here just last week with Gwen, and you're not—"

"You're Dallas. She told me you might come back."

The lava in his belly reignited but without the same gusto. He steadied his voice, eradicating any note of malevolence.

"Who told you I might be coming back?"

She dropped the reins and worked the bridle over the horse's head. "The woman you stayed with last week. She was sent here to be me." She patted the animal's neck after he dropped the bit from his mouth.

The horse went right to the grass, ignoring Dallas.

His fingers tingled, aching to close into fists. "I don't understand. Why did you need to have someone become you?"

She turned to the saddle, lifting the flap. "My ex-husband and father wanted me out of harm's way during the Robertson trial." She loosened the buckles holding the girth in place. "Doug wanted me to stay with him, but my father knew if I left, Robertson's people would hunt for me. Then one day, Doug came to me with a plan to have someone who looked like me, and could care for my horses, pretend to be me until things blew over. With Robertson's men and the feds watching my decoy, I disappeared. I wasn't crazy about the idea, but I went along with it to make my father happy."

Her almost shy quality was a far cry from the assertive woman he'd known. His Gwen would have looked him dead in the eye and challenged him. This woman didn't have her fight.

Dallas shook his head as the genius of the switch washed over him. It was the perfect way to guarantee the real Gwen's protection, keep the FBI at bay, and make sure an apprehensive Ed Pioth stuck to his promise to testify. It was what he would have done if presented with the same situation. The one thing unsettling him was where they had found someone so perfect, and so well trained to pull off the job.

"Who hired the decoy? Where did you find her?"

Gwen lifted the saddle from the horse's back and set it on the gate. "Perhaps you should come inside." She released the latch.

The horse took advantage of his freedom and trotted toward the barn.

Dallas scanned the landscape, searching for other cars, other people, anything to tip him off that he'd been set up or lied to again. The job hadn't felt right from the moment Carl had brought him in, and there was no reason to believe anything had changed. The girl could be a plant, work for the feds, or even Robertson. He had to remain vigilant.

He waited for Gwen to close the gate and then followed her to the house, noting the way she casually strolled, held her head in an almost dreamy pose, and didn't appear to be in a hurry. There was none of his Gwen's fire.

They climbed the porch steps, and Dallas took an interest in the two large dogs at the far end.

"Are those your dogs?"

She opened her front door and her shiny hair swept across her shoulder. "Harley was mine, too. I heard about what happened to him when I got back."

Dallas followed her, hell bent on finding answers.

He walked inside the house and stopped when he saw the pictures on the walls. They were everywhere, and mostly of Gwen—the Gwen standing in front of him. Her father and brothers were with her in most of the photographs. A few were of her in a wedding dress. Next to her stood a groom with a slight build, red hair, and round pink cheeks.

"It's different." He motioned to the home and peeked up the staircase, noting more photos. "It wasn't like this."

She released a willowy sigh. "It's still not back to the way it was. Robertson's men destroyed everything when they went through the place. Ripped up the sofa, mattresses in the bedrooms, damn near wiped out the pantry and kitchen. It took Carl's men two days to clean it up. At least my pictures were safely tucked away in storage. I just got them all back up. It was one of the first things Rainn told me to take down."

He turned to her. "Rainn?"

"Rainn Lin. The woman who replaced me."

The last vestiges of his resistance to a fake Gwen shattered like glass smashed by a hammer. To hear her name brought home the reality of the scheme. He sent people out to deceive others, was an expert at what he did, and yet, here he was—hoodwinked.

Gwen glided into her living room. "My ex-husband and Greg Caston were good friends. Doug knew the art business was just a sideline for Greg. His real business was running an organization of spies like yours."

Dallas reached for the doorframe. "You know what I do?"

She stopped at the kitchen entrance. "Rainn told me. Doug contacted the person who took over Caston's organization. That's who came up with the plan to replace me with a specialist."

She's a specialist?

The betrayal sent a cold shockwave through him. Everything about her suddenly made sense—she was like him. It would explain her precision with a gun, her interrogation techniques, her combat training, and the way she seemed to stay one step ahead.

He dug his nails into the wooden doorframe. He'd dealt with Caston, and thought he knew most of his people. He'd never gotten wind of another player in the game after his death.

Dallas raised his head to ask her more questions, and the light coming through the living room windows stopped him. It landed on the new red sofa, dark oak coffee table, and the red rug across the polished hardwood. Knickknacks of horses crowded the coffee table, framed pictures cluttered the mantle, and the ocean view painting above the fireplace had become a wooded valley landscape.

Dallas released his grip on the doorframe. "Where did you go?"

Gwen fidgeted, lacing her fingers. "Houston, to stay with Doug. I made the switch with Rainn right before the feds showed up. She was chosen because not only did she look like me, but she could also ride and take care of my horses."

He shook his head, feeling like an utter fool. "There were signs something was off, but I never pushed to get answers. I never followed through."

She peered at her clasped hands. "When Carl contacted my father and told him he was bringing you on board, Rainn almost walked away. She knew of your reputation and didn't think she'd be able to pull it off."

Dallas wiped his sweaty palms together. "Well, she did pull it off. She did a bang-up job of outwitting me."

"Don't blame Rainn. She didn't tell me about everything that went on between you two, but I had an idea something was up. When I got back and saw her face, I figured it out."

He rested his shoulder against the doorframe, still smarting. Silence stretched between them, adding to the knife twisting in his back. He needed answers Gwen couldn't give him. He had to go to the source.

"Where is she?"

"I don't know. After you left, I flew in from Houston. We made the switch at my father's house. I haven't spoken with her since."

"What about your husband? Does he still have a contact number? I need to speak to whoever he dealt with."

Gwen came up to him, a frown spreading across her full lips. "What difference would it make? She's like you, a shadow that disappears when provoked. She won't let you find her unless she wants to be found."

He tipped his head closer and put a menacing edge to his voice. "I can find her. Just give me a place to start."

She crossed her arms, and for an instant, she was the defiant woman he had protected. "I won't do that. I owe her."

The wheels turned in his head, fishing for an angle to play. "If Carl Bordonaro ever finds out what you and your father pulled …"

"But you won't tell him, will you, Dallas? We both know who orchestrated the whole charade with the feds, and who set up Robertson, and who killed him. A man like that is a better friend than an enemy, and for me, Carl is family. Who do you think he'll believe? Me or you?"

He saw Ed Pioth staring back at him. It would seem her father had taught her more than how to fight—he'd shown her how to survive.

"You're just like your old man."

She shrugged, appearing colder. "You don't grow up surrounded by men like Carl and my father without having something rub off."

A round, gray tomcat trotted down the stairs and passed right by Dallas's feet.

He looked down and scowled. "I see Lawrence survived."

Gwen laughed, a deep bellow, sounding nothing like his Gwen.

"It would take more than a bunch of wise guys to off old

Lawrence. He'll outlive us all."

Dallas missed the light, airy sound of his Gwen's voice. "I should go."

"I hope one day you find Rainn." Gwen walked next to him as they approached the door. "I have a feeling you two have unfinished business."

He smirked but didn't offer his thoughts on the matter. Instead, he held out his hand after she opened the door.

"You have a good life."

"You do the same, Mr. August."

He made his way back to his rental car, no longer interested in the country air or the open sky. The acid tearing a hole in his stomach needed blood to appease it—Rainn's blood.

He walked through the gate, and as he shut it, he took one last look around the farm.

I'm going to find her.

The bitch had taken him for a ride and become a threat to his business. He would treat her like the others who'd tangled with him in the past—he'd cut her off at the knees.

CHAPTER THIRTY

Dallas gripped the railing of the balcony attached to his stuffy two-bedroom suite at The Airport Hilton and looked down at the dismal rectangular pool eight floors below. The depressing sight, bleachy hotel air, and orange upholstered furniture only compounded his frustration with not getting a flight out of the city. He'd refused Lance's offer of a place to stay and booked a room close to the airport, eager to catch his early morning flight. Besides, the night in the hotel would give him time to plot his revenge against Rainn.

He'd sent Stokes the task of finding her in a very long email. But what would he do with her once he did? His mind flipped through a possibility of bloody scenarios, but nothing felt satisfying, nor seemed very wise.

He trudged across the plush carpet and arrived at the complimentary tray of alcohol left on top of the small fridge. He grabbed the bottle of vodka and a clean glass.

Dallas stared at the ugly orange sofa in his sitting area. He'd stayed in a lot of hotel rooms, but this had to be the most abysmal.

He'd barely poured his drink when a knock on the door distracted him.

Dallas figured it was a complimentary basket of some sort to make up for the lousy suite.

He went to the door and discovered it wasn't room service—it was Carl Bordonaro.

His pasty complexion had not improved, but his presence worried the shit out of Dallas.

"Lance told me I could find you here." Carl Bordonaro gave him a brisk going over. "Sorry you couldn't get out until mornin'."

Dallas waved him inside. "To what do I owe this visit?"

Carl peered at him through his thick glasses as he walked in the door. "I assume you're here because of my fruit basket."

Dallas returned to the vodka he'd left on the coffee table. "Are you the one who made sure Gwen and her father were safe at last or was that someone else's doing?"

"Prison's a nasty place, filled with angry and violent people. All kinds of things can happen to men there."

Dallas added more vodka to his glass. "What about Brewster and Crawford? Was that for the FBI's benefit or Robertson's?"

Carl sobered as he made his way to the fridge. "Does it matter?"

Dallas kept his attention on Carl as he selected a can of ginger ale. "How did you find out the Gwen Marsh I was protecting wasn't the real Gwen Marsh?"

"When you brought her to my house on Esplanade Avenue. I saw the surveillance videos and knew it wasn't Gwen."

An uneasy flutter gripped his stomach. "Surveillance videos?"

Carl made himself comfortable on the sofa next to Dallas. "Got the whole house wired, everythin' except the bathrooms. You can learn a lot about people that way."

Dallas picked up his drink. "I don't know if I should be embarrassed or pissed off."

Carl popped open the ginger ale and took a sip. "Ed was protectin' his daughter. I can respect that. He's family, so I can forgive him a few little white lies." Carl patted Dallas's thigh. "You held up your end of the deal and didn't rat me out to Dan Wilbur. I knew he would threaten you to get to me, and you proved you're loyal. That's what I needed to know."

Dallas held his drink inches from his lips. "Is that why you hired me? Was this a test?"

Carl ran his finger around the top of his can. "You and me run worlds where trust is a rare commodity. The people we hire need to prove they can keep our secrets. Without that, we got nothin'. Now that I know I can count on you to keep my secrets safe, we'll be doin' a whole lot more business together in the future."

Dallas set down his drink, and sagged into the sofa. "This has been your operation all along. Me, Gwen, Robertson, Brewster, even Dan Wilbur. You knew what everyone would do before they did it."

"But I didn't know about that girl you like so much." He pulled a card from his suit jacket and placed it on the coffee table. "Maybe this will make up for that."

Dallas scanned the address printed in bold letters. "This is Greg Caston's gallery in New York. Why give me this?"

"I got it from Ed. Now you have a place to start so you can find her." Carl stood, holding his can. "I gotta go. Can't be in one place too long these days. See me out."

Dallas edged around the coffee table. "You want me to go after her?"

Carl laughed, sounding like a little boy as he walked across the room. "She's the competition, ain't she? And you always got to keep your eye on the competition."

Dallas followed him to the door, suspicious. "But she outsmarted me. She beat me to Gwen's secret. Maybe you should hire her."

Carl stopped at the door. "No need. You got her to hand everythin' over to you. If you hadn't been there, who knows where all of that information might have ended up?"

Carl reached for the handle, and Dallas put his hand on the door.

"I have to know. What was in Earl's safety deposit box? What did so many people have to die for?"

"Pictures," Carl said with a shrug. "Of Earl and his family."

Dallas lowered his hand and slumped forward, letting his disappointment slacken his face.

"Pictures? That's it?"

Carl turned the handle. "And Earl's books," he added with a grin. "He kept accounts of every transaction he ever made, from his first numbers operation in the French Quarter to the days when he ran one of the big casinos. Now all that's protected, and all those other interested parties won't be goin' anywhere near Gwen's farm again thanks to you." Carl opened the door. "I owe you."

Dallas shook his head, not sure how he felt about Carl's gratitude. "I guess that means you'll be in touch."

Carl patted his shoulder. "You know it."

After Carl left, Dallas set the lock and rested against the door, gazing into his suite. He'd always been a stickler for control over his assignments, and it was a new experience for him to discover he'd handed over that control to another without knowing. He didn't like the questions and doubts the assignment had left with him, but there was one thing he had to discover—who was Rainn Lin?

He returned to the sofa and picked up the business card on the coffee table, debating how to proceed.

Dallas dug his cell phone from his jacket pocket and scrolled through his contacts until he found the number he needed.

"Watchya need, Boss?"

Cleveland's deep baritone lifted Dallas's spirits.

"There's been a change of plans. After you pick me up at the airport tomorrow, I'll need to go to the Chelsea Art District. Tell Stokes to cancel my morning appointments."

"Sure thing." Cleveland paused. "You buying some new pictures for the penthouse?"

"No, I won't be buying anything." Dallas closed his hand around the card. "I'm going to check out the competition."

CHAPTER THIRTY-ONE

A black Mercedes G-Class SUV eased in front of the Greg Caston Galleries on West 25th Street in the Chelsea Art District of Manhattan. The three-story renovated warehouse had a glass entrance and windows covering the entire façade. The bright lights from inside the gallery shone through the first two floors, but the third floor was dark.

Cleveland viewed Dallas in the backseat through the rearview mirror. "You sure you wanna go in there? After everythin' that happened in Mr. Caston's gallery in N'awlins, you might be takin' a big chance."

"I need to find out who is running this operation so I can get some answers."

Cleveland shrugged his broad shoulders. "It's your ass."

After climbing out of the car, Dallas strolled toward the building. He pulled the collar of his coat closer as a brisk breeze from the nearby Hudson River blew past. When he reached the glass entrance, a slender Asian woman with a welcoming smile, long, silky hair, and fiery dark eyes opened the door for him.

"Welcome to Caston Galleries."

She jutted out her lower lip, giving a hint of the grit he suspected she kept sequestered behind her professional mask.

"My name is Nia. How can I help you?"

In a fitted, black silk dress and stilettos, Nia had to be one of Greg Caston's people. She had the look of someone well-aware of her surroundings, cautious of strangers, and with a beauty that could turn any head. Everything he looked for in a specialist.

Dallas removed his gloves, taking his time. "Nia, I'm looking for your boss."

The slight arch of her eyebrows told Dallas what he needed to know—he'd roused her curiosity.

"Perhaps there's something I can help you with. The gallery manager is out at the moment, but I am—"

"I'm looking for your other boss." He leveled his gaze on her, letting her know he meant business. "The one who lives upstairs in the penthouse."

Nia's perfectly calm expression never wavered, but the rise in her pulse stretched the veins in her neck enough for Dallas to notice.

"I'm sorry, but Mr. Caston—"

"Is dead. I know that." He reached into his coat pocket and pulled out his business card. "I need to speak to the one who took over for Mr. Caston." He handed her the card. "Give him this. He'll want to see me."

Nia took the card and read it. She then looked up at Dallas, her jaw ajar.

"Of course, Mr. August. Please wait here."

Nia hurried across the gallery floor and went through an unmarked door.

Dallas perused the works on the walls, keeping an eye out for the small camera lenses connected to the monitors of the person living upstairs. He lingered over the large oil paintings of the New York skyline. The reds, orange, yellow in the sky sharply contrasted the water in the river. He liked it. Perhaps he would buy one for his office.

Intermixed with smaller pieces of important local historic buildings, he found some abrasive watercolors of nude men in a variety of compromising positions.

Dallas strolled through the first floor, occasionally glancing at his watch and wondering what was taking so long.

Nia suddenly reappeared on the gallery floor, her expression as stony as any of the statues around him.

"If you would come this way, Mr. August."

She crooked her finger and then gracefully turned on her high heels. She walked across the stone floor, barely making a sound.

They arrived at a door with *private* etched in a brass plate across the top.

She opened the door and stepped through, her gaze as cold as the icy room.

He followed her with a confident stride, assured whoever had been watching him from the cameras in the gallery already knew who he was.

A narrow hallway done in gray with dark-tiled floors echoed his footfalls. He arrived at a security desk with monitors built into a semi-circular console. The guard behind the desk, dressed in all black and with a .9mm pistol strapped to his side, had arms almost as big as Cleveland's.

Nia stepped aside as the broad-chested guard came around the desk and faced Dallas with an intimidating glower. He said nothing but motioned for Dallas to raise his arms.

The pat-down was quick but thorough, and something Dallas expected. No one got into his offices without getting cleared by Cleveland. It was the reason he'd left his gun back at his penthouse.

Once done, the security guard nodded to Nia.

She motioned to a pair of silver elevator doors with a

manicured hand. "If you take the elevator, it will take you to the penthouse."

"Who's waiting in the penthouse for me?"

"The person you came to see," she softly said and turned away.

Nia headed down the short corridor, and the guard returned to his station behind the desk. Dallas heard the click of the door to the showroom and then walked toward the elevator. A slight flutter cropped up in his stomach as he pressed the call button.

The silver doors opened, and after stepping inside, he faced the security guard. The bulky man didn't appear interested in him, which gave Dallas some assurance that the person waiting in the penthouse wasn't nervous about their meeting, just curious.

In the elevator car, he hit the P button on the console, knowing what awaited him. He ran through what he remembered of the penthouse layout, preparing for any surprises.

On the ride up, he tried to picture his counterpart. He knew Greg Caston would never have trusted just anyone with his organization. Like Simon La Roy, the man had been a ruthless and manipulative bastard who had prided himself on being able to extract secrets from the rich and powerful. Greg Caston would have made sure that whoever succeeded him was just as cunning.

The elevator came to a halt, and the doors slowly opened. Dallas waited, his head held high, ready for answers.

A spacious loft apartment opened before him with large windows at the rear that overlooked the Hudson River. The red-brick walls had been left bare, but new hardwood floors had been installed, adding to the contemporary ambiance. He walked into a living room filled with white leather furniture. To his right, an open kitchen boasted gray granite countertops and stainless-steel appliances. A set of thick wooden stairs, with buffed iron railings, rose to a loft bedroom walled in glass. He could make out the king-sized bed surrounded by chrome and leather furniture.

"I never thought you would come here."

The feminine voice sent a shudder down his back. It sounded so familiar, but it couldn't possibly belong to the same women he'd sworn to destroy.

No longer interested in creating an intimidating impression, he spun around.

She appeared right behind him, a few feet away and staring at him with more wonder than hostility. He blinked, but when her image didn't fade, he realized she was no mirage. It was Gwen or Rainn. In black pants, a red silk shirt, high-heeled pumps, and wearing makeup, she was nothing like the woman he'd known.

The heaviness expanding in his chest made breathing unbearable. His mouth tipped open, but then the emotions he'd fastidiously controlled since leaving New Orleans exploded.

"What the fuck are you doing here?"

His hands itched to wrap around her throat, but that wouldn't get him anywhere—not yet, anyway.

She inched closer, not appearing daunted. The light coming through the windows danced on her flowing, silky hair.

"You asked to see the guy in charge." She waved her hand down her figure, acting just as brash as the woman he remembered. "That would be me."

"You?" He laughed, a little too loudly—more shocked than amused. "Caston left his organization to you?"

"Technically, he left his fortune to his son, Joshua, which includes the galleries, but not the organization. That he left to me." She turned, heading deeper into the apartment. "I was his right hand for almost three years, just like you were Simon's."

He arched his back, debating what to do. Killing her seemed a bit extreme at the moment, considering there were a lot of questions he needed answered.

"All those looks of innocence, the moments when you seemed so vulnerable, your tales of trauma and victimhood that never happened—you were playing me the entire time without giving a damn about the consequences. I spotted the holes in your stories, but I didn't want to buy you weren't Gwen Marsh because it made no sense. And then when I met the real Gwen, saw she wasn't you … You made everything that happened, all the death and suffering, pointless." He stopped and lowered his voice. "You got a lot of balls, lady."

She tipped her head. "Don't sound so high and mighty when you're no different. We were on that farm to do a job—you needed the information Gwen had, and I decided to play with you before I gave it away. You're pissed because I beat you at your own game."

Sweat popped up on his brow as he yearned to let into her, but something held him back—she was like him. If she had worked for his organization, he'd be damned proud of what she'd pulled off. But Rainn was the competition, and her skills remained a problem—one he had to handle carefully.

He ushered his calm and concentrated on the woman who held information vital to the survival of his organization. Until he got what he needed, he had to stay in control and not let her get to him. But he couldn't help but notice that her eyes, once a source of so much beauty and warmth for him, now evoked bitterness and hate. She didn't show any resemblance to the woman he'd held in his arms. The Gwen who had reduced his high walls to rubble was gone.

Dallas unbuttoned his coat with shaking hands, resolving to

shut the door on who she had been and get down to business.

"How did you get involved with Caston?"

She rested against the back of the sofa and motioned to him. "I got the idea from you. You don't remember meeting at Quantico, do you?"

He wiped his face, sick over the realization. It all made sense, her tactics, her accuracy with a gun, even her coldness—she had started like him.

"You worked for The Bureau."

"I was going to go to medical school, but I didn't want my father's life as a physician, so I joined up." She twisted her hands together, appearing slightly nervous. "We first met at the training facility in Virginia, but you were too into your partner, Carol Wilbur, to notice anyone else. A few weeks later, Carol was killed, and you resigned. I heard about your teaming up with Simon La Roy. That was when I contacted Greg and offered my services."

He walked up to the sofa and flung his coat across it. "What else have you been keeping from me? Is your name Rainn Lin, or is there something else I should be calling you?"

"My real name is Rainn Lin. My father was from China, but my mother was American. I was born in New York and fell in love with horses when I was four. Like Gwen, I rode competitively, and my mother also died when I was young. Unlike Gwen, my father died when I was in college." She blew out a disgruntled breath. "And was never the asshole Ed Pioth is."

"I sensed something was off from the moment we met. The way you didn't want to cook for me, the missing pictures in the house, even your bedroom never felt like you. And the scar on your wrist?" He pointed to the red scar poking out from beneath her sleeve. "You didn't get that by catching your arm on a nail, did you?"

"You were right. It was a knife wound from a fight I got into a few months back on assignment." She tilted her head, observing him. "So why are you here, Dallas? What else do you need to know?"

He rushed toward her, his stomach a ball of fire. "Why me?"

Rainn stepped away from the sofa, keeping some distance between them. "I didn't hire you, Carl Bordonaro did. If I'd known he was going to bring you in, I would have never taken the job."

Her smirk showed all her feistiness. Dallas didn't realize how much he'd missed it. But how much of what he saw was Gwen or Rainn?

"Why did you take the job?"

Rainn stopped in the middle of the living room and put her hand to her brow. "Because Doug Marsh came to me, asking for help. You know how this business works. We can't afford to alienate our clients."

The air around Dallas felt so brittle that it could snap at any moment. Or perhaps that was him. With his nerves frayed to the quick, anything was possible.

"Why didn't you hand over the key from the beginning? We could have avoided the entire fiasco and saved ourselves from having this meeting."

She took a step closer, gentling her voice. "I was going to, and then Carl Bordonaro hired you. I wanted to see you, see if you were still the specialist that everyone admired. Then once you arrived, I realized if I just gave you the key, I'd compromise my position and put Gwen in danger. So, I kept my secret until I knew she would be safe."

He gripped her forearm, squeezing. "You could have gotten me killed."

"But you didn't get killed."

She chuckled, and the saucy sound cut through him like a razor blade.

"Admit it, Dallas. You're like me. Beneath the exteriors, we're both calculating people who are very good at what we do. We should be proud of our accomplishments."

He pushed her away. "Deceiving people is nothing to be proud of."

"Isn't it? It all depends on one's perspective. Secrets are a commodity that will never lose value. The world runs on them, men build empires with them. They can topple governments, and can even turn a Hollywood hopeful into a star. What we do may not be right or popular, but it is necessary." She gazed into his eyes. "We are secret brokers, you and I. And leopards with the same spots should always stick together."

Dallas went over every facet of her face, attempting to figure out her intentions. Rainn wanted something. She wouldn't have allowed him into her penthouse unless there was something in it for her.

"What are you suggesting?"

She raised her chin, showing the obstinacy he'd come to know. "I want us to join forces."

"You and me?" He snickered. "You must be joking."

"Why not?" She pouted, reminding him of their fights on the farm. "Let's face it, our business is getting tougher. I've had to set up more getaways for my people than ever. I've had too many specialists getting hurt or even killed because of revengeful targets. Technology is advancing, and we're struggling to keep up. We could pool our resources, share our specialists, and come up with strategies to stay alive together."

"We run competing businesses." He turned away, uncomfortable with her proximity. "We can't work together."

She eased in front of him. "Simon La Roy and Greg Caston ran competing businesses—not us."

"They hated each other," Dallas countered, raising his voice.

"But we don't." Rainn rested her hand on his jacket lapel. "What would it take to convince you that this could work?"

Dallas removed her hand. "I'll keep that a secret for the time being."

She was so close that her sweet scent tempted him. Unable to resist, he moved closer, wanting to kiss her and see if it was still there—that longing, gnawing, insatiable desire for her.

He believed she would retreat from him, but instead, Rainn eagerly curled her arms around his neck.

Dallas became lost in the sheen of her hair and the lure of her velvety skin. Then he kissed her, tenderly at first, but as the taste of her drove him mad, he crushed her to him.

After everything she did to you? You can't give in.

Without a second thought, he stepped out of her embrace.

She stared at him, her lips parted as their red color faded. "Why are you stopping?"

He unwrapped her arms from around his neck, proud of his self-control. "It can't go anywhere between us." Dallas went to the sofa and picked up his coat. "You're not a target."

She rushed after him and caught his arm. "Does that matter? You don't want a relationship any more than I do. It's safer this way, for both of us."

He shook her off and put on his coat. "Safer for you, perhaps, but not for me."

Dallas concentrated on walking away and not appearing too desperate to be free of her, but he was desperate—he was so close to giving in it scared him to death.

At the elevator, he pressed the call button, and the silver doors parted.

"What about my offer to join forces?" she asked behind him.

Once in the elevator car, Dallas faced her, keeping up his forbidding scowl.

"I'll be in touch."

CHAPTER THIRTY-TWO

The dull, dreary gray clouds hanging over the New York skyline reflected Dallas's sullen mood. He sat at his desk, unable to escape his throbbing headache. Lack of sleep—he'd tossed all night—and the turmoil Rainn had created in his life mounted with every passing hour.

The constant calls, tedious conversations, complaints, and juggling of specialists and temperamental clients didn't help his foul temper. The workload left him little time to think. He had to figure out what to do about Rainn.

He didn't know what had shocked him more—Rainn was in charge, or that she wanted to join forces. Simon La Roy would have scoffed at the suggestion. But Simon had been well-established in the business. Dallas was not. He would have to fight to maintain the integrity of his organization. Perhaps Rainn had been on to something. Times were getting tougher for his unique brand of services. To survive, he had to get creative.

"Your three o'clock is here," Stokes announced, barging into his office.

Dallas almost toppled the coffee mug in his hand—his fifth one so far.

"What three o'clock?" He set his coffee aside and reviewed his computer calendar.

"The recruit. The former MI-6 agent."

Dallas sagged into his chair. *Oh yeah.*

He needed to get his mind off Rainn and back on his business. "Sure. Send her in."

Stokes rested against the doorframe. "She's impressive."

Dallas swiveled his chair around to level a discerning eye at his assistant. "Impressive? You thought Bridget was impressive."

"She's young. Give her time. And you can't blame her for not reading a man right. You're no wiz with women."

He refrained from giving Stokes the satisfaction of punching back with a few choice words. He opened the file on the recruit on his computer and did a quick review.

"I don't need another dead specialist on my hands. You know what a mess that is to clean up. Make sure you teach Bridget what she needs to know."

Stokes eased up to the desk. "You want me to train her? Shouldn't you do that?"

"Overseeing a specialist's training is the job of the second-in-command." He pointed at him. "That's you. My job is to keep this entire enterprise afloat." Dallas stood. "Just don't sleep with this one."

Stokes chuckled. "What can I say? Women love me."

"You just don't love them." Dallas removed his gray suit jacket from behind his chair. "That's what makes you such a good specialist. You don't care who you sleep with."

"Oh, I care. I just don't let them get under my skin like you."

Dallas paused while slipping his jacket over his shoulders, the barb fueling his unraveling temper.

"Sometimes, you can be an asshole, Stokes."

"Ah, there's the brutish Dallas August I've come to know." He waited for Dallas to finish putting on his jacket. "When were you going to tell me about your visit to Caston's gallery?"

Dallas hid his discomfort while he adjusted his sleeves. "How did you find out?"

Stokes hiked his eyebrows. "You think you could waltz in there and not set tongues wagging. I got calls, a lot of them."

He'd been so obsessed with finding Rainn that he'd given little consideration to the consequences of their meeting.

"I went to meet the new head of his group. A woman named Rainn Lin."

Stokes's rigid posture relaxed. "I heard rumors he had a woman as his second, but I never knew her name."

An incredulous Dallas leaned against his desk. "Well, we know it now. And it's presented me with a new dilemma. Rainn wants to join forces. My organization and hers working together."

Dallas waited for his reaction and was a bit dismayed when his assistant's chiseled features didn't register a smidgen of concern.

"Sounds like a good idea to me. We've been at odds with Caston's group for years. It's about time we ended the rivalry."

"That's not what Simon La Roy would have done," Dallas maintained.

Stokes's throaty laugh sounded surprisingly genuine.

"Simon's dead, and you're not him. You'll never be him. You've always strived to be a better boss than he was, and you are."

A lot of things would suffer from associating with another organization, but there were a few benefits. It would allow him to keep tabs on Rainn. She knew too much about him, and keeping her close was better than second-guessing her intentions.

"I'll think about it," Dallas finally conceded.

Stokes went to the office door. "I'll get the recruit."

"What's her name again?"

"Nicole," Stokes called over his shoulder as he exited the

office.

Nicole. The mention of Nicci's given name didn't send him into a pit of despair. Perhaps the pain of their past was behind him. Or maybe someone else had set her aside in his mind.

The suggestion ignited spasms in his neck.

Don't even go there.

A woman with auburn hair and deep gray eyes glided into his office. Dallas's brain locked up the moment he saw her face. She had the same flawless porcelain skin, refined features, and long legs that had enthralled him with Nicci Beauvoir.

"Mr. August, I'm Nicole La Grande," she said in a British accent.

He struggled to get his sluggish mind working again. Dallas silently chastised his loss of composure. He couldn't afford to fall apart in front of the woman. It went against what any specialist wanted from their boss—a detached, decisive leader who could make the call whether someone lived or died.

He took her hand and showed her to the leather chair by his desk. "Welcome, Ms. La Grande. I'm glad you could make it today."

He noted her snug blouse, the slit in her skirt, and her high heels. She had dressed to impress men at a bar, not for an interview.

She took her seat, and Dallas got a better look at her sharp nose, deep red lips, and stunning cheekbones.

"You were MI-6." He took his seat. "Why not go to the CIA? Why me?"

"I was told me you were the best. And the money I would make with you is far more than anything a government could give me."

Dallas nodded in agreement. "Yes, we pay better, but I expect

299

my specialists to give everything they have to get the required information."

Nicole eased back in her chair, crossing her shapely legs and letting the slit in her skirt reveal her slender white upper thigh. "I have no problem with doing my utmost for the assignment, Mr. August. I know what it takes to get what I want."

Dallas liked her brazen self-assurance. It reminded him of another specialist he knew.

"Yes, I can see you'll fit right in."

Dallas shut his office door after concluding his brief interview with Nicole La Grande. He returned to his desk, confident she was perfect for his organization. She had the looks, brains, and savvy to carry out any assignment. If she could use her assets to get the job done had yet to be determined, but he would break her in slowly as he did with every new specialist.

He settled into his chair, questioning which seasoned specialist he would have shadow Nicole on her first assignment. Dallas faced his computer about to find someone best suited for her skillset when his phone rang.

No number flashed, meaning someone was blocking him. That wasn't good.

Dallas's fingers tingled as he listened to the harsh ringing. Unable to stand the suspense any longer, he picked up the phone.

"Who's this?"

"Hello, Dallas." Rainn's sultry voice came over the speaker.

Dallas's blood turned to ice. *What is she up to?*

"I didn't expect to hear from you so soon."

"I was just checking in."

"I'll bet." He picked up a pen, looking for something to do with his hand. "Why are you calling me?"

"I wanted to sweeten my offer by discussing an assignment. Something we would both have an interest in."

Dallas hesitated as he considered. It could be a trap, or she was genuinely interested in going into business together. With Rainn, it was hard to tell. He tapped the pen on his desk, deciding to string her along.

"I haven't made my mind up about your offer."

She sighed. "What will it take to convince you we could accomplish a great deal together? Look how well we fit. It's like we were molded for each other."

He ignored the reference to their night together, wishing he could forget it. "What kind of assignment are we talking about?"

"It's not safe to go into too much detail over an open line." She was quiet for a moment, and then she asked, "Is your heart pumping yet? Is your blood racing? Admit it, you're addicted. The rush of a new assignment is your drug of choice."

He threw the pen on the desk, knowing he would never be able to resist her offer. Years of living in the shadows had corrupted his mind and destroyed any chance of his having a normal life. His time with Nicci had proved that. Rainn knew what it took to entice him—intrigue.

"Where are you?"

"I'm at Greg's gallery in Chelsea." Her voice held a trace of ruthlessness in its honeyed notes. "Come by tonight after we close. We'll talk then."

CHAPTER THIRTY-THREE

The windows of the three-story brick warehouse were dark, but in a side service alley, a glaring spotlight illuminated the two glass doors at the entrance. Dallas's heart revved as he stepped from his Mercedes SUV. Then the flash of a single light appeared in a third-floor window. She was ready for him.

"You sure about this, Boss?" Cleveland asked from the driver's seat. "Maybe I should go in with you."

He stood by the open car door, amused by Cleveland's constant mothering. "I won't need you. I can handle this."

"I'll wait out here just in case. You've already been beat up once by this woman. She ain't safe."

Dallas straightened the knot in his tie, keen to send Cleveland home. "She didn't beat me up. Go back to the penthouse. I'll text when I need you."

Cleveland smashed his lips together, looking menacing, but Dallas wasn't intimidated as he shut the rear passenger door.

Without another thought about his overzealous security guard, he headed down the service alley, shielding his eyes from the bright spotlight.

A camera mounted on the side of the building tracked him as he walked by. The hairs on the back of his neck tickled. If he'd been set up, it was too late to back out now.

He reached the thick glass doors, and as soon as he touched the handle, a loud buzzer sounded. Before entering the building,

Dallas searched the frame. Another security camera sat positioned above his head.

He stepped into a short hall with black tile floors, gray walls, and spotlights set into the ceiling. Right ahead was the familiar circular desk and the array of monitors keeping an eye on the gallery and outer doors.

A guard in all black came out from behind the desk. This man was shorter than the previous one he'd met but still loaded with muscles. He also carried a .9mm strapped to his hip.

The guard waved him down the corridor to the silver elevator doors.

"Ms. Lin is waiting for you, Mr. August."

Dallas looked the square-faced young man in the eye, glad his suspicions about not receiving another pat-down were correct.

"Thank you."

He strolled toward the elevators, weighing his odds. They seemed better than he'd hoped. If Rainn hadn't trusted him, her guard would have found the concealed semi-automatic Sig in his jacket pocket.

Once inside the elevator, he relaxed his shoulders and pictured his reunion with Rainn. The thought of putting a bullet between her eyes crossed his mind. But then images of her slim hips beneath him chased away his lust for revenge. That had been the way of things since their last meeting—one minute he wanted to kill her, the next he daydreamed about sleeping with her.

He'd convinced himself that killing the competition would be reckless, but a relationship with Rainn could be just as catastrophic. The elevator ground to a halt and Dallas's indecision simmered.

She's going to be the death of me.

When the doors opened, the lights along the Hudson River

sent rays of yellow, white, and red along the thick rough-hewed beams set in the ceiling.

She came from the kitchen, gliding forward in a lapis gown gathered at the waist. The beaded bodice and flowing skirt accentuated her hourglass figure and reminded Dallas of a princess in a Disney movie. Her black hair sat atop her head in a messy bun with several wisps strategically placed around her oval face.

The overall effect bewitched him. *Well, I certainly can't shoot her in that.*

"Did you get dressed up for me?"

"We had a small function at the gallery tonight for a few VIPs. Impractical for our meeting but necessary since my last guest only left twenty minutes ago." Her gaze swept over his suit. "Coming from work?"

Dallas strolled past her, irritated with his inability to stay mad at her. "I'm sure you already know the answer to that question."

He went to the windows and admired the lights on the water—anything to avoid looking at her. Dallas regrouped, reminding himself not to let his guard down.

Stick to business.

"I can see you're in a great mood," Rainn commented behind him. "Bad day?"

Dallas inspected the bare walls, not about to discuss his day with her. "For someone who lives above an art gallery, why don't you have any art on your walls?"

"Greg used to have expensive pieces hanging when he lived here." She gathered up her long skirt and strolled toward the kitchen. "But I sold them. There was no point keeping them hidden away up here when they could be earning a profit downstairs."

He put his hands behind his back and watched her. "You're not into art?"

"Greg was the art fanatic." She slid behind the black granite breakfast bar. "I have no interest in it."

"Then why are you running his galleries?"

"Because I ran his organization exceedingly well, and he realized I would take care of his galleries in the same way. A business is a business."

He stepped up to the bar, encouraged by her sudden honesty. "What else do I need to know about you?"

"I'm thirty-six. I have an older brother who lives in Washington and works for the Department of Homeland Security. I've never been married, never come close, love horses, hate people, and until I joined the FBI, I thought I wanted to save the world. Then I learned how shitty the world really is. After four years of no pay, boring details, and getting shot once, I ended up with Greg." She twisted her lips into her quirky smile. "Anything else you want to know?"

He leaned against the bar, fixing his gaze on her. "Yes. Why am I here?"

Rainn turned away and opened a cabinet above the sink. After collecting two old-fashioned glasses, she retrieved a bottle of vodka from the countertop.

The *swish* of her dress reminded him of the wind moving through the trees at Gwen's farm. The stab of her betrayal returned, rejuvenating his distrust.

Rainn set the glasses in front of him, catching her lower lip between her teeth. "I need your help."

"My help?" Dallas snorted with disbelief. "After the shit you've pulled, you expect me to help you?"

She cracked the seal on the bottle. "Why not listen to what I have to say and then you can make up your mind?"

Dallas scowled, irritated with her being so logical, and then gave a curt nod.

Rainn poured out a measure of vodka into each glass. "I'm having a problem with a client."

"A problem?" Dallas grimaced, reminded of his never-ending troubles with clients. "I've heard that before. What does this client want?"

"To destroy me. He has an eye on taking over my company, and he has information he can use to push me out and set himself up as your biggest competitor."

He gauged her expression, trying to discern if it was all a lie or real. He couldn't make up his mind.

"Why don't you let him have it? It would be ideal for me, and then you would be out of my hair for good."

Rainn smirked and turned to the refrigerator. "The individual asking for the information knows a great deal about me, Greg, and the organization. He's threatening to blackmail my clients and expose my specialists to the authorities. If that happens, I'm as good as dead." She opened the freezer and seized a handful of ice. "He wants me to work with him as his second. And if I do, he would run one of the two most powerful organizations in the business." She added the ice to their drinks. "And he plans to go after yours next."

Dallas's mouth went dry. The organization was all he had. He'd given up everything to own it and keep it safe.

He kept his emotions in check as he picked up his glass. "Who is this client?"

"Darryl Keen." She snapped up her glass and held it before

her lips, watching him. "He's known as the Whiz of Wall Street and—"

"I know him." His gut twisted tighter. "He arranged a meeting shortly before Carl asked me to go to New Orleans. He wanted a plant for his offices. He had a leak, or so he claimed."

She shot back her vodka and then set her glass on the bar.

"He wants me to put a specialist in your organization. Someone to collect the information he needs to cut you out."

He peered into his drink. "What kind of information is he looking for?"

"Come with me." She took his hand and coaxed him from his stool. "I have to show you something."

He set his glass aside and let her lead him away. The warmth of her soft hand eased the tension constricting his chest. It didn't quell his rage, but it soothed him to have her near.

She urged him to an alcove set into the walls. A roll-top desk with a large brass lamp sat next to a bookcase packed with black binders dated by month and year.

Rainn reached for a binder dated 2017. She held it to her chest and opened it.

He examined the plastic sleeves containing CDs—two to a page. There were dozens of discs crammed into the binder.

"This is how Greg kept track of the secrets his specialist collected." She motioned to the bookcase. "There were thousands of assignments stored on these discs, along with information on the specialists who performed them. When I took over, I had the discs erased and the information housed on a backup drive for privacy." She shut the binder. "Greg was pretty sloppy when it came to security. And now we're paying the price. Somehow, Keen got hold of what was once on these discs. He has all the information on this organization."

Dallas browsed the almost two dozen binders. It was a lot of information, and anyone could do significant damage with even a small amount of it.

"Greg had a similar set up like this in his New Orleans gallery. I saw it when I was there last year. Was the same information housed there?"

"Yes." She sighed and set the binder back on the shelf. "But that's not all he had there."

A tickle teased the back of his throat. "What do you mean?"

She went to an open laptop on the desk and typed something onto the keyboard. "The police never found the surveillance videos when they searched Greg's New Orleans penthouse after the murders. Luckily, I got to them before they did. Or I thought I did. It seems someone beat me to it."

She hit the enter key and a video, grainy and hard to decipher, popped up on the screen.

In the video, Caston sat at a table with Darryl Keen and another man he didn't recognize. He was lean with wavy hair and had a square face with heavy jowls.

"Who is that?"

"Devon Robertson." She pointed at the screen. "The three of them had several meetings, none of which were logged into any of Greg's appointment books. I never knew about them until I saw this video."

Dallas's stomach became a knotted nightmare. He wiped his face as Devon Robertson's image seared in his memory. What the hell had he gotten himself dragged into?

"Where did you get this?"

"Keen gave it to me when he visited me on the same day you

confronted me about the Marsh job. He made it quite clear this is what he plans on showing to the feds if I don't cooperate."

Dallas rubbed his chin, trying to figure out Keen's motives. "Which means the FBI would have cause to get a warrant and tear apart your business."

"And find my clients, who are also many of yours. You know the people we deal with and the ramifications could destroy many lives, not to mention the economy, national security ... There's no end to what could happen."

Dallas's chest caved as if smacked by a powerful blow. "It would only be a matter of time before the FBI came after my organization."

She nodded and deleted the video. "I either work with Keen or he will go to the feds with all Caston's records."

Dallas's mind was a flurry of questions. "But how did Keen get any of this information?"

"I wish I knew. And believe me, I've tried to find out. No one in my organization admits to ever knowing anything about him, Caston, or Robertson ever being seen together."

A long breath escaped between his clenched teeth. "Has he given you a timeframe? Some window we can use to find a way to turn the tables on him?"

"There's a showing at this gallery next week for a new artist. He will be there. If I don't give him my final answer by then, he will go to the feds."

Dallas crossed his arms, going over everything he knew about Keen. "Why is he doing this now? Greg Caston's been dead for a year. Why show his cards?"

"Robertson is dead. He showed up soon after his death was announced. My bet is Robertson knew something or had something to keep him from moving ahead with his plans to take over this company."

He tapped the blank computer screen. "So whatever Robertson had is what we need to uncover."

She leaned in closer. "So how do we proceed?"

He scratched his head. "We put someone on the inside with Keen. Someone who can get close to him. That would at least give us a plant to feed us information."

"Can't be anyone in our organizations. We can't risk him knowing about them. We need an outside person, not someone in our business."

He tapped his lower lip as an idea percolated. "Someone newly hired, not from this country, and has never worked inside the US before."

She stared at him. "You have someone."

"A new hire from MI-6. She could get close to Keen and he would never see her coming."

She caressed the sleeve of his jacket. "I like this. You and me, working together. See? I was right. We should join our organizations."

He withdrew his arm, wanting to keep some distance between them—at least for now.

"Maybe we should worry about getting Keen out of our lives before we talk about becoming partners."

"I like the sound of that—partners." The right side of her mouth tweaked upward as she inched closer. "I believe we would work well together because we're the same. We only give a damn about one thing—our organizations."

He met her fleeting smile with a cold stare. She was right, of course. The business was the one thing they had in common, and they would do whatever it took to protect what they had.

"If we're going to work together, we'll have to make some changes."

"What kind of changes?" she asked in an uncertain tone.

He dipped his chin and frowned at her. "No more lying. To beat Keen, we need to be honest with each other."

She moved in, keeping her gaze on him. "I'm listening."

"That should be rule one for this relationship. You don't lie to me, and I don't lie to you—at least about business. Rule two is we share all information about specialists and assignments, so we don't have any conflicts."

She rested her hand on his jacket. Her fingers glided over the bulge of his gun. "Rule three should be we're to trust each other."

"Are you sure you want to make that a rule? Because you're not very good with trusting people."

"Neither are you." She played with the end of his tie. "That's what makes us so good together. We already know what we are. We don't have to play games."

He pushed her hands away. "We can't complicate matters by throwing you and me into the mix. We need to remain objective. We should make that rule three—no relationships."

She pouted. "I don't like the sound of that."

His determination to keep her at bay floundered with every passing second. She was no longer Gwen Marsh, the woman in need of protecting. She was Rainn Lin, a woman he needed to defend himself from. He still found her attractive—devastatingly so—but he could not give in to his desire when there was so much at stake.

"If you and I are to work together, there can be nothing between us. We have to concentrate all our efforts on Keen. We can't afford distractions."

"And after Keen is gone?"

He adjusted his jacket and eyed the elevator doors, eager to get away. "We'll see."

"So, how do we seal this deal?"

He held out his hand to her. "The old-fashioned way."

"How about ..." She tipped her head toward the stairs to the loft bedroom. "We do something a little more binding."

He took her hand, slapped it into his, and shook it.

A bitter smile slinked across her lips. "Why do I feel like I'm getting the raw end of this deal?"

"I think it's time you and I both tried something different. First, we trust, and then maybe, if you're good, we can try something more binding."

Rainn sighed, letting her shoulders sag, but then she nodded. "I'm game if you are."

Dallas took a step backward, encouraged. "I'll be in touch."

He walked away, heading toward the elevator, his confidence surging. He had resisted her. He could be in the same room with her without shooting her or taking her to bed. He had remained in control. Something he thought he'd lost when he'd first gazed into her extraordinary eyes.

Dallas pressed the elevator call button, and the doors opened. He stepped through the silver doors, grinning.

I've still got it.

EPILOGUE

The stiff tuxedo collar tugged against his neck as Dallas climbed from his limo at the entrance to the Greg Caston Galleries. The first two stories were aglow, but the black windows in the third story sparked that luscious rush of adrenaline—she wouldn't be hiding in her penthouse tonight.

He passed waiters carrying silver trays filled with flutes of champagne. Guests in black-tie and colorful ball gowns mingled about the entrance, but Dallas didn't bother perusing the faces of New York's Upper East Side. He had business to attend to.

He snapped up a glass of champagne offered to him by a cherub-faced waiter, and then walked purposefully into the gallery, doing his best to get lost amid the crowd. He sipped his drink, admiring a few of the extreme, barely there gowns worn by women hoping to get everyone's attention.

"You bastard," Rainn grumbled as she came up to his side. "I saw you drooling over the half-naked women."

Dallas glimpsed the dance of bubbles in his glass. "Why, are you jealous?"

"And what if I was? What would you do about it?"

"Remind you of our rules—particularly number three." Dallas followed the outline of Rainn's emerald green satin gown. "Nice dress."

She sighed. "It's a shame I can't count on you to rip it off me later."

Dallas swallowed hard, fighting not to picture what she'd look like without that dress. He concentrated on the guests in the gallery.

"What have you got on Keen so far?"

Her demeanor changed, and her flirty smile melted. "Arrived ten minutes ago with his wife and an assistant. They're on the second floor."

Dallas raised his glass to his lips, hiding his mouth from the crowd. "And my specialist, Stokes?"

"He's in the main gallery on the first floor with a striking woman draped on his arm." She paused and frowned at Dallas. "Did you have to pick someone so obvious?"

"Nicole is the perfect bait. Let's see where Keen leads us once we work our way into his world."

He started toward the gallery, but Rainn held his arm, making his champagne slosh.

"Then what?"

He let his drink settle. "I don't know. I'm making this up as I go."

Rainn laughed, crinkling her nose. "You?"

Dallas inched closer, enjoying her tinkling laughter and the temptation of her red lipstick. "Yeah, I guess you're rubbing off on me."

Rainn patted his arm before letting it go. "Just don't get killed. Then who would I have to share my secrets with?"

"Your secrets?" He stifled his chuckle, keeping up the grim line on his lips. "You're not the kind of woman who shares her secrets."

"I only keep my secrets from you, Dallas. To the rest of the world, I'm an open book." Rainn nodded toward the gallery.

"Keen is waiting."

Dallas peered at the champagne bubbling in his glass. "A year ago, when I took over Simon's business, I never pictured I'd have to fight to keep it. I always thought I would walk away one day, but it seems, I can't."

"Our kind doesn't walk away from the thrill. We live for the rush, the intrigue, the hunt for secrets." Rainn hooked his arm. "Not to worry. I won't let you spend the rest of your life, doubting your decision."

He examined her profile while her words ignited his interest. "Do you plan on being there for the rest of my life?"

"Of course. You're hopeless without me."

Dallas's enthusiasm for the subject dimmed. "Perhaps we should talk about this after the party."

"Debate about it, you mean," Rainn countered.

Dallas gave her a curt nod. "That too."

She shot him a dirty look and strolled away.

He marveled at the sway of her hips, remembering their night together, and wondering how long he could resist her. Perhaps he'd finally found a woman who could embrace that different kind of happiness Lance had once mentioned.

Rainn accepted what he was and would never want to change him. In a way, Dallas had become indebted to her. She'd shown him that he wasn't cut out to be a boatbuilder or a father or a husband. Because of her, he'd embraced Simon's business, making it his own. He was a secret broker. Good or bad, for better or for worse, Dallas August was right where he wanted to be.

About the Author

Alexandrea Weis, RN-CS, PhD, is a multi-award-winning author of over twenty-seven novels, a screenwriter, ICU Nurse, and historian who was born and raised in the French Quarter of New Orleans. Having grown up in the motion picture industry as the daughter of a director, she learned to tell stories from a different perspective and began writing at the age of eight. Infusing the rich tapestry of her hometown into her novels, she believes that creating vivid characters makes a story moving and memorable. A member of the Horror Writers Association and International Thriller Writers Association, Weis writes mystery, suspense, thrillers, horror, crime fiction, and romance. She lives with her husband and pets in New Orleans where she is a permitted/certified wildlife rehabber with the Louisiana Wildlife and Fisheries and rescues orphaned and injured wildlife.

www.AlexandreaWeis.com